THE BENJAMIN STEPS

A Mystery

Ian Pert

To Viv

Prologue

February 1945

The dog had run on ahead. Daniel Prideaux followed with his head down, hands deep in the pockets of his oilskin. The rain was horizontal, so fine it was like mist. He was used to the weather, this was real Cornwall, not the picture postcard sunshine that you might get for two months in Summer.

The dog had disappeared: he'd gone into Park an Jowl, sniffing out new scents in the hedges. As Daniel reached the gate he saw headlights coming towards him from the town and he stopped to let the car pass. The road was narrow: there were ditches draining water from the mines on either side of the carriageway, reducing its width so it was only just wide enough for a car.

There was no sign of the dog. He whistled, there was no answering bark. Reluctantly he took out his torch so he could find the catch on the gate. The batteries were low, replacements were difficult to find these days, and the beam was dim. As he was opening the gate the beam flashed over the water in the ditch and he noticed it was unusually dark. Puzzled, he crouched down to get a closer look. The water was red.

"Oh my lord," he said, opening the gate and running into the field, calling urgently for the dog. He was remembering the saying:

Adits run red…

The torch had now died completely and he had to walk the field, calling all the time for the dog. There was no response. He found him half an hour later, lying on his side under the dark of the cliff, breathing heavily, groaning. It was an unearthly sound, and it chilled his soul. Beside the dog was a small pool of the same dark water Daniel had seen in the ditch. The dog looked up when he saw his master and tried to get to his feet but he was too weak. Daniel picked him up and hurried out onto the road and back towards the farm, covering him with the oilskin. No-one must see. No-one must find out.

He was trying not to think of the rest of the saying:

... cattle be dead.

1

July 2010

The long passage down the centre of the cottage felt different. The parquet was hidden beneath a thick carpet, and the wooden panelling below the dado had been removed. There was none of the sharp echo she remembered as a child. Julia was thankful: it helped her maintain her detachment.

The living room, which took up most of the front of the cottage, was unrecognisable. It had been shabby and comfortable, full of surprises, like the coins and sweets which used to fall out of her father's pockets and lodge in the folds of the chair covers. Now it had been sanitised: cool, clean and impersonal, a photo from the Ikea catalogue.

At the far end of the room were the French windows which opened onto the terrace. She unlocked them and stepped out into the heat. It was late afternoon but the sun was still high and the air motionless, full of the scent of roses and jasmine. Down the middle of the garden the lawn sloped away to the stream and pond, and the little wooden bridge which led to the bottom gate onto the public footpath. It was the way they used to go to the cove, just a few hundred yards further down the valley. She couldn't see the beach, only the blue of the ocean. On the horizon a tanker was moving north.

A faint breeze ruffled her hair, and she heard the rustling of leaves in the trees at the foot of the garden. She stepped off the terrace and walked slowly down the lawn. The turf was springy under her feet, and she remembered rolling down it with her friend Charlotte, her mother shouting at them to stop before they tumbled into the pond. They never did, they always went in an arc and dropped into one of the flower beds on either side of the grass. The beds were still there, full of marigolds and asters and freesias. Half way down she passed the little pool in the right hand bed, still fed by a trickling flow from the old clay pipe which led from the mine. She and her father had dug out the pool and the channel which took away the overflow. Under the water were the pebbles she had put in to make the water chuckle as it raced down the slope.

She followed the stream down to the foot of the garden where it ran into the big pond, dark in the shade of the big willow. On her left was the bridge over the main stream which flowed lazily in, creating slow eddies which swirled and dissipated as they spread across the surface of the water. The bridge was rotten and unsafe now.

Turning to make her way back up the slope Julia was able to see the whole of the front of the house. Wheal Mawgan Cottage. It had once seemed to be the most exciting place in the world, but now it just looked ordinary: a white pebble dashed bungalow with UPVC windows below a grey slate roof, sitting on a terrace cut into the hillside. The terrace was all that remained of the head of the mine. The front had been paved and her father had planted some bushes in big pots to make it look alive. Behind and to the right of the cottage was the heavy green door of the garage, once the main entrance to the mine.

High on the corner wall was a CCTV camera looking across the terrace. They were all over the block of flats where she lived in Hackney, watching the dusty walkway outside her door and the playground opposite where the dealers hung out after dark. She hadn't expected to find cameras here. Everyone was paranoid now, it seemed.

She strode back up the slope and went through to the back of the house, where the two bedrooms lay. Hers was full of suitcases and unopened cardboard boxes. He hadn't unpacked, he couldn't have been back here very long. She squeezed through to reach the window, which looked out across the back yard at the bare rock face beyond. It was stark and sombre, but she remembered enjoying this room, lying in bed looking up at the glow-stars on the ceiling, imagining that was the sky and she was with the Revenue, preparing to ambush smugglers as they unloaded barrels of rum from a rowing boat on a moonlit night.

Childish nonsense. She went quickly into the second bedroom, where he'd been sleeping. It too had the same bland furniture as the rest of the house but it felt lived in. There were clothes strewn over a chair, shoes under the unmade bed. The room was stuffy, smelling of dirty washing and the faint whiff of aftershave. She had once loved its smokiness, and the way it seemed to move ahead of him. On the bedside table was a small brown bottle of prescription pills. Beside the bed on the floor were a scuba diving magazine, an ordnance survey map of the area, and a science fiction novel: *A Canticle for Liebowitz*. A story about history repeating itself and the dangers of science. He had once tried to explain it to her but it was boring and she had fallen asleep on his shoulder.

She moved on to the kitchen. The layout was familiar: fitted units down one wall, the sink under the window at the far end. That was where her mother used to stand, watching Julia playing on the lawn as she washed up. A small table stood against the opposite wall. On it were the remains of a half-eaten breakfast: toast, a dish of butter going soft, a glass of orange juice, and a cup of coffee with a skin on it. A copy of the Guardian was open and folded over at a Sudoku puzzle. There were three chairs, one tucked neatly under the table, the other two on their sides, thrust out of the way by the sink. This was where it must have happened.

Julia righted the chairs and took the butter dish to the fridge. It was full of fresh produce: salads, fruit, milk, eggs, and a supermarket cod steak with a sell-by date of the following day. He hadn't had a chance to eat it.

While she was clearing the remains from the table there was a knock at the door. She opened it and there was Charlotte, her large frame filling the doorway. She was wearing a voluminous green dress and sandals. Her mass of black hair framed a fleshy face. Her eyes, always kind and expressive, filled with tears as she bustled in and enfolded Julia in a suffocating hug. Julia was slight and barely reached Charlotte's shoulders: it was like having a huge fur coat draped around her.

"You poor thing," said Charlotte. "I'm sorry I missed you. I got caught in traffic. I didn't want you coming in here on your own."

Julia bore the embrace for a few moments then pulled herself away.

"It's OK," she said. "Is this where you found him?"

Charlotte nodded. "He was on the floor. He was conscious but it looked serious. I went with him in the ambulance but he had another attack and died before we reached the hospital."

She started crying again and Julia took her hands. "I'm sorry it had to happen to you," she said. "It must have been awful."

It sounded completely inadequate but Charlotte seemed to appreciate it, putting her arms round Julia's head and pressing it briefly to her bosom. Julia suffered it for a few moments then gently released herself.

"Let's go into the front room," she said.

They sat at opposite ends of the sofa. Julia found her hand automatically slipping down into the gap between the cushions, feeling for coins. She snatched it back when she realised. Charlotte was busy with a handkerchief and didn't notice.

"While we were waiting for the ambulance he told me he wanted to see you," she said unexpectedly.

"It's far too late for that." Julia felt her anger rising. "Did he say why?"

"He knew how ill he was. That was enough, surely."

"Not after what happened."

"I suppose so," Charlotte said unhappily. "I still don't understand it. He was such a lovely man."

"Once, maybe."

Julia stood up abruptly, disturbed by Charlotte's tears and

her own confused feelings. Charlotte was right: he had been lovely, and she had once been happy. But when they drove away so suddenly it was as if he was leaving all his warmth behind with the furniture.

She went over to close the French windows.

"I didn't know he still owned this place," she said. "I thought he hated it."

"It was empty for a long time. I was very lonely without you here. Then he began letting it out as a holiday cottage. It was busy until the recession hit. The last couple of years have been very quiet."

"Is that why he came back? He sold up in Guildford to live here on the cash?" She felt bitter. He had told her he would never return.

"It wasn't that," Charlotte replied calmly. "He was here incognito. He wouldn't even let me tell my mum. If anyone asked he was an author looking for peace and quiet."

"Another lie. What was he really doing?"

Charlotte heaved herself up from the sofa and joined Julia by the window.

"I don't know. He kept to himself most of the time. He would sometimes come along to the farmhouse for a drink or a meal, but we always talked about other things. But he was definitely up to something. I think he knew he didn't have much time."

"He knew he was ill?"

"Oh yes. He had a scare a few weeks ago: I had to take him to A&E."

They stood looking out across the garden for a long time, then Charlotte roused herself.

"I've brought the post," she said, handing over a bundle of mail.

"They're all addressed to Peter Foster," said Julia as she flicked through. "Is that the name he was using?"

Charlotte nodded. Julia continued sorting through the post. Amongst the envelopes were flyers from estate agents, painters and decorators, political parties. There was also a free local newspaper. The headline across the front page read *Autumn*

Opening for Polwerran Park; below was an artist's impression of a roller coaster.

At the bottom of the pile was an envelope marked Private, with her name handwritten in a script she recognised immediately.

"What's this?" She asked.

"Oh, sorry, I should have told you. He asked me to give it to you if anything happened to him."

"I know who it's from. I want to know what it is."

"Why don't you open it and find out?"

Julia stared at it, feeling apprehensive. Why this sudden interest in her after so many years? She ripped it open. Inside was a single sheet of paper.

Statement of wishes of Malcolm Philips, to be carried out on the occasion of my death.

My body is to be cremated. I want no ceremony. No flowers, no speeches. Anyone who wishes to mark my death may make a donation to charity.

I want Julia to scatter my ashes from the Benjamin Steps.

"What a nerve," she said, showing it to Charlotte. "He spends fifteen years freezing me out and now this."

Charlotte read it quickly.

"It is a bit cold, isn't it?" she said as she handed it back. "It doesn't sound like him at all. And it's a shame about the funeral. He deserves something better than that."

"It's his choice," Julia shrugged. "I'll organise it, then I'll scatter the ashes from these steps. Where are they? Somewhere round here?"

"I don't know. I've never heard of them."

Julia looked at her in disbelief. Charlotte's family had lived on the farm for decades, they knew everything about the area. Julia searched her own memory of living here, exploring the hillsides and coves for hidden caves and secret passages. A romantic sounding name like the Benjamin Steps would have stuck, but it hadn't. She knew nothing about them either.

2

Charlotte stood up to leave.

"I'd better get back to the children. Would you like to come over for dinner later? After they've gone to bed?"

"That's kind of you but not tonight. I'm really tired. I'll unload the car then crash."

"Why don't you sleep with us? You might find it difficult here. I can easily make up the bed in one of the spare rooms."

There was a plea in her voice and Julia glimpsed her loneliness. The three children would keep her busy when they weren't out at school, or in bed at night, but since Nick's accident there was no-one else for her to talk to. This was a remote valley, there wasn't another house for half a mile.

Julia had to choose her words carefully. They were close friends, despite living three hundred miles apart. They had met when her father arrived on a two year posting to the naval base and bought the cottage from Charlotte's parents. The two girls went to the same junior school in Polwerran, both outsiders who were never going to fit in: Charlotte big and clumsy and assuming everyone was her friend, and Julia the opposite, small and skinny and perfectly happy with her own company. The other kids started bullying them, and their lives were miserable until Julia's father persuaded her to learn self-defence. Once a few of the bigger girls had experienced lying on the ground looking up at the sole of her shoe they soon found other people to pick on. She made them stop bullying Charlotte as well, and they'd been unshakeable friends ever since. They phoned each other regularly, and met once or twice a year when Charlotte came to London. Julia never visited Cornwall.

But she was still a solitary person, and needed her space. She loved Charlotte like a sister but she knew that living with her for more than a few days would kill their friendship. Charlotte would start mothering her, treating her like one of her children, and Julia would lash out like a frustrated teenager.

"I need to be here," she said. "There are things I have to work out. I won't be far away," she added, seeing the disappointment in Charlotte's face.

"I suppose so," said Charlotte wistfully. "Just remember you can always change your mind later. And come for dinner tomorrow instead. Talking of tomorrow, have you worked out all the things you need to do?"

"Not yet," admitted Julia. "I've never been in this position before."

"Well, I have. There's a lot of work and it's easy to overlook something. I've still got the list I made when my grandfather died. I'll pop it through your letterbox later. The first thing you have to do is to get hold of the medical certificate from the hospital. Ring them. You can't just turn up. The same with the register office."

Julia followed her to the door. As they stepped out into the sun Charlotte seemed to notice Julia's Fiesta for the first time.

"What on earth have you got in there?" she asked. The car was packed with bags and cases, and Julia's bike was strapped onto a rack at the back.

"I didn't have much time to choose what to bring," said Julia, feeling rather defensive. "I just piled in everything I could think of."

"I'd better come back and give you a hand unloading then."

"Don't worry." This was exactly what she wanted to avoid. "I'll manage. It won't take long."

Charlotte set off along the short path back to the farmhouse. Julia watched her go. Despite being very overweight she moved quickly and lightly. Julia hoped she was going to be all right: she looked like a strong candidate for a heart attack herself.

Charlotte was right, Julia had brought far too much. Suitcases of clothes, her laptop, Kindle, biking gear, walking gear, scuba kit, the contents of her fridge in a cool-box, and all the paperwork she needed to plan next term's classes. There was no room in either of the bedrooms so everything went into the living room, except the bike which she left in the hall.

Julia woke early the next morning with the strange feeling of knowing but not knowing where she was. It was quiet after the continual traffic rumble of Hackney. She found herself remembering the sounds of the house: the swirl of the wind in the chimney, the skittering of leaves in the yard outside her window. There was something else, very faint. She lay very still, breathing slowly and silently as she tried to isolate it, just as she had always done when a new sound came into the valley. It took a while but she caught it eventually. It was the tinkling of a wind chime. She knew exactly where it was – hanging from the willow at the bottom of the garden, beside the pool. She and her father had put it up, over twenty years before, and it was still there.

They had been a team: he was the boss and she was the apprentice, steadying his ladder, holding the hammer or the screwdriver, running errands. He always explained what he was doing so that she could learn. Together they had dug the channel for the little stream that ran down the side of the garden. They did everything together, but when he was faced with the biggest problem of all he had run away from it without a word of explanation.

Wide awake now Julia jumped out of bed. She found Charlotte's note on the hall floor and read it in the kitchen while she made a coffee.

There was a lot of work: the list of arrangements to be made and people to be contacted seemed endless. But Julia had no immediate plans, just a vague promise to do some walking with a couple of her fellow teachers, later in the summer when they'd all got some energy back. Her only firm commitment was to Andy at the Karate Club: she had promised to lead the self-defence summer school in a month's time. She'd better warn him so he could start looking for another tutor in case she wasn't back.

Charlotte had scribbled a note at the bottom of the list, squeezed into the margin. *When you call the mortuary they may ask you if you want to view his body. Be ready with an answer – they will need time to prepare him.*

Prepare him? Julia shuddered. Charlotte could be alarmingly direct at times. Her immediate reaction was no, she had refused to have anything to do with him for years, seeing him dead would be hypocritical. On the other hand she would never have another chance. She was still undecided when she noticed Charlotte had written another note on the back: *If you're not sure say yes. You can always change your mind when you get there.*

At nine o'clock Julia rang the hospital and arranged to visit the mortuary that morning. She fixed an appointment at the register office for later that day.

The road to the county hospital took her back through Polwerran. At the top of the hill on the way in she passed a large building site with a sign outside proclaiming "*Polwerran Park. A new future.*" This was going to be the theme park which was all over the front page of the local newspaper. As she approached the entrance to the site a truck laden with debris swung out onto the road in front of her. She followed it down the hill into the town, keeping well back to avoid the bricks and lumps of concrete which were threatening to fall into the road in front of her. The town square was now a narrow one way street and the truck had to inch round it, mounting the kerb as it negotiated the corners.

Polwerran looked dead. It had lost its harbour in the nineteenth century when the inlet on which it stood had silted up with waste from the mines. It became a market town, she remembered the colourful stalls which used to occupy the middle of the square, but they had gone, it was now an empty car park. The Victorian fountain, where the town kids used to play, was dry and covered in graffiti. Most of the shops had closed: only a newsagents, a dirty looking café, a betting shop and a small supermarket remained. The back entrance to the Ship, the old hotel, sat on the lower side of the square, looking tired and run down, the paint flaking off the stonework and the heavy wooden gates to the old stableyard.

What a dump, she thought. Polwerran was always going to struggle to survive against more attractive towns like St Ives, but it now seemed to have given up completely. She hoped the theme park wasn't too late.

Beyond the town Julia was finally able to pass the truck, and put on some speed. Halfway to the A30 she passed a modern industrial complex, looking out of place amongst the old farmhouses and ruined mines. The yard was full of trucks bearing the green and grey livery of Pascoe's Pasties. A huge billboard showed the familiar beaming face of Gordon Pascoe taking a bite out of one of his creations. They were on sale everywhere. She had tried one once, it was just good enough to be edible, but how he managed to sell so many was a mystery.

The mortuary was in a separate building at the back of the Hospital. A middle aged woman guided Julia to a small side room. It was bright with off-white walls and a large frosted window lit by the sun. The only furniture was a pair of simple hard backed chairs and a bookcase with no books, just a vase of artificial roses on the top shelf. Her father's body was laid out on a stainless steel trolley in the middle of the room, covered in a sheet which left only his face visible.

"I'll leave you," said the woman quietly. "You can stay as long as you like."

After the door closed Julia hesitated a moment then walked over to the side of the trolley. The room was cold, and she shivered in her thin summer dress. She should have brought a cardigan. His face was smooth and waxy white, his eyes closed. She was glad of that, she couldn't bear to see his defiant, defensive expression again. He had lost his frown. His hair was a little thinner, and had a stubble on his chin as if he hadn't shaved. Julia had read somewhere that this was natural. The beard appeared to grow after death, but that was just the skin shrinking.

She wished she could feel something, some empathy with him, but all she felt was frustration. She had thought she wanted nothing more to do with him, but she was wrong. She still needed an explanation, but she was never going to get it now. He had won.

She remembered the rows. Trying to get past his evasions, losing her temper and goading him into anger. They said unforgivable things to each other, and they remained unforgiven. Even now she couldn't say sorry.

The dead stillness of his body was starting to unnerve her. Julia leaned over to look at him for the last time, her face beside his.

"You should have trusted me," she whispered. "It was all I ever wanted."

She stood up and left the room without looking back. The administrator handed her an envelope with the medical certificate and a plain plastic bag containing his belongings. She took it out to her car, put it on the seat beside her and drove away quickly, still feeling the chill of the morgue.

The register office was full of noisy happy wedding parties and Julia felt out of place as she waited for her appointment, unable to get the arguments with her father out of her head. Driving back to the cottage she could feel the wall around her emotions starting to crack.

Outside the house Julia sat in the car, unwilling to open the door and face their old home again. The memories were overwhelming. But she couldn't stay where she was – Charlotte would see her from her kitchen window and come over to investigate. Julia couldn't bear that, so she walked quickly back along the drive and onto the path down to the sea.

The track was familiar: a couple of hundred yards following the stream as it wound through the woods, then out onto the cove. A great bank of shingle hid the beach beyond, the cliffs rising up steeply on either side. The stream curved round to the right, skirting the shingle, but Julia went straight ahead to the top of the bank. It was strewn with debris: dried seaweed, lengths of old rope, netting, cuttleshells and branches of wood smoothed by the waves and bleached by the sun. Dad would have loved it.

She sat down by the water's edge, watching the little waves dumping onto the pebbles. The sun was hot and the air still, but the beach was deserted. It was just a small, unattractive slope with no sand, difficult to find and anyone who did soon decided it wasn't worth the effort. But Julia liked it. She had learned to swim on this beach, doggy paddling between her mum and dad. She could feel the memories coming back again. She couldn't seem to escape them.

She took off her shoes and walked down to the water. The sea was cold, and the chill calmed her. She waded further, until the water was up to her waist, the dress billowing out around her. She took a few more steps, the beach shelved steeply and she was soon up to her armpits. She ducked under, drawing her knees up so she floated, feeling the tension beginning to flow out of her body. Surfacing, she looked round. There was still no-one on the beach, and no-one on the cliffs on either side. She pulled her dress over her head and threw it high onto the shingle, above the high water line, then turned and dived. She swam underwater for as long as her breath held, then set off across the bay at a fast, steady crawl. The water felt cool and fresh, very different from the chlorinated water of the Leisure Centre. She relaxed her breathing and let her body stretch: this was a distance swim not a sprint.

Julia swam for half an hour, back and forth across the bay, keeping within the line of the headlands to avoid the lethal currents of the Channel, only stopping to change direction. She was a strong swimmer, and the discipline of coordinating her breathing with the long regular strokes took all her concentration. As she finally made her way back to the beach, swimming slowly and easily, her head felt clear, her body tingling from the exercise. She put on the sodden dress and her shoes and trudged back up the path.

In the cottage she threw the salty wet clothes into the bath, showered and changed, then retrieved her father's belongings from the car. His clothes she put straight into the laundry. A smaller bag contained his keys, some loose change, and his wallet. She took it all into the kitchen and started working through it all, making notes of everything as she went.

The wallet was large, too big for a trouser pocket, old but well made. The leather was scuffed and creased at the corners. Inside there was a notes compartment with £60 in twenties. In the front were credit and debit cards, a bus pass and a National Trust card. Stuffed into the spaces behind the card slots were some receipts and a shopping list.

As she closed it she felt something crackle. Curious, she examined it more closely. Some cheap wallets had cardboard inserts to make them stiffer, but this one wasn't cheap. Eventually she found a compartment she hadn't seen at first, hidden at the back of the notes pocket. The flap was a close fit and difficult to move, but by moistening her fingers she was able to get a grip on it. Lifting it she found a photograph. It was creased as if it had been there for a long time. She put it on the table and smoothed it out.

The picture was of a family group. It was wonky and out of focus and there was something not quite right about it: it showed her father with one arm around her and the other on a small child. She put it down in disgust, it seemed a perverted thing to do, but a detail caught her eye and she took it up again, realising that she'd been mistaken. The clothes were out of date. She turned it over, and on the back was a pencilled note: Wheal Mawgan, May 1994.

"Oh, fuck," she said out loud. Julia wasn't the woman in the picture, she was the child. The adult was her mother Olivia, relaxed with her arms folded, waiting patiently for the ordeal to be over. It was the first picture of the three of them that she had ever seen. Olivia had hated having her photo taken, and there had been no family groups on the shelves in the cottage. There had been none in the house in Guildford either, which was no surprise considering what had happened.

It had been taken on the terrace, just a few feet from where she was sitting. She recognised the French windows. Seeing the image of her mother she was suddenly aware of how like her she had become: tiny thin body, short sandy hair and eyes that didn't like the sun. She was like her in other ways too: they were both quiet and serious, in contrast to her father, who was relaxed and easygoing. And untidy. Behind the wall in that photo the house would be chaos: bits of rubbish from the beach waiting to be turned into mobiles or "art" to be dotted around the house, mud from the garden or tar from the pebbles brought in on his shoes, tools from some DIY job which he hadn't got round to putting back in the garage. She could still hear her mother's sharp voice nagging at him to tidy up. It never did any good. But when he was away aboard ship testing one of the gadgets they were developing at the base, and the house was spotless, they both missed him dreadfully.

Julia noticed spots of water appearing on the photo and she wiped them away before they could damage it. She looked around to see where the water was coming from, then realised it was her: she was crying. She wasn't an outsider any more, dragged unwillingly into his affairs. He hadn't been indifferent to either of them. He was carrying their picture.

She wiped her eyes. It was nearly time to join Charlotte for dinner, but before she went there was one thing she had to do. In the living room she found a small print in a cheap plastic frame, took out the contents and replaced them with the photo. She took it into her bedroom and put it on the bedside table. Before she left she took another long look at it. There were many truths in that image, truths she wasn't sure she wanted to face.

3

"Malcolm Philips was my buddy."

The Reverend Beckinsale's high lisping voice slithered round the crematorium like an angry snake. There was an uneasy stir in the tiny congregation, these were not words they were expecting. Julia knew what he meant, and it cut through all her defences.

She had planned a short, simple service, with no excess of emotion. A couple of prayers, a generic eulogy, a standard hymn then it would be over, her duty done. She had nothing to mourn. Not even his will, which had arrived the day before, could change her feelings. Charlotte had brought it with the rest of the day's post, a plain envelope with a Guildford postmark, containing a single sheet of A4 paper.

"To Charlotte Ounslow I leave £1000 for being such a good friend," Julia read out.

Charlotte broke down, reaching for a tissue to wipe away her tears, not noticing Julia's expression as she read the rest of the will. In one terse sentence, devoid of either affection or explanation, he had left everything else to her.

Julia had looked at the paper for a long time, hurt by the contrast between his warmth for Charlotte and the impersonal simplicity of his words to his daughter. Finally she had carefully put the will back in the envelope and put it away with the rest of her letters. He wasn't going to buy back her respect like that.

She had kept herself busy in the days leading up to the funeral: cleaning the cottage, closing her father's accounts, packing away his belongings, steadily removing all trace of him from the house.

Only once did she weaken: in the back yard she found a piece of driftwood, a small branch worn smooth by the sand and the tide, slightly bent like the elbow of a small child. It was the sort of piece he was always rescuing from the high tide line to make mobiles to hang on the patio. She had taken it to a florist and it was now almost invisible at the back of a small bouquet of flowers.

The flowers were in front of her now, resting alone on the top of his coffin, picked out by a shaft of dusty sunlight shining through the crematorium window. The chapel was almost empty, the small group of mourners barely filling the first two rows of seats. Charlotte was beside her, sniffing noisily into a handkerchief, next to her was Charlotte's mother Monica, cool and elegant. Behind them were her father's old commanding officer from the base, now retired to the coast a few miles away, a cousin from Lincolnshire, and a dozen local people that Julia didn't recognise.

Beckinsale's squeaky voice drifted into a meaningless sermon on the value of friendship and the congregation settled down to listen in polite silence. For Julia, however, his words had opened another wound. She was ten, helping her father rinse out his scuba gear in the bath. She had been too young to dive herself, but he had taught her the theory: neutral buoyancy, the effects of water pressure, the magic of the regulator which gave you air at the right pressure regardless of how deep you were. *One day you'll be my buddy,* he had said. Not this effeminate little vicar. Me.

Five years facing the teenagers at the Holy Innocents, with their instinct for weakness and uncertainty, had taught Julia how to hide her feelings. But this was hard. Beckinsale could not have picked a better metaphor for everything she had lost. She had to find a way to get through the rest of the service without breaking down completely. The answer surprised her.

Confront it, she told herself. *Treat it like a scientific problem. You've spent fifteen years angry with him because of what he did. You never once thought about why.*

In his wallet he had kept a photo of the three of them. Julia looked at every day. It nagged at her, suggesting that she had been wrong about him, that her father's situation had been more complicated than her ten year old mind had been ready to accept.

Unquestionably, he had let her down. In the middle of the crisis, without any explanation, he had changed. He stopped searching, he wouldn't answer her questions, becoming defensive when she persisted. He ignored her ideas for new places to look, like the unmarked mineshafts which she and Charlotte had found in the woods and on the cliffs. When, finally, he told her to pack it was an order, sharp, not to be questioned. Her love for him died in those few weeks, and for the first time he frightened her.

In the seat beside her Charlotte was starting to fidget. The Reverend was going on too long. Julia dropped her eyes and studied her hands.

He had told her they were never coming back, and yet he had, in secret. When he became ill he had asked to speak to Julia, but he had died before Charlotte could pass on the message. She would never know what he wanted to say.

But even as she thought that Julia felt a tickle in her stomach. Her subconscious was telling her it wasn't true. She closed her eyes to concentrate. She immediately felt Charlotte's hand grasp hers, she wanted to shake it away, it was distracting her thoughts, but she stopped herself; Charlotte was kind and she meant well.

Put yourself in his position. He needs to get a message to his daughter, he asks Charlotte to tell her he wants to speak to her. But since leaving home Julia had blocked his every attempt to contact her: she ignored his phone calls, binned his e-mails, shredded his letters unopened. Had he been hoping that a plea coming from Charlotte would have more success? Perhaps, but he was a realist, he would have known it might not work.

So how would he make contact with her? Was there any way he could be sure to catch and hold her attention?

Julia opened her eyes and stared at the coffin in astonishment.

I want Julia to scatter my ashes from the Benjamin Steps.

He'd set her a puzzle.

"We will now sing *The Lord is my shepherd.*"

The vicar's words cut briefly into her thoughts. She stood, not joining in the singing. She was nine again, and it was Christmas 1993. It had been cold and sunny, no snow. Her present from her father, amongst the pile of parcels below the tree, had been a simple envelope. Inside was a small piece of paper with a handwritten question on it. *What's the biggest weed in the world?*

Julia had looked at him in disgust. This was a Christmas present? But she had known the answer: a willow. There was one at the bottom of the garden, they had hung the wind chime on it. He'd given her an encouraging nod and she had reluctantly trotted down the lawn. Why couldn't she have a Gameboy like everybody else? But she knew she had to find out what he had planned for her. Pinned to the back of the tree was a second envelope. She could no longer remember the details, it was something mathematical which led her pacing up towards the rockery and another note. And so it went on for another half hour. She would never admit it but she was enjoying it. Finally she was pushing back the door to the garage and claiming the beribboned box on the workbench. It was a chemistry set. It was the start of her deep interest in science.

He had always known that Julia could not resist a problem, and would worry at it until she solved it. She never gave up. Now he had given her his last.

Am I making this up? She asked herself. *Was he really trying to drag me back into his life?*

Of course he was. The request was exactly the sort of thing he would write. No explanation, no elaboration, just a simple challenge. *Find the Benjamin Steps*, he was whispering to her, *they're important.*

The hymn finished, and they remained standing for the committal. As the curtain closed round the coffin Julia knew she could simply ignore all of this: go through the motions of finding the Steps, sell the cottage and move on. No-one would know what she had rejected. But her father had known her too well.

"You're on," she said quietly, before turning her back and leading the congregation out into the sunlight.

4

Before she could begin to honour her promise Julia had first to endure the reception.

"There's no point," she had said. "No-one knew he was here. They're not going to join in a celebration of his life."

Charlotte was adamant. "They will, Julia. He knew a lot of people, and they'll want to pay their respects. Don't worry, I'll organise it."

Julia was right: there was only a modest queue of people making their way up to the farmhouse. She recognised none of them, but most seemed to know her, nodding sympathetically and muttering condolences as they shuffled past and into the hall.

The guests were gathered in the parlour, a large sitting room which took up the whole of the right hand end of the ground floor. Julia remembered it as gloomy and stuffy, the only light coming from a bay window at the front, but now there were windows on all three sides and the room was bright and welcoming. By the side window a middle aged woman was sitting stiffly upright, a cup of tea in her hand, looking at her as if trying to attract Julia's attention. She hadn't been at the cremation, although the look of authority on her face was familiar.

"Sorry I missed the funeral," the woman said as Julia approached. "I had a puncture. Wretched lorries, spilling nails all over the town centre. Price of progress, I suppose."

Julia recognised the deep voice of her old headmistress.

"Mrs Jeffries? How lovely to see you. Are you still at the school?"

"Until I die."

She didn't seem to realise how inappropriate her remark was. Julia had a sudden vision of the last time they'd met: in the Study, sitting on one of the chairs normally reserved for adults, looking up into Mrs Jeffries's face scowling at the speakerphone as she ordered Monica to come and pick Julia up. Julia impatient to start looking, afraid of what her father would say when he discovered how she had failed him.

"Sorry to hear about Malcolm," Mrs Jeffries went on. "He was a good man. It must be difficult for you."

Julia muttered a thank you.

"Come and see us at the Circle," said the woman. "We can have a proper conversation."

Julia remembered the Circle, a local women's organisation, like a WI. Her mother had dragged her there a few times. She was saved from having to reply by the arrival of another guest, a tall, gangling middle aged man.

"I'm sorry my dear," he said to Julia, "I have to leave. Domestic crisis."

Julia took the outstretched hand. "Thanks you for coming," she said. She recognised him from the crematorium, Jim Feathers, secretary of the Historical Society.

"Laura," he said, turning to the headmistress. "Are you coming to the meeting on Wednesday?"

"Of course I am. It's my playing field."

Julia took the opportunity to slip away. The heat and noise in the room was making her feel sick. She made her way to the kitchen and escaped through the back door.

She walked quickly away from the house into the silence of the garden. It hadn't changed since she'd last seen it, fifteen years before. She found herself beside the little stream which bubbled out of the ground and seemed to flow upwards towards the hill before dropping silently into a deep dark pool. Its sides were smooth and unbroken and she and Charlotte never found out where the water went. Next to the pool was a palm tree, it had been the first Julia had ever seen. They would never sit under it in case a coconut fell on their heads.

The path took her to the kitchen garden, between the palm and the well which never had any water. Julia walked slowly between the beds of potatoes and carrots and beans, hearing the murmur of conversation from the house and the sad cry of the seagulls. When she reached the well she picked up a pebble and tossed it in, hearing the sharp clicks as it bounced off the sides, then the hollow clatter as it hit the bottom. She was out of practice: she and Charlotte used to send stones to the bottom without them ever touching the sides. She sat on the low wall, trying to remember what it was like to feel joy from throwing a pebble.

Visible beyond the far hedge was the roof of Mawgan Cottage. Moss was growing on the slates. Julia felt a sudden desire to be there, to stop moping and do something. The riddle her father had set her was waiting to be solved. She hadn't the slightest idea of where to start, but none of his puzzles had ever defeated her completely, this would be no different. She trusted him to that extent. The answer was somewhere in the cottage, in a place where she hadn't yet looked.

She caught the smell of cigarette smoke. Sitting on a bench, almost out of sight behind the vegetable patch, was Monica, Charlotte's mother. Julia strolled over to join her. Slim and erect, with short immaculately cut dark hair just turning to silver, she sat with an unforced elegance. Her black suit was silk, simply cut. I hope I look that good when I'm her age, Julia thought.

She smiled as Julia approached, and moved to one side to make space for her to sit.

"Come out for a bit of peace?" She asked.

"It's too stuffy in there," Julia said as she sat down. Monica offered her a cigarette but she shook her head. Charlotte had once stolen one from her mother's packet for them both to try, down on the beach in a sea breeze, unable to keep a match going long enough to light it. They had been too embarrassed to try again.

"I do miss this garden," Monica said. "I remember watching the two of you playing here."

Monica had been cool and unflappable even then, despite bringing up a young daughter and managing the house single handed. She and Truscott had divorced a couple of years before Julia and her parents moved into the cottage. Now she lived in a bungalow further up the valley.

"What will you do now?" Monica asked.

"I have to deal with the estate. I'm his executor."

Monica looked at her in surprise. "You two weren't speaking." It came out as a question.

"It's true, though," Julia sighed. "He's left me everything."

Monica stubbed out her cigarette.

"You've got a lot of work ahead of you then. What will you do with the cottage?"

"I haven't had much time to think about it."

"Sell it," Monica said firmly. "It's worth a fortune. It's a lovely quiet spot, and it's got a fascinating history. It was once the mine office. Parts of it are over two hundred years old."

"I never knew," said Julia. "Dad would never let me go into the mine." It was the one thing her father had absolutely forbidden her.

"I'm not surprised. It goes for miles, tunnels and shafts everywhere you look. You could easily get lost in there. But for a prospective buyer of the cottage it all adds to the romance. Everyone wants a place like that."

"Here? It's not exactly fashionable, is it?"

"It will be soon. When Polwerran Park opens prices in this area will rocket. Hundreds of new jobs, a lot of them for professionals like accountants and engineers. People who'll want to live somewhere a bit special."

"You seem to know a lot about it," Julia smiled.

"I've seen it happen. We appointed a new transport manager a while ago and it took him six months to find somewhere decent to live."

"We?"

"The Bakery. Pascoe's Pasties," Monica looked at her in surprise. "I thought you knew. I'm the Finance Director."

Julia had no idea.

"Of course, I was forgetting," she said hurriedly. It sounded feeble and Julia felt embarrassed at her own ignorance.

"I see," said Monica, with a wintry glance across at the farmhouse. "My daughter didn't think it was worth telling you. I'm also FD for Zenith, we're building Polwerran Park, but I don't suppose she told you that either."

Oh God, thought Julia, now I've started a family row. She knew Monica worked for Gordon, but Charlotte had given the impression it was a lowly job, like a secretary. Monica's achievement was impressive and Charlotte should have been proud. Julia changed the subject.

"You've lived here a long time, haven't you. Have you ever heard of the Benjamin Steps?"

Monica thought for a moment as she lit another cigarette. "No, why do you ask?"

"That's where dad wanted me to scatter his ashes, but I don't know where they are."

Monica shrugged. "Does it matter? He's not going to know, is he?"

"Perhaps not, but I will."

Monica gave her a shrewd glance. "I wish you luck then. When you do decide to sell let me know. I can get you a buyer without all the expense of estate agents."

Julia thanked her, and they sat in silence for a few moments. Monica had reminded her that she had a hard decision to make, and there wasn't much time: in a few weeks she had to be back in London for the start of the new term. But the cottage was a link with her father, one that until a few days before she didn't know existed. In spite of all that had happened between them she couldn't contemplate breaking that link now.

Charlotte called from the farmhouse. The vicar was leaving. Julia excused herself and hurried back.

"Thanks for running the ceremony," she said as they shook his hand.

"It's my job," he said simply. "I do wish he'd come to see me, though. We used to be good friends."

"I know. Scuba buddies," said Julia. "I'm sorry."

His departure seemed to be a signal and soon most of the guests took their leave. The last to go was Monica.

"Come for a drink one day," she said, embracing Julia. "I'll call you to fix a time."

5

Back in Mawgan Cottage Julia changed into jeans and a T-shirt. It was time to start. But where? Her father's papers had told her nothing, the only place she'd been unable to look was on his laptop. It was in front of her now, on the kitchen table, fairly new but dirty with fingerprints all over the screen, and impenetrable. He'd password protected it, the only clue a yellow post-it note just above the keyboard, the neat blocky letters in red felt tip teasing her: *dadoes*.

That wasn't the password. She had already tried it, and all the variants she could think of: upper and lower case, substituting a zero for the o, a 5 for the s, and so on. She hadn't expected to succeed, it was too obvious. He wanted her to find an association. When she had been ten the word *dadoes* would have had a meaning, but not now. She had kept those memories buried for fifteen years, she was afraid they might be lost forever. The room gave her no help: the bland furniture and décor belonged to another house, not the place where she had grown up. The shelves of books and magazines and videos, where all the knowledge was, were gone.

dadoes. Her mind remained blank, and after a few minutes she gave up thinking about it. *Go and do something else*, she could hear her father saying. *Let your subconscious scratch its head for a while.*

Not yet. There was a small chance that it really did have something to do with dado rails. There was only one set in the cottage, waist high on the walls of the hall. They were now painted magnolia, blending in with the emulsion on the walls so that they were hardly noticeable. It was as if the decorator hadn't liked them but hadn't the energy to take them out. Julia used a torch to examine them closely. The paint was clearly several years old, there was no sign of any recent tampering. There was nothing for her there.

It always started like this, with nothing making sense. She had to let him guide her, immersing herself in the problem, eliminating the obvious answers. The solution lay in something they had shared, here in this house. What was he passionate about? Gardening, woodworking – he'd installed a workshop in the garage, making mobiles from driftwood - walking, scuba diving. He was always active. Dado rails were made of wood, maybe it was something to do with his workshop. Julia hadn't explored that yet. It was late, the sun was going down, it would have to wait until the next day.

Back in the lounge she stood by the door, looking past the stacked boxes to the patio doors beyond. She could see him: in his hands seaweed and bits of rope from lobster pots which had broken free in the storms. Sand under his feet and tar on his fingers, mum shouting at him for bringing all the muck into the house. His conspiratorial wink to Julia. She was going to have to explore all of this.

"You bastard," she called out. "Why don't you leave me alone?"

No longer detached, she was beginning to feel the grief she should have felt at the funeral. These memories had nothing to do with the problem she was try to solve, she should get rid of them, move on, but they were too strong. She had lost her family, here, in this house, in this room.

"Oh fuck," she said, sinking to the floor, unable to stop crying. "Fuck, fuck."

Julia cried into the night, barely sleeping. The next morning she felt drained, moving round the kitchen like a zombie, feeling nothing. Her car was outside, she could drive off, back to

London, back to her life. Someone else could deal with all of this.

Then she saw the laptop again, and the red lettering. *dadoes*. Finally a faint frightened recognition. Rain, and darkness and neon lights. Julia stood very still, trying to pin it down. Where? What were she and her father doing? She remembered feeling scared but not admitting it.

Her mobile rang, and the image vanished. Cursing, Julia picked up the phone. It was Charlotte.

"Are you all right? I thought you handled yesterday very well."

"I'm fine."

"I've got your post. I'll bring it over in half an hour. You're not going out, are you?"

"No, I'll be here," said Julia wearily.

She disconnected and tried to retrieve the picture from her mind, but the vision had gone. Her subconscious would have to scratch its head a little longer. It was time to start outside.

The garage with its workshop was cool, a cavern in the hillside full of tools, smelling of paint and oil and sawdust. The other kids from the junior school would gape at it in wonder, Julia nonchalant. This was where she and her dad worked together, she knew how to use everything, except the big mitre saw, she would have to be a few years older before he would show her how to operate that.

The outer sliding door was old, green paint flaking away, but its heavy wooden planks were still strong and secure. It had a mortise lock with a hook which clamped onto the door frame. Julia unlocked it, the door pushed back easily, the rollers from which it hung recently greased. She switched on the lights, fluorescent tubes suspended from the bare granite ceiling. The railway track which had once carried ore out of the mine was still visible in the concrete floor.

The space was big, even with her father's Toyota Prius parked inside there was plenty of room in which to work. Julia remembered the workbench along the left hand wall, her dad at her shoulder guiding her hands as she sharpened one of his chisels on the grinder, sparks flying through the air like a Catherine wheel that had jammed. He had made a small wooden box for her to stand on so she could reach the worktop. The grinder was still there, and the wooden panel on the wall where the saws hung.

That part of the workshop hadn't changed since Julia was a child, but the rear wall was different. It had originally been bare breezeblocks, with a faded blue door in the centre. It led to the mine and her father always kept it locked. She had peeped in once: the darkness was so complete she had felt it would swallow her up, in the distance she had heard unearthly booming sounds, giant trolls deep underground ripping out the tin ore with their bare hands and flinging the rocks into massive railway trucks. His prohibition was unnecessary, she had been far too frightened ever to step inside.

Now most of the wall was covered by a brand new workbench, with only a two foot gap at the right hand, where her father had parked his motor mower. Drawers and cupboards covered the space below the new worktop, while above sheets of plywood masked the wall. Shelves ran the length of the wall, with power points on the left hand side.

Julia heard quick footsteps behind her and Charlotte appeared in the doorway, breathing heavily.

"The post," said Charlotte as Julia came over to join her.

"Thanks. And thanks for organising the wake yesterday. It must have been a lot of work for you."

Charlotte was dismissive. "It had to be done."

She looked round in surprise.

"So this is what he was doing."

"What?"

"Building that," she pointed to the new worktop. "He spent a lot of time in here but I had no idea what he was up to."

"He made it himself?"

"Yes, the last time I was here you could still see the old door into the mine."

She walked through to the rear of the garage.

"Lovely workmanship," she said.

"Why, though?" said Julia, half to herself. She noticed for the first time how clean it was. There was no sawdust on the surface, no splashes of paint or oil, no marks of any sort, just a fine film of dust.

"I don't know. He never told me why he was here or what he was doing. He hinted that he hadn't been well and he was recuperating, but he was never specific."

"And all the time he was quietly extending his workshop."

Charlotte didn't seem concerned. "He liked his projects, didn't he?"

Julia was running her hands across the surface. "I wonder what this one was."

She had checked the drawers and cupboards, they had revealed nothing, just more tools, pots of paint, and the usual paraphernalia of a workshop. No work in progress, no diagrams, nothing to suggest a reason for all the work.

"I'd better get back," said Charlotte. "I've got some bread in the oven. Do you want anything from Polwerran? I'm going in this afternoon."

"Not yet," said Julia. "I'll probably go tomorrow. I'll have some letters to post by then."

"Go in the morning and stop off at the Circle. I'll be there, we can have a coffee."

Julia was doubtful. She remembered her mother dragging her to the old brick built community centre next to the church. An unwelcoming, dimly lit entrance hall panelled in dark varnished oak, the draughty corridor where she had been forced to sit during the interminable meetings, the unfriendly faces of the older women as they queued up at the hissing tea urn.

"It's where everyone meets. Laura Jeffries is usually there in the mornings, and I know she'd like to see you. There wasn't much chance to talk after the funeral. The building is a lot more pleasant than it was," Charlotte saw the expression on Julia's face "Mostly."

"*Mostly?*"

"We still have our patron," she made the word sound like an expletive.

"Who?"

"I thought you knew."

"I don't live here, Charlotte. How would I know?" Charlotte could be maddeningly vague at times.

"You're just his type," Charlotte eyed her critically. "Best to be prepared."

Julia took a deep breath but Charlotte held out a hand like a policeman stopping a car.

"Gordon Pascoe," she said.

"The pasty man?" said Julia, surprised. "That's his bakery on the road to the A30, isn't it?"

"It's not just pasties," said Charlotte. "He owns most of the town. And because he's given the Circle so much money he thinks he can drop in whenever he likes. And he's not there for the coffee."

"Ah," Julia saw what Charlotte meant. But fending off a middle-aged groper didn't worry her. "OK, I'll be ready. Now you'd better get back to your baking."

"Oh heck." It was the nearest Charlotte ever got to swearing. "It will be burnt."

She hurried back to the farmhouse. Julia turned back to concentrate on the garage, hoping she wasn't letting Charlotte drag her too deeply into Polwerran's petty affairs.

The new workbench was bothering her. It didn't seem necessary, and that meant it was significant.

Julia found the car keys and reversed the Prius out onto the hard standing, next to her Fiesta. She wanted to see the whole space. She found a kneeler amongst the garden tools and sat on it in the middle of the floor, hugging her knees, her eyes level with the top of the new workbench. She let her gaze wander over its surface, taking in the Ikea drawer fronts with their brushed aluminium handles, the shelves stacked with pots of paint and plastic boxes of nails and screws, the racks of chisels and screwdrivers, the power tools on the worktop.

Why didn't it cover the entire wall? Why leave a gap on the right?

Then she noticed that the electrical outlets were all bunched up to the left: three double sockets spaced no more than a couple of feet apart, serving perhaps a third of the working surface, nothing at all for the remaining two-thirds. It seemed a curious thing to do. It wasn't to save money, he'd already spent a considerable amount on making the bench, he would hardly stint on adding power to make it all useable. Julia walked slowly back to the bench, feeling a stir of interest.

There was nothing remarkable about the power sockets, ordinary surface mounted boxes with round steel conduit between them to carry the power cables. There were no wires protruding from the last box, nothing to suggest that he'd been planning to extend the line of sockets across the whole bench.

As she leaned on the worktop her fingers felt a slight ridge in the surface. She looked more closely, brushing away the dust to reveal a fine line, running straight from front to back. Where it met the front edge it continued down to the floor; at the rear it went up all the way to the top of the shelving unit. She ran her fingers along the front of the worktop until she found a second ridge. Another line about 30 inches to the right of the first.

The lines disappeared when she stepped back. They were so fine they were only visible if you were up close. Julia found some small paint tins and used them to mark the front and back of each line. Now it was clear. The marked out section was exactly in the centre of the rear wall, covering what had once been the entrance to the mine.

Her father hadn't blocked off the door, he had hidden it. He was going into the mine and concealing the fact.

"Good work, daddy," she breathed. She had found the first clue, she was in the game.

Julia now understood why the bench didn't cover the entire wall. She wheeled the mower out of the space on the right, found a torch and examined the side of the drawer units. *Yes.* Just visible where the side of the carcass met the brick wall was the spine of a long hinge. With a ruler she compared the depth of the bench with the width of the space beside it. They matched.

The right hand section was designed to swing into the gap. Once that was out of the way the centre section had a space to swing into, pivoting to the right to reveal the entrance behind. That was why the power sockets stopped where they did: running the conduit along the entire wall would prevent the door opening.

But how to open it? There was no handle, or latch, or keyhole. The middle unit was bolted to the wall behind; the right hand unit had no bolts but it was still held rigidly in place. Perhaps there were concealed levers, but she could find nothing. They looked like completely ordinary cabinets. Julia found a spanner and tried to undo one of the bolts: if she could take the unit off it might be easier to find out how the door opened. But the bolt just turned without loosening. She tried others with the same result.

It was now lunch time. Julia drove the car back into the garage and locked up. Not being able to open the rear door was frustrating, but she hadn't expected it to be easy. She would succeed eventually. If he could get into the mine, then so would she.

6

Charlotte had been right: the Polwerran Women's Circle was much more welcoming than Julia remembered. The hallway was still panelled in oak, but it had been stripped of all the dark brown varnish and now gave the entrance a warm, airy feel. The steps which led to the front door were freshly swept and lined with pots of flowers and shrubs. Julia chained her bike to the rack beside the entrance and stepped cautiously in. A large baize noticeboard carried adverts for babysitting, a trip to the Eco Park and second hand goods: a fridge, several prams, and children's clothing. An A4 sheet with the words *Save the School Field* in heavy red letters, carried the date of a meeting two days hence.

Beyond the hall a brand new café area stretched along the entire rear wall of the building. At the right hand end was a serving counter stocked with sandwiches and cakes, a gleaming chrome espresso machine and a water boiler for tea. A large silent TV on the wall was showing Jeremy Kyle with subtitles. The dozen or so tables were all occupied and there was a low buzz of conversation. Most of the women were young, many with buggies. The shriek of toddlers came from a side room. At the opposite end of the cafe, furthest from the counter, was a group of older women, and amongst them Julia saw Charlotte, waving to her. At the same table was Mrs Jeffries, the head teacher, facing into the room, sitting erect like a queen looking down on her subjects.

The room went silent as Julia threaded through the tables to join Charlotte. It reminded Julia of the effect she had when she walked into a classroom at the Holy Innocents, but this wasn't the wary respect of teenage pupils, it was hostility. Indifference she expected, she was an incomer, not to be spoken to or trusted; but this felt personal. They were looking at her as if they'd seen her before, and not liked her then.

Julia didn't recognise any of them, however. Behind the animosity all she saw was despair, a generation brought up on benefits.

"Welcome to the Circle," said Mrs Jeffries proprietorially, as Julia took a seat next to her.

"Thank you," said Julia, forcing herself to smile, not feeing in the least bit welcome. She tried to find something positive to say. "This looks fabulous. It wasn't like this when I lived here before."

"We had it build five years ago. We've got a crèche, a women's crisis centre, a gym, as well as the old meeting room upstairs. It's everything we need."

"It looks like it," said Julia, looking round again. "Mr Pascoe must have spent a lot of money on it."

"He gets his reward," said Charlotte.

"Charlotte doesn't approve," Laura said to Julia. "She thinks he exploits the girls, but they're a lot more savvy than she thinks. I know, I taught them. He does pick up girls, but they know exactly what they're doing."

"They're mostly married with kids. It's immoral."

"It's life," said Laura complacently. "It happens all the time."

"It doesn't have to," Charlotte said. "Oh, and have you heard about Ben at the newsagents?"

Laura looked up sharply. "Not him as well?"

Charlotte nodded in grim satisfaction. "His rent has gone up again. He thinks he'll have to close."

She turned to Julia. "That's how Pascoe operates," she said. "He buys up a freehold, pushes up the rent and forces the tenant out of business, then leaves the premises unoccupied. He does that a few times and the town starts to look run down. Fewer people come in to shop, the remaining properties struggle to survive and eventually they fold, so he buys them, and eventually he owns everything."

Julia was puzzled. "What would he want with a dead town?"

"You've heard about our theme park?"

"Oh, I see. Once that's built the town won't be dead anymore."

"And he'll make his fortune," said Charlotte. "I'm not sure about anyone else."

"He's entitled to make some money," said Laura. "If it weren't for him this place would fade into nothing. We're an unattractive town with no jobs and no amenities, and the highest rate of drug usage in the county."

"We haven't benefitted from his pasty business," Charlotte retorted. "He doesn't employ anyone from the town. He's got Poles and Bulgarians and Pakistanis, probably illegal immigrants as well, people he pays a pittance and sacks whenever he feels like it."

"Your mum works there, doesn't she?" Julia ventured.

"That's different," Charlotte cried. God, that touched a nerve, thought Julia. What's the matter with her? She tried to change the subject.

"I'm dying for a coffee. Can I get one for either of you?"

"I'll go," said Charlotte. "You have to be a member to buy anything here. It will have to be instant though. That monster is another of his gifts and no-one knows how to work it properly."

She marched off to the counter.

"Mr Pascoe is an unlikely saviour," said Laura quietly when Charlotte was out of earshot. "He can still be sly and underhand, and we have to watch him. At the moment he's trying to persuade the council to sell him my school playing field, so he can build a hotel. We have to stop that. But he's the only one actually doing anything to help the town."

Charlotte had picked up her tray and was making her way

back towards them.

"It can be uncomfortable doing the right thing," said Laura quietly. "I don't think everyone here fully understands that."

"How long has he been…" Julia searched for a diplomatic way to ask the question. "…helping you out?"

"At the Circle? Over 20 years now. It's strange how people surprise you. I remember when he first arrived, little better than those yobs who hang around the fountain. Just another Pascoe, peddling drugs. Not as bright as his father, but with a certain charm, I admit. I never thought he'd amount to much. Certainly not a successful businessman."

"Another of your pupils?" Julia asked.

"I'm not that old," Laura retorted. "And the Pascoes were never local. They're Falmouth people."

"Charlotte has her own reasons for hating him," said Laura quietly. "Though I suppose you knew that already."

The coffee was vile. Julia felt out of place amongst these sordid preoccupations. She had expected that someone in Laura's position would be much less forgiving of the behaviour of a predator like Gordon Pascoe, however important his money was to the prosperity of the town. Charlotte's attitude was disappointing too. Julia was used to her cheerful side, she had never before seen her friend so bitter and negative. And what was she supposed to know about Charlotte's feelings towards Pascoe?

Julia just wanted to leave. She was forcing down the coffee when Charlotte leaned over.

"He's here," she said.

A change had come over the room. The murmur of conversation had become tense and expectant. Heads were down, everybody talking with a forced casualness, but Julia sensed they were all aware of the well built, powerful man standing in the doorway. He was wearing an expensive linen jacket over an open necked shirt. He paused, as if to emphasise his presence, before moving casually to the nearest table and greeting the two women occupying it. He pulled over a chair and sat down, talking casually to the mother while holding out a finger for the child to play with. He was relaxed and smiling, his eyes never leaving the woman or her child, but Julia saw that he was completely aware of the effect he was having on the room, like an actor playing out an intimate scene for the benefit of an entire audience.

He turned and spoke to the other woman at the table, then with an expression of regret stood up and moved on to the next table, leaving the two women to continue smugly sipping their coffees. The anticipation in the rest of the room was growing. Even Julia caught herself wondering what she was going to say when he reached their table. He was the only remotely attractive man she'd seen since she arrived in Polwerran, charming and confident, and undoubtedly successful. Stop being ridiculous, she told herself, he's older than your father was. But she still wished she'd taken more care with her clothes.

"Look at them all," said Charlotte. "Behaving like fifteen year olds."

"Shush," said Laura. "He's coming over."

Julia had her back to the room and didn't look round, continuing to drink her coffee until she felt his presence at her shoulder.

"Gordon, a pleasure," said Laura. "We have a newcomer. This is Julia Philips."

Julia turned to greet him. When he saw her face he looked puzzled, his practiced smile briefly vanishing before he was able to recover. It was all over in a second, Julia didn't think anyone else noticed. She shook his hand, calmly returning his gaze, which now looked a little forced.

"Julia is here for her father's funeral," said Laura.

"Malcolm. Of course. Such a good man," murmured Pascoe.

Julia nodded, not trusting herself to say anything sensible.

"Do you expect to be here long?" He enquired.

"Until I've sorted out his affairs."

"I hope we see you again."

With that he released her hand, nodded to Laura, then turned and left.

"Well," said Charlotte. "You got away with that. He's normally onto anyone new like a cat on a mouse."

"It's who you're with," said Laura drily. "He'd have had to endure the two of us. We've crossed swords before."

Julia said nothing, busying herself finishing her drink. It wasn't Laura and Charlotte who'd deterred Mr Pascoe, it was Julia herself. She had frightened him.

7

Freewheeling down towards the square Julia was still puzzling over the incident when her thoughts were interrupted by the sound of car horns. Threading her way through the stationary traffic she saw the cause: an articulated cement carrier struggling to turn from the square into the narrow street, shuffling back and forth as it tried to manoeuvre into position. Facing it, trying to turn into the square was a tipper truck laden with bricks and rubble. The driver was impatient, inching forward, making the situation worse by reducing the room available to the cement lorry.

Where are the police? She thought. They should be sorting this out. She finally squeezed past the truck and onto the square. At that moment the tipper driver finally lost his patience, revving his engine and swinging the truck left, mounting the kerb to get through the small gap left by the reversing cement lorry. He hadn't seen Julia. Suddenly aware of the danger she leapt out of the way as the truck loomed above her. She pulled at the bike but there was someone behind her on the pavement. She tripped, and before she could get back to her feet the bike was wrenched out of her hands, and with a sound like crumpling paper the truck crushed the rear wheel and frame.

She looked up in shock, unable to speak, the front wheel of the truck inches from her foot.

"You all right my lover?" A middle aged woman was peering

anxiously into Julia's eyes. Julia looked back blankly.

"They lorries didn't ought to be going this way," continued the woman. "I told my husband. Someone's going to get hurt."

Julia shivered as her mind began to work again. Half a second slower and those wheels would have crushed her leg. The driver had climbed down from his cab and was looking at her apprehensively.

"You OK?" he asked. Julia managed a nod. The woman turned on him.

"You should be ashamed of yourself," she said. "You've all been told not to bring they things through here, but you keep doing it. Now look what's happened. This lady could have been killed."

He ignored her. "Sorry love," he said to Julia, "I'm only doing my job."

Julia finally recovered her voice.

"I'm calling the police."

"They won't be interested. No injuries, just a bike. They won't send a car from Truro for that," he handed her a pre-printed sheet of paper. "These are my details. I'm working up the hill. Polwerran Park."

He climbed back up to his cab and drove off before she could ask anything else.

"They're all the same," said the woman. "Someone ought to stop them. Don't you be picking that up," she saw Julia reaching for the bike. "My husband will help you."

"I can manage," said Julia, snatching up the remains of the bike. If the police weren't going to do anything then she would. The frame was so buckled it was impossible to wheel, so she slung it over her shoulder and set off up the hill, the crossbar digging into her shoulder and the inside pedal rubbing against her thigh.

The building site was half a mile away, up a long hill, and by the time she reached the gate Julia was hot and sticky, her jeans covered in oil from the chain. Dirt from the frame had left dark streaks on her T-shirt. She dropped the bike in front of the security guard standing by the barrier.

"I want to see Mr Pascoe," she said.

"He doesn't work here."

"The manager, then." The guard looked at her dubiously.

"What's it about?" he asked.

"What do you think it's about?" she said, pointing at the bike.

"Oh, a claim."

He sounded relieved. "We've got a system for that. Just come into the security office and fill out the form."

He stood back, inviting Julia into his office, but she didn't move.

"I want to speak to someone in authority," she repeated. "I want an explanation."

"You can't at the moment. They're all busy."

"There's been an accident," Julia was controlling her anger. "Someone could have been killed. Now get me the manager."

He looked at her for a moment, as if weighing her up, then reluctantly turned and spoke into a walkie talkie.

After a brief conversation he told her to wait. Julia stretched to loosen her muscles, stiff from carrying the remains of her bike up the long hill. The hill continued to rise in front of her, but the whole of the northwestern face had been sliced off by years of quarrying to leave an ugly dark cliff. To her left, on the slope down towards the sea were the remains of the Park Estate, now out of sight behind a small village of portakabins. It had been the roughest area in the town, rows and rows of shoddy terraced houses and flats patrolled by weasel-faced boys on bikes. You never went into those roads alone. There had been a green with a playground in the corner. She and Charlotte had tried to play there once but the weasels had chased them away.

Now it was all being demolished, the bricks and rubble carted away in huge open trucks like the one that had run over her bike. Workers in bright yellow helmets were making their way in and out of the cabins. A van was unloading folding chairs into an empty cabin, while two men were wiring an electric cable to a junction box on its side. Further down a lorry carrying bundles of steel rods was parked beside the road. In the distance she could hear the revving of a heavy diesel engine and the crash of falling masonry.

Over the noise of the engines she gradually became aware of raised voices. Beside the lorry carrying the steel a man with a control box in his hand was operating a crane fixed behind the cab. A long girder was hanging from it, moving out towards a stockpile next to the truck, a second man holding it to guide it into place. The shout had come from a third man, who had just joined them. Taller than the others, he was gesticulating forcibly, pointing at the crane and then at the side of the truck. The girder stopped in mid air, then swung slowly back to the truck and dropped gently down onto the flatbed. The driver moved to the side of the truck, appeared to fiddle with a panel low down beside the crane and a stabiliser bar emerged. Julia saw what had happened. The lorry driver had been trying to save time by unloading his steel without stabilising the truck. With the crane at full stretch the weight of steel could have tipped it over. The taller man checked that the stabilisers on both sides were properly deployed before nodding to the driver to continue unloading.

As he came away there was a look of disgust on his face. He looked in his mid 30s, perhaps ten years older than Julia, with sandy hair visible under his yellow helmet.

"What's this?" he asked as he approached. He had a soft Scottish accent.

"The remains of a bicycle," said Julia. "Thanks to one of your trucks."

He gave her a sceptical look.

"Anyone hurt?" he asked, glancing at the wreckage.

"No."

"Good."

He nodded towards the guard. "This man can deal with your claim."

He turned to go, striding towards a heavily built man who had come out of one of the portakabins with a cigarette in his mouth. Julia looked at his back in disbelief.

"WHAT'S YOUR NAME?" her voice rang out across the

cabin village. There was a sudden silence. All eyes turned to look at her.

The man stopped, then turned to face her.

"What business is of yours?" he demanded.

"You are in charge here?" she held his gaze.

"Yes."

"Then tell me your name."

He hesitated, and in that moment she knew she had him.

"Munro," he said quietly.

"Why are your trucks going through the middle of the town, Mr Munro?"

He looked surprised. "They're not," he said. "They go across country."

"My bike was run over in the square."

"Then it couldn't have been one of ours."

"It was, Mr Munro. The driver admitted it. He gave me his details."

Munro glanced across at the security guard, who gave a tentative nod.

"Jesus."

Another tipper, laden with debris, ground up the slope. He flagged it down.

"Which way do you go to the landfill site?" He asked the driver.

"Through the town and out onto the A30."

"Why aren't you following the traffic plan and going round?"

"I don't know anything about any traffic plan. I take the shortest route."

"Well, I'm telling you to go round."

"And who the fuck are you?"

"Connor Munro. I'm the project manager."

"What project manager? My contract is with Kevin Fisher."

"Kevin takes his orders from me, and I'm telling you to follow the rules, or you won't work on this project again."

Julia looked on, astonished at his lack of tact. Munro seemed to have the interpersonal skills of an Rottweiler. The driver's face darkened as he leaned out of the cab.

"You do that sonny and you won't have a project," he said loudly and distinctly. "We have a union here, remember."

There was an impatient toot from a car behind. Munro glanced round quickly, and Julia was surprised to see a vulnerable look in his eyes.

"Kevin," he called, and the large man flicked away his cigarette and ambled over. Munro met him half way. After speaking for a few moments he came back to the driver.

"We need to sort this out." He spoke more calmly. "Carry on as you were for the moment. You'll get fresh instructions later. Just be careful. There was an accident this morning," he pointed to Julia's bike. "It's lucky no-one was injured."

It was the first sensible thing Julia had heard him say. The driver looked at the bike and the scowl left his face. With a nod to Julia he put the lorry into gear and drove out of the site and down the hill towards the town.

Munro turned back to Julia.

"Give your details to the guard," he said. "We'll pay for the bike."

"What about the traffic?"

"I'll deal with that."

"You'd better," she said. "I'll be watching."

8

"Someone is going to get killed," said Connor Munro. "You can't send big trucks through those streets."

He was standing behind the offices with Kevin Fisher, looking down over the site. Kevin was rolling another cigarette in his nicotine stained hands. There was a film of sweat on his face. The girl with her mangled bike had gone.

"No-one's going to get hurt."

Fisher's voice had an unhealthy gravelly wheeze.

"The locals keep out of the way, they know how important this is. It's only the incomers we have to worry about, and there aren't too many of them. No-one come here for a holiday."

"That girl didn't sound local."

"Probably wasn't. Schoolteacher I reckon, with a voice like that. Had you by the short and curlies, didn't she?"

Connor didn't want to be reminded of it. He wished he could wield his authority as easily. When he first saw her he thought she was just a teenager. That was before she spoke.

"Why take the risk?" He said. "Just send them the other way."

"It takes too long. We're already three weeks behind because of the storms, and we're right up against the Aquantas deadline. Miss that and the project is dead."

Connor knew about the storms; two weeks of hurricane force wind and billions of pounds of damage across the county, but they had saved his career. His predecessor Alex had broken a leg when the winds had overturned a Portakabin on top of him, and Connor was the only one available to take his place.

"Tell me about Aquantas," he said.

"They're supplying the rides. Biggest manufacturer in the world, and they know it. This may be the biggest theme park in Southern England but to them we're just another customer. You get your delivery slot and if you're not ready that's tough, you go to the back of the queue. Two years. No exceptions."

He lit his roll up, inhaled and coughed.

"I tried to get more trucks, but the council's requisitioned everything for their own clear up. I'm left with four. Not great, is it? If I send them the long way I only get three round trips a day out of each. Through the town they can manage one more. That's a third more capacity."

"Why not look further afield," said Connor. "It's not difficult. You could get them from Scotland if you had to."

"The boss won't authorise it, it's too expensive. Rates have tripled in the last month because of the demand."

He pulled a piece of tobacco from his mouth.

"It's none of your business anyway. We run the construction, not you."

"I run the project. You may be the main contractor but the grant money comes through my company, and I have to sign off that everything is being done correctly. At the moment it isn't."

"Don't get snotty with me. You're not in London now. If you stop us because of fucking health and safety everyone in this town will want to see your blood. If you don't believe me go and tell them in the Ship and see what reaction you get."

Connor had no doubt Kevin was right. Polwerran needed the employment and the visitors' cash. Cutting a few corners wouldn't worry them as long as it got the job done. He looked out over the site. Beyond the remains of the old quarry, overshadowed by the cliff, were the ruins of the green, the grass turned to mud by the heavy traffic, interspersed with islands of concrete where steel rods sprouted like rusty weeds. The green sloped down to the abandoned estate, a warren of boarded up terraces silently awaited their fate. Two JCBs were clawing down the first row of houses and loading the rubble onto a truck. As he watched the JCBs stopped and the truck drove away. The site was silent.

Where's the urgency? He asked himself. "There's got to be a better way than this," he said aloud.

"It works," said Kevin. "If you can come up with something different I'm sure the boss would love to hear it. In the meantime I've got a building site to run."

He ground out the butt of his cigarette and ambled slowly back to his office

Connor watched him go with a familiar feeling of helplessness. Another enemy. He had once been famous for his tact, always getting what he wanted without even raising his voice. Trainees would be assigned to work with him to see how it was done. Not any more. Since Swithunsgate and his disastrous run in with Conco every discussion seemed to turn into a confrontation. Conco, the biggest contractor in London, now refused to work with him and Connor found himself unemployable, stuck in the office, running costing models for new bids which never featured him in their management teams. When his boss Tony had called him in he'd been convinced that it was to give him the sack, but with Alex injured Connor was unexpectedly given one last chance.

His first reaction had been to turn it down; of all the jobs this was the one he didn't think he could face, it would be a constant reminder of that terrible day. Tony had been sympathetic, considering the trouble Connor had caused, but pointed out that if he didn't deal with his problem it would destroy him. There was also the more prosaic need to pay the mortgage on his Battersea flat, so Connor reluctantly accepted.

Once on site he began to feel more positive. This was to be Stevie's great legacy, not the shopping centres and office developments which drew crowds around the world, or the grand public buildings that had won him the Stirling Prize. It was The Ultimate Theme Park, the project that had obsessed him all his life. Now it was Connor's job to make it happen. His fingers found the little red Lego brick that he always carried in his pocket. He pushed it into his palm and closed his fingers tightly around it, squeezing until it hurt.

It brought him back to the present. He was right, somebody in the town was going to get hurt if the contractors carried on as they were, but being right wasn't enough when the party in the wrong was a powerful construction company. He could use the regulations to force Kevin to do things differently but he knew that the warnings were real. A building site was not a good place to be if you were unpopular. He would have to work out a viable alternative, then persuade the contractors to adopt it. The first stage in doing that was to familiarise himself with the site.

His eyes were drawn once again to the cliff. It puzzled him. Overpowering, permanently in shadow, it seemed to suck the life out of the whole area. He'd noticed it in the people working round him: silence, nervousness he'd never seen on a building site before.

What am I missing, Stevie? Not even you could make an exciting venue out of this dark depleted quarry. Unless... His eyes went to the top of the cliff, one hundred and fifty feet above him. That's where I need to be. He set off along the road as it curved round the back of the hill until he found a narrow dirt path leading to the top. It started gently, becoming more steep in the middle of the climb, but Connor was fit and he strode on without breaking sweat. Approaching the summit he paused to look around. He wanted to see it the way a punter would. Below him on the opposite side of the road was a field full of cows. That was going to be the car park. Customers leaving their vehicles would make their way back to the entrance, buy their tickets and board the Polwerran Puffer, a narrow gauge steam train which would take them up onto a bridge over the road, curving back and climbing across the slope of the hill, reaching the summit just above where he was standing. He continued the last few steps.

At first all he could see was the grass, sloping up to where the white portal would be. Through the arch the train would burst out onto a high slender pier, where everything would be revealed. The park below, stretching into the middle distance, towards the ocean, shimmering in the sun, dotted with white sailed yachts, container ships and tankers on the horizon. At the far end of the park the lake, with powerful water jets on either side framing the distant view of the sea. Closer in the railway track would run past the wave pool, the lido and scuba experience pools, the snakelike waterslides, the massive granite tower of Engine House, the dramatic swooping water coaster and the endless fountains, before dropping to ground level beside the River. This wasn't going to be just a theme park, it would be a visual experience unlike anything else in the country. Tourists would come just to ride the train. Stevie had turned the dark, menacing cliff into its greatest asset.

A gust of wind at his back reminded Connor that the cliff was still dangerous. He stepped away from the edge, and brought his mind back to the present. The rides and fountains were a long way into the future. The site was just a mass of trenches with white concrete at their bases, and forests of concrete posts, steel reinforcing rods protruding from their tops. In the middle distance were the beginnings of deep excavations for the swimming and diving pools.

Connor took out his phone and photographed the site, then turned back down the slope to continue his exploration at ground level.

His mind was still taking in what he had seen as he walked down the gentle slope towards the warren of deserted streets. Abruptly he found himself at the barrier around a massive hole: this was to be the diving pool. Looking down the hideous memory came back to him, and he turned away quickly, almost running into the quiet of the empty terraces beyond. When he was out of sight he stopped, taking deep breaths to calm himself. It's always going to be like this, he told himself. Reminders everywhere, you'll just have to get used to it.

He set off into the dark and narrow streets, canyons between the terraced houses, dislocated, with no sense of place, like a film set after the crew had left for the last time. There were no front gardens, just concrete and brick, with sheets of corrugated iron masking the doors and windows. He wandered deeper into the complex until he reached the centre, a forlorn circle of grass, waist high and smothered with nettles. This was going to be levelled to form part of the lake, the piers of the water coaster rising from its bed.

He felt he was being watched. A movement out of the corner of his eye caused him to turn quickly. A fox was standing just a few feet from him, poised in mid stride, its eyes fixed on his. Then it started, and disappeared into the forest of weeds. It wasn't Connor that had caused it to panic, it was a sound. Connor heard it too, a thump, like something falling on a floor, coming from one of the empty houses. There were too many of them, all close together, to tell which one it had come from. Now it was silent and still. Connor strained to listen, but there was nothing. Something for Security to deal with, but Connor had no radio and there was no signal for his phone. He made a note of where the sound had come from and hurried out of the complex to the perimeter road beyond.

Below him was the barbed wire fence surrounding the abandoned naval base. A row of decaying Nissen huts blocked his view of the sea. He turned right to follow the road along the fence. The houses here were in a poorer state than any he'd see so far, with broken gutters, missing roof tiles and moss growing up the walls. In one place there was no house at all, just an untidy gap at the end of a terrace, the outline of rooms visible in the end wall of the adjoining house. All that remained was a concrete floor covered in weeds and strewn with discarded furniture and rusting fridges.

The road took him around the edge of the estate and back to the top of the slope, at the opposite end of the cliff, where there stood a four storey block of flats. The ground surrounding the red brick walls was littered with beer cans and discarded syringes. He turned away quickly and strode quickly back under the cliff towards his office. He didn't like this place. It felt sullen and angry. He would make sure the park was built, but it wouldn't be a success. It made him shiver, it would do the same to others. The euphoria of seeing the glorious panorama from above would vanish. Like him, they would find themselves repelled by the stern granite face of the cliff.

9

Connor's office was on the first floor of the portakabin complex. Simply furnished with a desk and table for meetings, it had a solitary window which looked out over the site entrance. On the walls were a plan of the site and project schedule, now out of date. The room was stifling, like the inside of a car left out in the sun. He left the door open to get some air circulating while he called Security and told them to investigate the noise he had heard, then spent the rest of the day going through e-mails. Most were rubbish: adverts that had slipped past the company spam filter, pointless CCs from colleagues paranoid about ensuring they'd missed no-one from their discussions, copies of circulars on the latest Building Regs, a reminder from Comms that the deadline for his 500 words of background on the project for the company blog was due in a fortnight, and a backlog of messages from contractors about delivery dates, quality problems, availability of specialist equipment on site, the list went on and on. They all had to be answered, leaving him with no time to think about the Aquantas deadline. But it was Friday, he had the weekend to work on it.

He was staying at the Ship, the only hotel within ten miles, a run down 18th-century coaching inn with its white pebbledash streaked with grey and paint flaking off the window frames. Connor went in through the stables, now the car park, checking as he passed that his car hadn't been broken into. The reception desk was at the end of a dim, shabby corridor with a threadbare carpet. Sally, the manager's daughter, was at the reception desk, her head down over a textbook. She was young, no more than about twenty, with a mass of black hair and bright intelligent eyes in an open, artless face. She looked up with an uneasy smile as he came in. She'd seen the hard look on his face; he made an effort to appear less intimidating. He glanced down at the textbook.

"Mechanics?" He asked.

"Exam on Monday."

"Sooner you than me," said Connor. "So boring."

"It's engineering," she said as she handed him his key. "It's supposed to be boring. You've just got to learn it. Will you be eating in tonight?"

"I suppose so." He hadn't given it any thought. "What's the choice?"

"Spaghetti and chips, pasty and chips, steak and chips, curry and chips..."

"Oh, God don't tempt me," he said. "What would you recommend?"

"Casa Toccata in St Ives," she said instantly. "Don't waste your money on this rubbish."

"Tomorrow, maybe. I'm too tired at the moment."

"In that case have a pasty. At least it's authentic. What time?"

"Make it seven. Oh, and I've got a favour to ask. I need to do some work over the weekend. Have you got a room I could use? It doesn't have to be big: just a decent sized table and chair and some wall space."

Sally thought for a moment. "There's the private saloon, but that's big and smells of beer. We could try the Board Room. I don't know what state it's in, no-one's used it for years. Want to take a look?"

She took out a key from the desk drawer and led him up the stairs to the back of the building. The board room was small, about ten feet square. There was a long oak table in the centre with heavy leather upholstered chairs on either side. The walls were panelled in varnished wood up to a dado at waist height.

Above was plain wallpaper which had once been cream, now it was nicotine brown. Black and white photos of mines and prosperous looking mine owners hung from the picture rail. Everything was covered in dust.

"I can clean this up for you," said Sally.

Connor was looking at the photos.

"This was before the tin ran out," he said, feeling some sympathy for the town for the first time.

"It didn't run out," Sally corrected him. "It's just cheaper to mine in Malaysia."

Connor moved to the window. "My God!" he exclaimed as he looked out.

Sally joined him. "How short sighted is that?"

They were looking out on the quayside, its mooring bollards disfigured with rust. Where the water should have been there was only silt and bare heaps of mine waste. The sea was out of sight beyond a bend in the inlet.

"They built a railway to supply the mines, so they didn't bother keeping the harbour clear. We're all paying for it now. We can't fish, build a marina, nothing. Our only transport is a bus once a day."

"You could dredge it."

"No-one will pay for it. There's no local industry interested in a new harbour, and the council won't stump up anything, as far as they're concerned regenerating this area begins and ends with building your park."

It was another confirmation of the importance of what he was doing.

"This will be fine," he said as Sally opened a windows to clear the stale air. "I'll fetch my papers tomorrow morning."

One of the old photos had caught Connor's eye. A Victorian gentleman with ferocious whiskers in frock coat and top hat standing next to a wooden railway truck full of ore. Behind him the tracks led through the black opening of a mine shaft. His weight was on one leg, the other bent slightly at the knee. His hand was on the rim of the truck. He was looking to one side of the camera, as if he didn't care for the photographer. His face was square, his complexion dark, his eyes hard.

"Worst of the lot, he was," said Sally. "Those are his tailings blocking the harbour. Jeremiah Truscott, esquire. He never cared how much ruin he left behind so long as he made his profits."

"Truscott? Any relation to Monica Truscott? I've seen her name on e-mails."

"Her great great grandfather," said Sally. "She's finance director at Zenith. They own this hotel."

"And the building site."

"So Gordon's your boss."

"No, he's the developer and builder, but I'm independent."

"How does that work?"

"It's complicated."

Sally eyed him coldly.

"Well, I'm only a girl but I might be able to understand."

"Mr Pascoe's company owns the land," Connor ignored the look. "He got planning permission for the park. Then he won the competitive tender for the building contract."

"To no-one's surprise," said Sally.

"The money for the park comes from the regional development agency. They won't give it directly to the developer, they appoint an independent project manager to handle the grant and report back that the money's being spent correctly. That's me."

"So Gordon works for you. Best of luck with that one. Nobody tells him what to do."

"We'll see about that," said Connor, with more conviction than he felt.

Next morning Connor drove back to his office and loaded his car with files and the site map. On his desk he found a copy of the Security investigation form: they had checked the perimeter fence and there was no sign of a break in. None of the houses showed any signs of a forced entry either. Connor put down the paper and looked out over the site. He hadn't been mistaken, there was definitely something going on. It had other implications, they could no longer simply tear down the houses, each would have to be checked first in case there was someone lurking inside. He wrote a quick e-mail to Kevin then finished gathering the files.

Back at the Ship Sally had cleaned the board room and the air felt fresh. Connor sat at the desk with the laptop still closed. The problem was simple to state. The site had to be cleared of rubble in four weeks. Kevin's approach would just about succeed: Connor had to find a way to do the same with only three quarters of the truck capacity.

He'd explored the main solutions with Kevin. There were only two routes to the landfill site: through the town and along the back road, half an hour longer. The drivers couldn't work more hours without breaching Department for Transport regulations. He couldn't hire extra drivers to work the trucks in shifts either, because the drivers were also the owners and they weren't going to let anyone else behind the wheel. The alternative of finding more trucks was still a possibility, but a last resort. Kevin had made it clear that if Connor wanted to do that he'd have to pay, and that meant finding funds he currently didn't have.

Connor was stymied. There seemed to be no solution, and he was forced to consider that Kevin's solution might actually be the best for everyone. Before agreeing that, however, he wanted to see if there was anything in the project plans which might help him.

A theme park had first been proposed 16 years before, in 1994. The MOD had announced that the naval base was to close and the Council produced a development plan for the area, which was already suffering from high unemployment. The plan was deliberately vague: it simply suggested an amusement park, something light-hearted to complement the more serious Eco-Park at St Austell. Bidders were invited to present their own ideas. It was then that Gordon Pascoe realised he had a distinctive asset: his company Zenith had a tract of land with a spring rising near the top of the slope, the water running down to the lower boundary in a pipe buried deep under the soil.

The stream was pure and the volume substantial, and the idea of a water-based park was born. The initial proposals were cheap and unimaginative, however, and they were rejected. However Pascoe was persistent and over the following years he produced more variations on his plan. He did not give up easily. Finally, after more than a decade, he succeeded. At an exhibition in London he saw a revolutionary concept for a water park. He invited the architect to develop a proposal for his project. This was accepted, the funds were granted, and detailed design work started.

Connor knew all about the concept, he'd helped to create it. He felt for the Lego brick in his pocket, a reminder of the last great model they had built together.

By late afternoon Connor had a much better understanding of the project, and a growing realisation of how important it was. The paperwork seemed in order, but he still had no solution to the demolition problem. His concentration was beginning to fade so he decided to take a break, a walk along the cliffs would clear his head. The map on his phone took him from the hotel to the disused quay, left and up the hill on a narrow road which ran parallel with the coast. At the top of the hill the road dropped down to cut through the remains of the naval base. Concrete blocks and rusting barbed wire prevented cars getting through but a narrow path had been opened for walkers. Away to his left were the derelict houses of his building site, and beyond them the bare rock of the cliff.

In front of him was the uncompromising West Cornwall landscape. There was nothing of the grandeur he'd seen from above the building site, just an exposed coastal strip where only grass and low shrub were able to withstand the Atlantic storms, the tiny fields with their grey stone walls, some growing root vegetables, others grazing cattle. Everywhere reminders of the industrial past, crumbling engine houses and heaps of mine waste. There was a forlorn beauty to it all, a gloom which the bright sun and cloudless sky could not overcome. This was a land which belonged to winter. His doubts about Stevie's judgement came back to him. Why would anyone choose to visit this derelict landscape?

Beyond the narrow path the road resumed, curving uphill again and winding between the fields. He passed rutted tracks leading into fields, then a newly surfaced drive blocked by substantial metal gates with CCTV cameras on either side. It was the first sign of prosperity he'd seen, unwelcoming though it appeared.

The footpath he was looking for was less than a hundred metres beyond, a dusty track which took him along the side of a field and out onto a headland. The ocean below him was calm, gulls bobbing up and down on the low swell. High above him a skylark twittered, invisible against the blue sky. He lay down, letting the warm sun relax his body. He dozed for a while, and when he awoke his head was no longer filled with spreadsheets and Gantt charts.

In the water below him he noticed a pod of seals, like a pack of large floating dogs, just off a small deserted cove. Watching them Connor felt a twinge of loneliness. This was the sort of place he and Billie used to explore. Not any more: she hadn't been able to cope with Connor's breakdown, their relationship much more superficial than either of them had guessed. Billie, a solicitor, was now killing herself in pursuit of Partnership. Marriage would have been a disaster, but he still missed her.

His map showed him a path to the cove further along the road, beside a farm track. It wasn't far away so he decided to try it. It was easy to find the track, a tarmac lane barred by an old wooden gate held closed by an electronic lock. On the top bar of the gate a faded sign announced that this was Mawgan Farm. Strands of barbed wire discouraged anyone from climbing over. On a post beside it were two mail boxes and intercoms, one for the farm, the other for Mawgan Cottage.

The hedges on either side of the gate looked impenetrable, but eventually he found a tiny gap a few yards to the left. He squeezed through, picking away the brambles until he found a recognisable track which wound down into a valley, passing through woods for a quarter of a mile before meeting a stream, the farm track on the opposite side. His progress was slow: the storms had brought down branches which hadn't been cleared from the path. In amongst the foliage were the ruins of a mine: an engine house covered in ivy, its chimney reduced to a short stump, and next to it a spoil heap where tentative weeds sprouted. Further down he passed a farmhouse and yard, although there was no sign that the farm was working: there was no mud in the yard and the outbuildings looked as if they had been converted into accommodation. An old Land Rover was parked in front of the farmhouse. Just beyond the farm the stream disappeared for a short distance behind a fence, a neat bungalow just visible at the top of the slope. After another ten minutes of walking the woods ended and he came to the open cove.

It was nothing special, maybe 30 yards across, with a flat expanse of grass and a shingle bank strewn with dried out seaweed, driftwood, bits of netting and plastic bottles. On the far side the bank shelved steeply down to the sea. There was no sand, which probably explained why it was deserted. It did look like a good place for swimming, though.

He sat down to watch the seals. For ten minutes they stayed quite close to the shore. He tried to work out how many there were: at least six, that's how many he counted on the surface at the same time. Then they all sank into the water simultaneously, and he didn't see them again.

Connor lay back, looking at the sky. He was a long way from the office redevelopments he was used to in London: noisy, chaotic, frantic pressure to complete every build so the owners could start earning rents from their fantastically expensive real estate. Sophisticated project management systems constantly analysing the schedule, looking for opportunities to save time and cost. Sites bounded by a mediaeval street layout, never enough space to store materials: goods arriving only when they were needed and immediately put to use. GPS transponders on delivery lorries so they could adapt build schedules in real time.

He sat up. His daydream had given him an idea.

He was so used to these tiny inner-city sites that he'd made the same assumption as Kevin, that the rubble had to be taken off site immediately. It didn't, it just had to be out of the way. The Park was vast, there had to be a place where there weren't going to be any foundations for the rides, where the material could be piled up temporarily. Moving the rubble from one part of the site to another would be a lot faster than taking it on a sixty mile round trip to landfill.

Buoyed by this idea he went quickly back to the Ship to study the site plan he'd stuck on the boardroom wall, looking for a space that wasn't covered by one of the rides. The tubes of the slides and the tracks of the rollercoasters covered most of the park, but there was one space where there were no rides: a maintenance area at the top of the site, where the block of flats currently stood.

An hour's work on the laptop satisfied him that the space was big enough. He went down to dinner knowing he had his solution.

The nightmares woke him at three in the morning. The same pattern: a barking dog leading him into foundations which became deeper and deeper, darkness taking over until he was looking into a void, an immobile, spreadeagled figure faintly discernible in the depths. He called out a warning, as he always did, and woke with his duvet thrown to the floor and the mattress visible around the crumpled sheet. As he was repairing his bed he glanced at the window: he'd left the blind open to let fresh air in and he could see bits of the square through the gaps. To his right a vertical section with the traffic lights on the road out to the building site. More vertical slices: the left hand side of the fountain, a solitary car beside it, a boarded up shop on the far left. Clouds obscured the moon, the only illumination came from the drab orange sodium lamps and the red, amber and green of the traffic lights monotonously regulating the non-existent traffic.

That wasn't true. Just for a second he'd seen something else, the glow of a phone. Connor put down the duvet and moved closer to the window. Probably someone out late, it was Saturday night after all. Then he saw it again, in the same place, up in the corner beside the lights, its owner hidden in the shadow of a shop front. The lookout for a burglary? Amateurish if it was, the phone was a giveaway.

Connor settled down to watch, hidden behind the blinds, his own phone to hand to call the police if anything developed. Nothing happened for ten minutes, but the light never moved. Then, faintly, Connor heard the sound of an engine. A moment later headlights shone into the square and a white van appeared, driving slowly through the lights, past the no-entry sign and continuing the wrong way across the top of the square. Another, darker van followed close behind. It stopped briefly, the passenger door opened and a figure slid in. When it had gone there was no further sign of the phone. The square was deserted.

Connor went back to bed. Whatever was going on had nothing to do with him.

10

"I've found a way," Connor announced when he was back in Kevin's office the following Monday. The air was hot and thick with smoke. On the wall behind the desk was a project chart, a calendar showing an ample blonde gamely holding a jackhammer which probably weighed as much as she did, and a large red No Smoking sign.

"We don't have to wait for every truck to do its round trip to the landfill site," he went on. "We just have to shift the rubble out of the way so we can put in the foundations."

"What are you suggesting?" Kevin was sitting at his desk with a pint mug of tea in his hand. "We dump it all by the side of the road?"

"No, where the maintenance yard is going to be."

"Last time I looked there was a block of flats there."

"Which is going to be pulled down. Do that now rather than at the end of the knockdown and you'll have a space. Your trucks will then have a ten minute round trip instead of three hours."

"Until it fills up."

Connor looked at him bleakly.

"It's big enough," he said. "I've done the sums. You have one truck ferrying rubble to the dump, the other three carry on as now, except they're going from the dump to the landfill. I'm surprised you didn't think of it yourself."

"We didn't need to," he said, slurping his tea. "We had a perfectly good system until you came along."

"We've been through that. What you're doing is illegal. The council could stop you today if they found out."

"They won't, unless someone is stupid enough to tell them."

He paused to make it clear who he was referring to.

"They'll look the other way; they need this park as much as anyone. And in case you hadn't noticed we can't demolish that block without a high reach excavator, and that isn't due until September."

"Bring it forward."

"Can't do that. It's on another job, and there's not another one within two hundred miles."

Connor had thought this might happen. "I've got some contacts in London who'll be able to help."

"Think of everything don't you? Have you cleared it with the boss?"

"Not yet, but he's got no choice. You do it this way or not at all."

Kevin looked at him in amazement. "Would you seriously close us down?"

"I'm showing you a legal way of doing it." Connor avoided a direct answer.

"If the boss agrees I'll do it. He'll be here later this morning, you can ask him then. Now fuck off out of my office."

Back in his own desk Connor sat with his head in his hands. He'd made a mess of it. He had lost the knack, just when he needed it most. But there was still time, if he could persuade Pascoe. First he had yet another difficult conversation this time with his own manager.

"I need a twenty tonne high reach demolition excavator."

"Why are you asking me?" Tony Buchanan sounded impatient. "That's for you to organise."

Connor took a deep breath. "There's one in Reading for the Corridor development and I know their knockdown is ahead of schedule, so I want to borrow it for a week. I need you to authorise the loan."

"What do you want it for? I thought Alex had Polwerran under control."

"He probably did, but since the storms they've lost time, which they're making it up by sending the rubble on a short cut through the local town. It's dangerous, I've already had one incident. I've worked out a safer way but it means bringing forward another part of the demolition. And that needs the high reach excavator."

"You're not overreacting again are you?"

"Someone could get killed," Connor snapped. "Imagine the headlines if that happened. Layzells putting profit before people. Then someone might discover that it happened before."

"Don't threaten me, Connor."

"I warned you Tony, but you just ignored me."

"I passed everything on to the contractors."

"Who did nothing. You didn't exactly push them did you?"

Tony was silent for a moment. When he spoke again he was more conciliatory.

"I'm sorry about what happened, Connor," he said. "But there was no proof, remember."

"You didn't need proof. You knew. I showed you."

"For God's sake grow up. If I'd pursued it they'd have blacklisted us. We'd have been bankrupt within six months."

They had had this argument many times before.

"I just want the excavator, Tony, that's all. Do you think you could manage that?"

"I suppose I'll have to," said Tony grudgingly. "I'll get back to you."

He disconnected. Connor stood up and looked gloomily out of the window. Tony was right. Dealing with a cartel of companies which controlled virtually all the construction business in the South East meant making unpleasant compromises.

In the car park below him Connor noticed a blue van, *Mather and Mather Hydraulics* stencilled on the side. A man he hadn't seen before got out of the driving seat, a notebook in his hand. Connor went down and introduced himself.

"Tom Mather." The newcomer shook his hand, a welcoming grin on his face. He was lanky, almost as tall as Connor but bony. "Just making a routine inspection."

"Can I join you?" asked Connor. "This is all new to me."

"Sure."

Mather walked him over to the circular concrete slab just inside the site entrance. It was about a metre across, with a manhole cover towards the near edge. Behind was a small metal box on a pole, and beside that a vertical steel pipe about 15 cm in diameter topped with a gate valve and a blanking plug. A thin copper pipe rose beside it, with an ordinary garden tap attached to its end.

"This is it?" Asked Connor. "The source of our water?"

"Doesn't look much does it? But once you're plumbed in it you'll be getting 5 million litres of pure water every day."

He patted the big pipe.

"This drops down to the spring, about 50 feet below us. We use the smaller pipe to take samples for quality testing."

He unlocked the metal box. Inside was a pair of electrical switches and a dial marked in metres/sec. He carried on talking as he noted the reading on his clipboard.

"Those switches control the valves. Complete your plumbing, connect up and flick the switches. That's all you have to do."

"How do you know the flow won't dry up when we start using it?"

Mather tapped his notebook.

"It's been running steadily at four metres per second since we started measuring a year ago. Your park isn't going to increase the demand, just divert it, so there's no reason for it to slow down."

He closed and locked the box, then turned on the copper tap. He let it run for a minute then put a plastic bottle underneath to collect a sample for analysis.

"All that water," Connor said, half to himself. "Where does it go?"

"It's in an old pipe which originally fed a stream, way down the hill where the old naval base now stands. But sometime in the nineteenth century someone sank a mine shaft, near your boundary, and it cut through the pipe. So now the water drops down into the mine workings, to God only knows where."

"It must be a very old pipe."

"From the style, I'd say about two hundred years."

Connor was impressed. "That would have been quite an undertaking. Digging a fifty foot deep trench what, four hundred yards long? Why did they do it? To drain the land?"

"Probably. Before they did it this would have been marshland, boggy, unhealthy, no use to anyone."

Mather was finished, and turned go back to his van. After he went with him Connor's mind was on the ceaseless flow of water below their feet. How many billions of litres of water had made their way out to sea, unseen and unheard?

As they were shaking hands a black Range Rover swept into the car park and came to a crunching halt beside them. Mather's eyes widened, he ducked into his van and started the engine. As he drove out a large, heavily built man climbed out of the range rover and strode quickly towards Connor.

"Who the fuck do you think you are?" Connor recognised Gordon Pascoe from the TV adverts, but there was no warm-hearted bonhomie in his expression, just cold anger.

"I'm the project manager," said Connor, making an effort to keep his voice calm. "And you, I take it, are Mr Pascoe."

"Don't try to be clever. You know who I am. This is my project. You just sit at your desk and keep the bean counters off my back while I build the park. You don't tell my staff what to do."

Connor straightened up, so his eyes were looking down at Pascoe's.

"I look after Health and Safety, Mr Pascoe," he said. "I have to tell the Regional Development Agency that the work is safe, and at the moment it's not. The trucks should be going round the town, not through it. You know it, Kevin knows it, but you're still doing it. There are kids on bikes and scooters on those streets. If one of them gets hit by a truck it could be fatal. You won't have a project after that."

"You think I don't know that? We're going through the town because we have to. I'm taking the risks round here, so these people might have a future. I don't need a little squirt like you telling me what I can and can't do."

"It's my job," Connor didn't flinch, "and if you'd listened to what I'm suggesting you'd know you can meet your Aquantas deadline without endangering anyone."

Pascoe eyes opened wide.

"I heard you were trouble," he said. If it were my choice I'd have you out of here so fast your feet wouldn't touch the ground. But it isn't, so you stay. You may think that's to your advantage, but it's not. You think about that."

He moved towards Kevin's office. "I'll have your plan, on paper, by five o clock today. Then I'll decide," he said as he left.

Connor watched him disappear into Kevin's office before following. Despite his bluster Pascoe was right. He controlled the build, not Connor, and it had been a mistake to try to force it on Kevin without his boss's approval. With a shrug he climbed the stairs to his own office and put together the plan for Pascoe's approval.

Gordon's response was quick. When Connor arrived at the site the following morning Kevin was waiting for him.

"The boss wants to see you," he said, a sly grin on his face. "He's in my office."

Here we go, thought Connor as he trudged up to Kevin's smoky cabin. To his surprise Pascoe wasn't alone. Sitting next to him at the meeting table was a smartly dressed middle-aged woman. She was reading a file, completely at ease in the grubby surroundings. She looked at Connor as he came in, her face unreadable. Connor sat opposite, tense, suddenly aware that this was going to be difficult.

"This is Mrs Truscott," said Pascoe. Now Connor understood. Monica Truscott was the Finance Director: this was about money. She turned back to her papers without offering to shake his hand. Pascoe looked at Kevin and dismissed him with a flick of his head. When the door had closed he turned to Connor.

"Take us through this again," he said, tapping the paper Connor had e-mailed the previous evening. Before he could start Truscott intervened.

"We've all read it," she said. "Where are the costs?"

"They won't amount to much," said Connor, aware that he'd slipped up again. "A possible cancellation fee for the high reach excavator, a few days extra pay for the drivers."

"It's all money," she said.

Pascoe leaned forward, elbows on the table. "You try to impose your idea of what's safe and expect us to pay?"

"It's not my idea," Connor replied, resisting the urge to sit back and let Pascoe dominate the table. "It's standard practice. We have to safeguard the public."

"Don't fuck with me Munro. What I'm doing will safeguard this town for years. The people expect disruption. They know they don't get something for nothing."

"They'd change their minds if someone was killed. You're cutting corners when you don't have to. My responsibilities include health and safety, and that's why I'm requiring a change in your approach."

As Pascoe began to reply Truscott raised her voice, cutting him off.

"That is your right," she said to Connor. "But I'm going to invoice you for the costs."

Connor shook his head.

"It's your problem," he said. "You pay. And that includes the girl's bicycle. You're lucky she wasn't injured."

He stood up to leave.

"Don't try to claim any of this on insurance," he went on. "You're operating outside the traffic management plan. That invalidates your policy."

Startled, Pascoe glanced quickly at Mrs Truscott, but she ignored him, looking steadily at Connor with an expression somewhere between respect and hatred.

Connor returned the gaze.

"I hope I don't find any more problems with this build," he said.

Back in his office Connor stood at his window watching Truscott walking quickly towards an Audi sports car parked near the gate, Pascoe striding along behind. They looked like a long-married couple in the middle of a row. She slid in to the driver's seat and started the engine. Pascoe had barely closed the door when she reversed sharply and accelerated out through the gate, cutting in front of a departing truck and causing it to shudder to a halt with an angry blare on its horn.

Connor went back to his desk. It had been a dispiriting meeting. They should have known about the insurance. What else didn't they know?

He spent another two hours checking the planning consents. The land had originally belonged to a local farmer, Daniel Prideaux, who had sold it to a company, Farwest 80. They had obtained planning permission for housing, vastly increasing its value, before selling it on to Zenith. Permission to reschedule the land from residential to entertainment had been a formality.

Connor was satisfied. At least that part of the project was legal.

11

He had more immediate priorities. The excavator was arriving from Reading on a low loader the following day. He checked with Kevin that it would be able to get through the site entrance and across to the block of flats. Two more JCBs arrived and joined the others tearing down the houses. Piles of bricks and tiles and wood were starting to build up, the tipper trucks unable to keep up with the pace of demolition. They would deal with that once the dump was available.

These were twelve hour days: exhausting, but it was Stevie's Ultimate Theme Park, it wasn't supposed to be easy. But after a week he began making mistakes. He was hardly sleeping, and struggling to concentrate. His antennae warned him his actions were becoming dangerous, so he forced himself to take a break. He threw a towel and bathers in his backpack and walked out along the coast to the little cove.

Once again he had the beach to himself. The air was hot and still, the sea calm, tiny waves flopping lazily onto the shingle. The sun was still high and after changing he lay down on his stomach to let its warm rays relax the tense muscles in his shoulders. He closed his eyes and tried to sleep, but his mind would not switch off, repeatedly presenting him with problems which after a few panicked moments he realised he'd already solved. He gave up, and went for a swim.

The cold water felt tangy and refreshing after the chlorinated pool in Battersea where he normally swam. After a short fast burst to get his circulation going he settled into a steady rhythm, emptying his mind of everything except the activity of swimming. After an hour he felt pleasantly tired and swam lazily back to the beach.

As he reached the shore he became aware that he was being watched. To the side of the beach, almost out of sight under the cliff, was a girl, sitting cross legged and eyeing him steadily. She looked familiar. As he reached for his towel he nodded to her, then continued to dry himself. He wasn't going to say anything: they were alone, and he didn't want to appear to be taking advantage of the situation, although her relaxed posture suggested she didn't find him in any way threatening.

"You were a bit too far out," she called over. "The currents beyond the headland can be lethal."

He tensed as he recognised the voice. It was the girl with the bike who had tried to humiliate him on the site. Julia Philips: he'd seen her name on the claim form.

"I'll remember that next time," he said.

"Oh, it's you."

Her voice hardened. "What's happening about my bike?"

Reluctantly he walked over to her. If they were going to have a difficult conversation he wasn't going to shout. She looked up calmly as he approached, her eyes scrunched up against the sun.

"I've passed it to finance," he said. "It was an unusually large claim."

"It was an expensive bike."

"I saw that. It was a custom build. Finance don't like those, they can't value them by just looking in a catalogue."

"Are you saying they won't pay out?"

"Of course they'll pay. It will just take a bit longer."

She snorted. "And in the meantime I'm left without a bike."

"That's the way it is," he said sharply.

She looked away, uncrossing her legs and leaning back on her arms, stretching out in a way he found disturbing. She looked very attractive. She was wearing a small strappy bikini, and her limbs were slim without being skinny. Her skin was pale, as if she was at the start of her holiday and had only just begun sunbathing. Her small body looked vulnerable, as if it could blow away in the slightest wind, but her face was hard.

"What about your lorries?" She looked back at him. "Still going through the square?"

"You mean you haven't checked?"

"I shouldn't need to."

"It would help if you did. You might then be able to speak with some authority."

"So you have rerouted them," she didn't seem to notice his jibe. "You should never have allowed them to go that way in the first place. Someone was going to get seriously injured."

"You think I don't know that?"

"You let it happen."

Connor could feel the stress building up again.

"What the fuck do you know about it? I'd been on site less than a week when you turned up with your fucking bike."

She looked startled, but before she could say anything he turned to go back to his towel, furious with himself for letting her goad him into losing his temper. As he went a small Jack Russell terrier ran up to him, yapping hysterically, nipping at his ankles. He tried to shoo it away.

"Is this yours?" He yelled at Julia. She shook her head.

"He's all right."

A large woman in a silver shell suit was crunching across the shingle towards him. Behind her, huddled at the top of the bank were a man and two children, a boy and a girl about five or six years old. They were laden with beach umbrellas, folding chairs, airbeds, and an assortment of bags.

"He just wants to play."

"Tell him to play somewhere else," said Connor, as it tried again to take a bite from his foot.

"No need to take that tone," she said. "Honestly, some people."

She picked it up.

"You come with me, Charlie," she said. "Leave the nasty man alone."

The dog lunged at her face. "Naughty Charlie," she laughed, waddling back to her family.

"I don't think much of this," she yelled out to her husband. "I thought you said you'd been 'ere before, and it was nice and sandy."

The father dropped the bags he was carrying. "I made a mistake, all right? But we're here now. I'm not carting all this lot back up to the car."

"It's all pebbles," the boy had a petulant whine, "I want to go somewhere where there's sand."

"Well you can't, so give me a hand with this stuff. We'll go over there."

He pointed to a spot in the middle of the beach. The dog was free again and was now attacking Connor's rucksack. He hurried over to rescue it. He was tempted to leave but it was too early to go back to the Ship and if he went to another beach he'd have to take the car, so he settled where he was. He lay down, closed his eyes and began deep breathing to calm himself.

The beach quietened. The dog stopped barking. Behind him Connor could hear the electronic zapping of Nintendos and the rustle of a newspaper over the gentle rushing of the sea. He dozed. When he woke the children had changed into bathing costumes and were playing in the shallow water, jumping on and off an air bed. He heard the crunch of feet on the shingle and opened his eyes to see Julia making her way down to the water's edge. She had a light, purposeful stride, arms swinging naturally as she walked across the loose pebbles as if they were springy turf. Her body was slim and well proportioned, With her upright stance she looked much taller than she was. She might have been a dancer. Behind him Connor heard a low "Cor!" from the father, and an admonishing "Gerald!" from his wife. Connor watched for a few moments as she swam away in an easy, powerful crawl, then closed his eyes again. She had no right to be so attractive.

He woke to the sound of music. A song by Des O'Connor filled the air. The dog began howling, and the mother shrieked with laughter.

"You got a lovely voice, ain't you Charlie!" she cried. Connor bore the noise for a few minutes before calling over to them.

"Could you turn that down, please?"

"Fuck off," said the father. "It's a free country," and he turned the volume up. Connor could see Julia, who was back on the beach now, starting to gather her belongings. The mother released the Jack Russell and it threw itself at Connor, yapping insanely. Connor caught it by the collar, then froze. Something wasn't right. He emptied his mind, both hands around the twisting whimpering dog, trying to pin down the feeling.

The children. He couldn't hear the children. He looked quickly down at the water. The air bed, which just a moment before had been on the beach was now 30 yards out in the bay, the boy half on, kicking with his legs, propelling it further out to sea. The girl was sitting in front of him, hitting him with something bright red. Oh, God, it was her water wings. She'd taken them off.

He ran down to the water's edge. The current was taking them away at an alarming rate, but if he shouted a warning they might panic. He would have to swim out and quietly coax them back. He dived in and swam quickly towards them. He used a crawl, breast stroke would have enabled him to keep the children in view but it would have been too slow. During one of his stops to get his bearings another swimmer drew alongside him.

"Swim towards the end of the cliff. They're about twenty yards away." It was Julia. "If anything happens, you take care of the boy."

Then disaster. The parents had realised what was happening and were standing on the shoreline screaming at the children to come back. The little girl seemed to pick up on her mother's panic and started screaming herself. The boy tried to turn the air bed around but as he did so a large wave hit them. They were both thrown screaming into the water. Neither appeared to know how to swim.

Julia was ahead of Connor and reached the raft first. The boy thrashed towards her as she searched for the girl, who had disappeared. Julia duck dived, surfacing empty handed. She dived again. Connor reached the raft and pushed it ahead of him, towards the boy. He ignored it, paddling desperately towards Julia, who had surfaced again, this time with the limp body of the girl in her arms.

Julia pulled the girl onto her back and started to tow her towards the shore. It was slow work and in his terror the little boy was catching her up. Connor had to act quickly: if the boy reached Julia he would climb all over her and all three of them might drown. He pushed the air bed towards the boy, but as he did so another wave caught him unexpectedly and he sank briefly, his mouth full of water. He fought back to the surface, feeling a brief moment of panic himself, and looked round frantically for the boy.

He was still heading towards Julia. "Grab the lilo," Connor hollered, forcing it in front of the boy. The child took hold of it, trying in his panic to pull himself up out of the water, but he didn't have the strength and kept slipping back into the water, moaning with fright.

"Just hold it," Connor yelled, "I'll pull you back in." He started back towards the shore, swimming on his back, pulling the air bed with him, making sure the boy was still hanging on. It took all his concentration, he couldn't see what Julia was doing.

Pulling the lilo and the boy, using only his legs to kick, seemed to take forever. He kept talking, telling the boy to hang on, they were almost there. As they approached the beach Connor could see the boy looking to his mother, who was still screaming hysterically on the waterline. He was starting to think about letting go.

"Keep holding," Connor told him, "we're nearly there."

When they finally touched bottom Connor quickly pulled the air bed round, grabbed the boy, now wide-eyed with shock, and handed him to his mother, who had waded in up to her shoulders. She cradled him, crying herself, her eyes following Julia as she came up the beach with the little girl in her arms. She put the little bundle down in the recovery position, on her side with mouth open, head down and chin up, and immediately put her lips close to the child's mouth to check for breathing. The mother rushed over, but Connor held her back.

"Look after the boy," he said firmly. "This lady knows what she's doing."

She nodded dumbly, and stood watching, her faced drained white, her son clinging to her leg. Connor took out his phone.

"No signal."

"Try mine," said Julia without looking up. "In my bag. You'll get a signal if you stand in the stream. Tell them the girl is breathing, just."

She raised her voice. "We need to keep her warm. I need dry towels, a blanket, Anything I can wrap around her."

Gerald, the father, seemed to come out of his daze and found a huge bath towel amongst their belongings.

"Anything else I can do?" he asked as he handed it to Julia.

"Get hold of this bloody dog," Connor called over. The Jack Russell was attacking him again. "Tie it up somewhere out of the way."

Connor ran to the middle of the stream, and eventually got a signal. He described what had happened and what Julia was doing.

"What is your precise location?" The operator was a calm mature woman, from the sound of her voice.

Connor described where they were.

"I'm requesting a helicopter," she said. "It will be with you in about fifteen minutes. Now listen carefully. Firstly, the casualties must be well wrapped up. The draught from the helicopter will be very cold. Use dry towels, coats, use your bodies to shield them from the wind if possible.

"Secondly, the pilot will assess the area for landing. I have a satellite map which shows a flat area just inland from the beach. Move everyone away from there. Get them onto the beach itself, just above the water line. Understood?"

"Yes."

"Thirdly, gather up all clothes, towels, plastic bags, umbrellas, pets, anything that could be disturbed by the downdraught. It's important that nothing loose finds its way into the engine."

"I'll do that."

"The last thing is this. If the helicopter starts its descent and you see anything which might cause a problem you must signal to the pilot. Face the helicopter, raise your arms above your head then cross and uncross them to wave him away."

"Got it."

"Very well. Now get everyone away from the landing site and make sure everything loose is secured."

She hung up and Connor set to work. In five minutes everyone was on the beach slope, together with their bags and the dog. A frozen little tableau: Julia bent over the girl, the mother clutching the boy, who was now sobbing gently, draped in his mother's cardigan, the father standing away from them, looking out to sea, the dog under his arm, an expression of utter despair on his face. The wait seemed endless, but eventually they heard the unmistakable thump of rotor blades and a few moments later a helicopter appeared from behind one of the headlands, turned and came slowly towards them. It looked huge and ugly, a grey body with a dull red nose, the aircrew just visible behind the flat sectioned windscreen. The noise in the confines of the cove was deafening.

Slowly the aircraft moved inland over their heads, keeping above the cliffs. Connor staggered in the icy downdraught. Then it came to a halt, turned through 180 degrees to face back toward them, and slowly descended. The draught became visible as dust and pieces of dried wood and seaweed were driven into the air and flew towards them. The wheels touched down, but the pilot seemed reluctant to commit himself and only slowly let the undercarriage take the weight, ready to take off if the shingle proved too soft. But the ground held and eventually the engines slowed and the helicopter sat down on its wheels. Two crew members immediately sprinted towards them in a crouching run and took over from Julia. Connor couldn't see what was happening, but he knew the best thing to do was to keep out of the way. He was starting to feel desperately cold, he was wet and still in his trunks, the draught from the helicopter blades, still rotating, was freezing. One of the crewmen spoke to the parents and they began frantically picking up their belongings.

The actions of the medics suddenly became more urgent. One ran back to the helicopter and returned with a stretcher and an equipment bag. The other seemed to be performing some form of resuscitation.

Oh shit, that poor child. They put her on the stretcher and ran her back to the helicopter. The family joined them, urged on by the crew, almost forgetting their dog in their hurry to get in. The engine picked up speed, the rotor blurred and the helicopter took off again, subjecting them to yet more downdraught. It flew back over their heads and out to sea before turning left and disappearing from sight.

It was all over, as suddenly as it had started. Connor sat down on the beach, his mind a blank. After the chaotic thunder of the helicopter the silence seemed just as loud, and only gradually did he become aware of real sound again, the thump as each wave hit the beach, the chuckling hiss of the foam as it ran back down the slope.

Julia was looking out towards the headland where the helicopter had turned from view, a blank expression on her face. Then she slowly sat down, pulling her knees up to her chin and wrapped her arms round her knees, pulling herself so tight that her hands turned pale. She was shivering, and that jerked him into life. He fetched a towel from his bag and draped it over her shoulders. She didn't seem to notice.

"Stupid, stupid people," she said. "Stupid, stupid." He

thought she was going to break down, but she didn't. He could see tears starting in her eyes but she controlled them. He sat down near her, his own mind still refusing to take in what had happened. He looked round at the empty beach, for a brief moment he couldn't remember where the family had gone.

They both remained there, staring out at the sea, for a long time. It was as if neither of them knew what to do next. Eventually he heard footsteps on the shingle behind them. A large woman in a red dress with wild black hair was marching purposefully towards them.

"Julia!" she cried. "What on earth is going on? Are you all right? Was that the Air Sea Rescue helicopter?"

Julia slowly unclasped her arms and stood up to face the newcomer.

"Hello Charlotte." Her voice was flat. "There was an accident."

She explained what had happened without a trace of emotion, speaking like a newsreader.

"I knew it," said the woman when Julia had finished. "I keep telling them to put up signs. It's such a dangerous beach for children. Come on, you'd better come back to the house. You're both shivering. You need a hot drink."

Connor was roused from his torpor. "I really need to be getting back to the hotel," he said.

"Nonsense, you're coming with me. Charlotte, by the way," she said unnecessarily. "We live at the farm up the valley."

"Connor."

She put an enormous arm around Julia and started to march her back up the beach, but Julia struggled free.

"I'm all right," she said sharply, turning to pick up her bag and clothes. Connor dressed quickly, stuffed his towel and bathers in his backpack and followed them. Julia had bits of seaweed in her hair. Connor felt completely unequal to the situation. Who the hell was this woman?

When they reached the farmhouse Julia disappeared into a bathroom while Charlotte led Connor into an enormous kitchen. It took up the entire side of the house, with windows on the front and side and a door at the back. There was a massive cooking range radiating heat, despite the warmth of the summer evening, and the room was sweltering. Condensation was running down the windows. The middle of the room was taken up by a huge table, covered with books and toys. At the far end three young children were sitting with colouring books. There were two boys who looked like twins and a younger girl. In the corner of the room a large German Shepherd was noisily lapping up water from a bowl on the floor.

"This is Connor," said Charlotte to the children. "This is Josh and Miles and Ginny. Connor and Julia have just rescued a little boy and girl from the sea."

"Did you come in the helicopter?" Asked Josh.

"No, I was already there."

"We like helicopters. We've been drawing pictures of them." He pushed a crayon drawing at him.

"Very good," said Connor automatically, trying to loosen his clothes, which were already starting to cling to his body. The drawing looked like a cross between a jumbo jet and a windmill. As he handed it back Julia came in, wearing a simple summery dress which made her look about fifteen. She sat down opposite him, avoiding everybody's eyes. The children looked at her warily before going back to their drawings. The dog padded over to Julia, its feet slapping on the tiled floor, and rested its head in her lap. She stroked it gently.

"Tea," said Charlotte emphatically, putting huge mugs in front of him and Julia. He took a dutiful sip, it was sweet and milky and tasted revolting.

"It will do you good," said Charlotte, seeing his dubious expression. "You've both had a shock. Those people were very lucky you were both there. Are you warm enough? I can fetch you both jumpers if you like."

"I'm fine," he said. He was starting to feel sick. "I really ought to be going. You've been very kind but I need to get back to my hotel."

"When you've finished your tea," she was treating him like

one of her children. "Are you on holiday? I haven't seen you here before."

"No, I'm working." Why can't she leave me alone?

"Oh, you must be at Park an Jowl."

The children stopped playing and crowded round him. Was it really the biggest in the world? How many rides were there? Did some of them really go underground? They started arguing over which ride was the best. Disaster Mine, Engine House, The Donkey. Their voices got louder, Miles scoffing at his brother's choice, and both of them shouting down their sister, who eventually burst into tears and ran to her mother. Charlotte yelled at them all to shut up, but they were too excited to pay any attention to her. Then the dog started barking, and suddenly Connor was watching another Alsatian, a guard dog on a building site, looking down into a huge pit, yipping and mewing piteously.

He had suppressed that image for years, but these insensitive people had brought it back. He pushed away the mug, grabbed his backpack and made for the door, narrowly avoiding the little girl. Out in the yard the air felt cool and fresh and quiet, but it couldn't banish that horrific sight from his mind. He looked around for the drive, but he was disorientated, he couldn't see past the outbuildings which seemed to surround him. He was starting towards the bottom of the yard, hoping to find an exit, when he heard the sound of footsteps behind him.

"Connor, wait." It was Julia. It was the first time she'd used his name. He stopped, unable to face her. He didn't want to face any of them, but she stood in front of him, her expression anxious.

"I can't stay here," he said. "I…"

Connor couldn't finish the sentence. He was trying to get the image out of his head, but the picture of Julia carrying the limp child would take its place. He wasn't coping, but then Julia came up to him and took both his hands in hers, pulled them gently together in front of his chest and clasped her own hands around his. Her eyes met his briefly before she dropped her gaze.

She stayed with him, not moving or speaking, holding him patiently. He had no idea how long they stood, but gradually his head began to clear and his breathing calmed. Finally he became aware of her: the warmth of her hands, a faint perfume from her hair.

She seemed to sense the tension leaving him, gently releasing her grip and stepping away, as if giving him back his space. It had been an extraordinarily sensitive gesture, but now he was confused, unable to make her out.

"Come and have a drink," she said.

"I can't go back in there," he said quickly.

"You don't have to," she said. "I've got my own place."

She pointed to a cottage which was just visible at the top of the slope. He had seen it from the path, behind the high fence. He still hesitated, unsure of her.

"You're not the only one who's had a shock," she said firmly. He caught another glimpse of the steel in her. But when she said that he couldn't refuse. She led the way behind the outbuildings and up past a long sloping lawn to the side of the cottage.

The cottage was small, with a door on the side wall leading to a long hallway which seemed to stretch the length of the house. Julia led him into a long sitting room, strewn with boxes, piles of papers, books, CDs, and clothes. At the far end of the opposite wall was a set of French windows.

"Excuse the mess," she said. "We'll go on the patio. I've got some whisky, or there's wine."

"Scotch would be wonderful."

She unlocked the French windows and went back in to fetch the drinks. It was peaceful on the terrace, all Connor could hear was the trickle of a tiny stream somewhere in the bed which ran down the side of the garden. The lawn looked lush, but it hadn't been mown for a long time and was beginning to look ragged. Far off to the right a shimmering patch of sea was visible between the trees.

Julia came out with a tray carrying a bottle of whisky, a jug of water and two glasses. He joined her at the table and took the bottle. It was good whisky: cask strength unfiltered Islay. He poured a measure and added water. Julia filled her glass and was about to drink it when Connor stopped her.

"You're not drinking it neat are you?"

"Why not?" She scowled at him. "I need this. Or is neat whisky only for men?"

"Not at all," he said. He felt relieved that she was showing her aggressive side again. "This stuff is overproof. It'll burn your throat. Take a sip if you don't believe me."

She hesitated, then slowly put the glass down and added some water. She turned away from him to look out over the garden. Connor sipped his own drink, alert now. He was starting to understand. This wasn't her home: she'd given an address in London. She was packing away someone's belongings, the garden was unkempt, she was drinking unfamiliar whisky. She'd lost someone, but her loss seemed to have made her angry, not sad.

He tried to lighten the mood.

"That stream is very relaxing," he said.

"It comes from the mine."

Her tone did not invite a reply. There were new sounds now, the croak of a frog, the distant bark of a dog, unidentifiable rustlings in the shrubbery.

She had finished her glass and poured another.

"I should have been watching those children," she said, "I could have stopped them."

"Their parents should have been doing that."

"That's no excuse. I'm supposed to look out for kids. It's my job."

"You're a teacher?"

She nodded. A movement in the air caught his attention: a black shape flitting erratically above the trees.

"Bat," he said.

"We get lots here," she said. "And owls. And foxes. They treat this lawn like a playground."

She drank some of her whisky.

"You're the one who saved them," she said. "I had no idea

what was happening before you ran down to the water. What attracted your attention? You were fighting off that Jack Russell when you just seemed to stop. You weren't even looking at the water."

"I get this funny feeling when something is wrong."

"What, like a sixth sense?" She sounded sceptical.

"No, I'm good at noticing when something important has changed, that's all. I just realised I couldn't hear the children. They had been part of the background noise, and suddenly they weren't there any more."

He had taken the little red Lego brick out of his pocket and was turning it over obsessively.

"Well, it saved the two of them," she said.

"You think so? The little girl looked bad."

"She's alive. More alive than she might have been."

Connor was holding the Lego brick under the table. He squeezed it so hard it hurt. *Why couldn't I have saved you?* he asked silently.

Julia's voice was suddenly businesslike.

"Would you like something to eat?" She asked. "I can make up a picnic."

He hadn't thought about food all evening but now he realised he was starving, and he'd missed dinner at the Ship. While she was inside he relaxed, putting the little plastic brick back in his pocket. He was beginning to respect Julia. She was prickly, but she was honest, and that moment outside the farmhouse was one of the most selfless acts he'd ever encountered. They had clashed because they both cared about the same things.

She brought out a tray of antipasti, cheese and bread, and a bottle of wine.

"We got off on the wrong foot," he said as they ate. "I'm sorry."

"That's OK," she said. "I didn't know you'd only just arrived. It must be exciting running a project like that."

He sensed that she was getting him to talk so she didn't have to, and he was happy to oblige. She listened dutifully as he described his job, but when he started describing the rides her expression became more alert.

"You know a lot about it don't you?" she said when he finished.

"I have to," he said without elaborating. He knew she had guessed something, but that part was personal. They continued eating in silence, as if neither of them felt it was necessary to speak just to be sociable. Connor could see they were both very private people, and he sensed that Julia knew it too.

It was dark when the finished, and Connor felt it was time to leave. Julia didn't object.

"I'll walk up to the road with you. I'll have to open the gate."

As they went back past the boxes and piles of books in the living room Connor said:

"This isn't a good time for you, is it?"

"I've known better," she replied.

They walked side by side up the lane to the road. Julia had a torch which she kept trained on the tarmac ahead of them. Above their heads the sky glowed with the long streak of the Milky Way. Connor had never know such darkness. As Julia unlocked the padlock he said:

"Is there any way we can find how those children are getting on?"

"I'll ask Charlotte. She knows people at the hospital. Thanks for keeping me company."

She turned, locked the gate and left without another word. He watched her go, her slight figure quickly merging into the night, leaving only the dancing light of the torch getting fainter and fainter until she reached the woods, the light flickering twice then vanishing.

12

Connor wasn't comfortable being a hero. The next morning at breakfast he looked up into Sally's delighted face as she served him yet another coffee and tried to smile in return, hoping she wouldn't notice the effort it took him. He didn't deserve it, he'd done what he had to do, that was all. If Sally really knew him she wouldn't be fussing over him. The congratulations were repeated on the site: the security guard, the drivers, people he'd never seen before came up to shake his hand. As soon as he could get away he climbed the steps to the solitude of his office, closed the door, switched his phone to voicemail and tried to bury himself in progress reports. He couldn't accept success, he hadn't earned it. Until he made up for what happened at Swithunsgate he never would.

He was engrossed in reports half an hour later when there was a knock on his door and Kevin lumbered in. The look on his face told Connor he wasn't there to offer his congratulations.

"We've got another problem," he said. "There's some concrete we can't get through. It's at the bottom of the site."

Connor put on his helmet and made his way quickly down the slope, through the creepy forest of abandoned houses to the bottom road. Kevin was going to follow a few minutes later. Guided by the stutter of the pneumatic drill he soon found the digger. It was attempting to break up the slab he had seen the first time he'd toured the site, on what had once been the end of a terrace.

"Never seen anything like it," said the operator, climbing down from his cab as Connor approached. "It must be four feet thick, and God it's strong. I've broken up wartime pill boxes which were easier to cut into."

"Why is it so big?" It wasn't just the slab for a house, it covered a substantial part of the garden as well. At the rear a trench had been excavated, and he could see the rough edge of the slab, bits of earth embedded in the concrete.

"Every other house sits on concrete a foot thick. Plonk the drill on it and it just cracks. Not this one. Watch."

He climbed back into his cab, swung the arm so that the bit was close to the edge, and started the drill. The staccato hammering produced no result other than a small puff of pulverised cement and a few chips of aggregate. After a minute he stopped.

"It's all like that," he said. "It's going to take weeks."

"Forget it then. We'll work out a different way."

The operator switched off his engine and for a few moments the site was silent. Then a pickup drove up and Kevin heaved himself out. He took out a pouch of tobacco and started rolling a cigarette.

"Got any bright ideas?" He said to Connor, a challenging smirk on his face.

"One or two," said Connor evenly. "A thermic lance would slice it up in a couple of days, that's one possibility."

"If you could get enough oxygen," said Kevin. "It's a hell of a lot of cutting."

"Good point." Connor conceded. "Have you got the site plan? I'd like to see what we're putting here."

Before Kevin could answer Connor's walkie talkie squawked. *"Security to Mr Munro, over."*

Connor unclipped the radio from his belt and acknowledged.

"Mr Munro, the young lady who had the bike is here again. She has a message for you. Says you'll know what it's about. Over."

Beside him Kevin grinned. Connor ignored him.

"Sign her in, and see if you can get someone to escort her

down here. I'm on the lower perimeter. Over."

"Will do. I'm going off duty myself, I'll bring her. Out."

While he'd been speaking Kevin had retrieved a site plan from the pickup. The JCB operator joined them and the three of them had just started examining it when a small car drew up and Julia got out, reluctantly putting on a yellow hard hat. Kevin and the JCB driver stepped back, instantly wary. Connor was disconcerted, she had the same hard expression on her face she'd had when they first met. For a moment he wondered if she'd seen through him and had reverted to the angry young woman who blamed him for the loss of her bike. But as she approached she beckoned to him to move away out of earshot of the others.

"Charlotte heard from the hospital," she said. "The boy was discharged last night. They're keeping the girl in but she's not in danger."

"That's a relief," said Connor. "Thanks for coming to tell me."

"It was on my way," Julia said. "I tried your phone but it was unavailable."

"No signal down here."

She was looking round, her eyes taking in the dead houses and weed strewn road.

"I know this place," she said slowly, as if she was remembering something.

"It was the Park Estate, the biggest housing estate in the town."

"No, I mean here. This spot. There were houses where that machine is," she pointed at the JCB. "My mother used to visit one of them. I came once. I think she was delivering a smoke detector."

"You lived here?"

"It was a long time ago."

She became brisk again. "I'd better go," she said.

"I'll walk you back to the gate," he said.

He went back to Kevin and told him to meet at his office,

then joined Julia again. She was gazing down at the remains of the naval base on the far side of the fence, a sad expression in her eyes. He waited, a little distance from her, until she was ready. Abruptly she turned, and without a word followed him into the complex of dead streets.

He liked Julia. She was genuine. She had bollocked him for losing her the bike, but then she'd seen the suffering in his face when he'd run out of the farmhouse and had somehow, he didn't know how, calmed him down without making any attempt to find what had caused it. She wasn't indifferent, she'd known he couldn't talk about it, and she'd respected that.

"I never liked this place," she said as the reached the centre with its overgrown circle of grass. "The kids were evil. I used to stick close to mum, they threw stones at us both. Charlotte would never come, even with the two of us there."

"It's spooky even now," said Connor, remembering the fox and the unexplained noises from the houses. "But not for long. A few more months and this will be under water. It's going to be a boating lake. And above us, the biggest water coaster in Europe. And here…"

They had reached the bottom of the green. "Will be Mine Disaster."

"That doesn't sound like a lot of fun."

"Oh, it will be. We…"

He stopped, embarrassed that he had said too much. He kept his eyes on the ground in front of him, but he could see Julia's quick glance at him. She changed the subject.

"When I asked at the gate they seemed to think I wanted that big man, Fisher. They said he was the manager."

"It's a common mistake," he said. "Kevin Fisher manages the main contractor: they're doing the demolition and most of the building. But I'm the project manager."

"That's just a title. What does it mean?"

"Do you want the dictionary definition? I make sure the project is delivered on time and on budget, and to the required standard."

"Slightly better," she said. Connor couldn't tell if she was amused or not. She waited.

"I do whatever I need to do to keep the project moving. It's mostly coordination. There are going to be a lot of contractors on this project. As well as the builders we'll have hydraulic engineers, security guards, landscape gardeners, shopfitters, Aquantas, which is the German company making all the slides and pools. It's going to be my job to make sure they all work together and don't get in each other's way."

"Wouldn't it be easier to give the whole job to the builders and let them sort out who does what?"

"A lot of projects do work that way," he agreed. "But rules for this particular grant say we do it this way, to cut out fraud and inefficiency."

"By adding a layer of bureaucracy?"

"What I do is not bureaucratic," he said, rather more sharply than he intended.

"What is it then?" She looked at him steadily, her eyes intelligent and questioning.

"Knocking heads together a lot of the time. Standing at the side of a hole which is in the wrong place with the man who dug it and the man who has to put something in it, trying to figure out what we're all going to do about it."

"That's up to the one who made the hole, isn't it?"

"Not necessarily; shouting at him isn't going to move the hole. Everyone has to calm down and accept the reality, and then we deal with it like adults."

Connor paused, remembering when it had actually happened. "When he sends in his bill, that's when we shout at him."

She laughed, and the amusement in her face was like the sun coming out from behind a cloud.

They continued in silence until they reached the gate.

"There's a fete next Saturday," she said as she handed back her hard hat. "The whole town will be there. Charlotte asked me to invite you. It's at the junior school. Sports day for the children, food and drink, and fireworks in the evening."

The thought of spending a day with these unfriendly people

filled him with horror.

"I'll think about it," he said, unable to think of a polite excuse. "I've got a lot on at the moment."

"You're the hero," she said firmly, "they'll want to see you."

She was eyeing him steadily, the unanswerable schoolteacher again.

"Will you be there?" he asked.

"What's that got to do with it?"

"You're just as much a hero as I am."

She shook her head. "You're the one who's going to save the town," she said.

Now he knew he'd have to go. "Oh, that sort of hero," he said. "OK, Tell Charlotte I'd be delighted."

"Good. I'll let you know if I hear any more from the hospital."

With that she turned and walked off, trudging resolutely out through the muddy gateway. Connor watched her go then noticed the security guard looking at him with a grin on his face. He turned abruptly and climbed back to his office, putting the image of her determined little figure out of his mind.

Soon after he sat down Kevin heaved himself in.

"We can leave that concrete alone," he said. "There aren't any foundations in that area. The architects avoided it because there's a mineshaft underneath. That's what the concrete is doing, blocking the shaft."

"What happened to the house that was there?" asked Connor.

"I dunno; does it matter?"

"I'm just curious. That concrete isn't the original foundation slab. It was put down later, after the house was pulled down. It didn't disappear into a sinkhole, did it?"

"Who cares?" Kevin said with a shrug. "With a plug like that it's not going to happen again. And before you ask, that's the only mine shaft on the site. I checked."

13

Saturday in the school car park was hot. Grey fumes hung over the circle of vans selling pasties, pies and fish and chips. The still air stank of cigarettes and burning onions. To one side was a long queue at the beer tent: inside Connor could see Sally pulling pints. In the middle of the circle were trestle tables where thin surly men in shirt sleeves were guarding pints, drinking with a determination that Connor had seen before in deprived towns and villages, places where the coal mine or steelworks had closed and taken the soul out of the town, and the only remaining pleasures were drink and tobacco.

He made his way past the school building, a single storey of concrete and glass, its windows festooned with paper chains of brightly coloured letters and drawings, to the playing field sloping up the hill beyond. The air was fresher here. Along the near edge were more tables, occupied by families eating lunch. Against the far wall were a bouncy castle and a sandpit full of small children, their innocent squeals of delight a relief from the grim atmosphere around the drinkers in the car park. The middle of the field was a running track for the children's races; white lines painted on the grass. Against the top wall was a dais with a row of empty chairs and a pair of heavy loudspeakers shaking the ground with 1970s rock. Next to it a VIP area had been cordoned off: well cushioned chairs, tables with colourful sunshades to keep the guests cool.

He saw Julia near the start line for the races, wearing the summery dress she had worn the evening of the accident on the beach. She smiled briefly as she introduced Laura Jeffries, the school headmistress, a large authoritative looking lady with a whistle on a lanyard.

"Know much about theme parks?" she said, eyeing him dubiously.

"Not specifically," said Connor, conscious that Julia was watching. "I've been responsible for projects much bigger than this one."

"People bigger than Mr Pascoe?"

"I'm sure we'll get on fine," he said, trying not to think about the argument they'd already had. "We both want the same thing, after all."

Laura Jeffries gave him a withering look.

"You *are* naive," she said, clearly unimpressed. "We'll just have to hope, won't we?"

She turned to Julia and began giving her elaborate instructions for the children's sports. Julia listened with her head down and her hands behind her back. Connor was amused to see her so submissive. Mrs Jeffries had probably taught Julia all those years before, and still saw her as a ten year old. He didn't think there were many people who could treat Julia like that.

The field was gradually filling as more families arrived. Amongst them Connor noticed Gordon Pascoe in the centre of a large group which was making its way to the VIP area. Gordon was smiling benevolently at everyone he passed; not everyone smiled back. Laura let out an audible harrumph as he left his party and strolled up to join her.

"Laura," he said, extending a hand. "As organised as ever."

"I hope it's not for the last time," she said shortly.

Pascoe's expression didn't change. "We all have to make sacrifices," he said.

"Not the health of our children," she retorted. "I will not permit that."

Gordon gave the slightest of shrugs, as if what Laura said

didn't matter and turned to greet Julia. His eyes passed over Connor as if he didn't exist.

"Delighted to see you again," he said, holding Julia's hand a little longer than he should have done. Connor felt a spasm of outrage at the familiarity. Julia nodded a thank you, coolly returning his gaze, which annoyed Connor even more.

He was not the only one annoyed. Just behind Gordon was his wife: permatanned with leathery skin, in a grey dress with necklace and bangles flashing in the sunlight. Her eyes were dark and unsmiling, her glance at Julia weary and resigned, as if she wanted to feel jealous but no longer had the energy.

There was an awkward silence, broken by the arrival of a press photographer, a young man with two well used cameras round his neck and a heavy bag over his shoulder. Pascoe reacted immediately, putting himself between Connor and Julia, an arm round each of them, switching on a beaming smile.

"Our heroes," he declaimed. Connor tried to shrug him off but Pascoe held his shoulder in a grip so tight it hurt. Astonished at the violence of the man he tried his best to smile at the camera. There was nothing else he could do. The pressman took a few shots then Pascoe released them, the warmth wiped from his face.

Then Connor noticed Mrs Truscott just behind Pascoe.

"Mr Munro," she said after giving Julia a friendly nod. Julia walked away to join Laura Jeffries and they were alone. "I've been talking to my opposite number at Conco, in London. Have you met him?"

Connor felt as if he'd been punched. "I haven't met him, no," he said carefully, wondering what was coming.

"He knows you. He was surprised when I told you were here. He thought you'd moved on, was the way he put it."

"I'll never work with Conco again, if that's what he meant."

"That was his implication. You caused some trouble."

"I did, and I'd do it again if I thought there was any risk to personnel. Did he tell you why I caused them trouble?"

"It was a short conversation," she looked him steadily in the eye. "I hope it's not an indicator of what else we might expect while you're here with us."

"It isn't, as long as no-one behaves the way Conco did. If that's too cryptic for you I suggest that when you next speak to him you ask about safety barriers. Now will you excuse me?"

He turned away before she could reply, not trusting himself to speak again. The only friendly face he could see was Julia, who was marshalling six year olds for the first of the afternoon's races. When she saw the expression on his face she glanced quickly across to Monica, who looked at him with a look of faint astonishment before turning to catch up with Pascoe.

"You know her?" he asked Julia.

"She's Charlotte's mother. Have you managed to upset her as well?"

"She'd doing her best to upset me."

"It seems to follow you around," she said. "You need a job. We could use an extra pair of hands."

He found himself holding one end of the finishing tape. He couldn't escape, but he didn't mind, it gave him something pleasant to do. The children were just having fun, there were no undercurrents of suspicion here. For the next two hours he was busy: timing races with the stopwatch, rooting around in boxes for spoons and ceramic eggs, escorting tearful losers back to their parents, most of whom seemed to have gathered outside the beer tent and greeted the arrival of their offspring with less than wholehearted enthusiasm. He noticed that children who were upset ones came to him for comfort, not to Julia. It had been the same with Charlotte's children. Julia's cool undemonstrative demeanour, which Connor found so refreshing, made the youngsters wary of her.

The sports had been going for an hour when there was an incident. Connor had taken over as starter. The Boys under 10s Fifty Metre Sprint had just finished and Connor was lining up the entrants for the girls' race when Laura Jeffries came up to him.

"Mr Pascoe wants to see you," she said. "You'd better go

now, he doesn't like to be kept waiting. I'll take over here."

Reluctantly Connor trudged up to the enclosure, wondering what he could have done to upset Gordon. The Pascoes seemed to have the central area to themselves. Two women, who looked as if they might be Gordon's grown up daughters, were sitting at the back with their mother. Two men were at a separate table laden with empty bottles. Gordon himself was sitting at a table to one side, bouncing a small girl of about five on his knee. He didn't look up.

He kept Connor waiting a full minute before gently putting the girl down and nudging her towards the women. As she trotted off Gordon beckoned to a large, overweight boy standing behind him. Connor recognised him, Darren, he'd come last in the previous race.

"Tell this man what you just told me," he said.

"I would have won but they tripped me up," the boy mumbled, his eyes on the ground in front of him.

Pascoe looked at Connor for the first time, a cold, emotionless stare. Connor began to feel angry: why the drama? It was obvious the boy was lying.

"Nobody tripped anybody," said Connor, controlling his voice.

"Yes, they did," the boy sounded desperate.

Gordon said nothing, and Connor had to continue. He had an idea.

"There isn't time to rerun the race," he said, "but I've got the winner's time. If you can beat it we'll give you a special prize. How's that?"

The child, now red faced with shame, said nothing. Gordon gave Connor a piercing look before addressing the boy again.

"You're telling lies again," he said. "Now, remind me which is going to be your ride."

"The Python," his voice was barely audible.

"That's right. You were going to be first through the Python."

Connor felt a lurch of disgust. Python had been one of their best ideas, a long water slide through the belly of an enormous snake. A snake that had eaten its lunch, so the rider would go through that as well. He and Stevie had spent hours working out what it would be, inspired by the old drawing of what looked like a hat but was actually a snake that had eaten an elephant. They couldn't see a way to make that work but then Stevie had thought of a python that had eaten another python, and maybe that in turn had eaten a third, so that the tube became narrower and the run faster as the rider went through each mouth. A beautiful concept which would be completely lost on this spoilt overweight brat.

Pascoe seemed to have the same thought. "You lost your race because you eat too much. Now go back to your mother. Any more lies and I won't even take you to the opening."

The boy ran off sobbing. Gordon picked up his wineglass and took a sip, looking out across the field. Connor was dismissed. As he turned to leave he noticed Monica Truscott again, sitting with Charlotte and the three children. He sensed that she'd been watching him.

When the sports ended Connor helped tidy up. Evening was approaching as they carried the last bags of equipment down to the school office and Laura invited him and Julia to join her for supper. Julia declined and left to go back to her cottage. There was no food service at the Ship that evening so Connor stayed, he and Laura bought salads from a health food stall and took them back up to the VIP enclosure. As they were crossing the running track Connor asked:

"What was your argument with Mr Pascoe about?"

Laura stopped walking.

"He wants to build a hotel," she said. "Where visitors to his park can stay. Unfortunately he wants to put it here."

"He wants to demolish the school?"

"He'd like to try," Laura snorted, "but not even he could get away with that. No, he just wants this field."

"But it's the wrong side of the town. Traffic through the square would be a nightmare."

"We noticed. When we pointed it out he said he'd pay for a

shuttle bus."

Connor had seen this sort of problem before.

"Why not put it next to the site?" he ventured. "Over the car park, for example."

"We can't. There's a covenant which prevents any building higher than one storey. There are no such problems here. The council owns this field and is prepared to sell it. All very profitable for Gordon and his friends on the planning committee, while the rest of us worry about childhood obesity."

Connor sympathised, remembering Pascoe's overweight grandson. The boy was still there, head down over a Nintendo. Around him the rest of Pascoe's family was becoming increasingly loud with drink. Only Gordon and Monica looked sober: Gordon bouncing a very sleepy four year old on his knee, while on the other side of the group Monica sat alone, her phone in her hand, a half empty glass of wine on the table in front of her. Why hasn't she left with Charlotte? Connor wondered. She didn't seem to be enjoying herself, nobody was talking to her now.

Just beyond Monica was another table with only one occupant, a tall thin man puzzling over a crossword. Nodding to Monica as they passed Laura took Connor to join him.

"Jim Feathers," he introduced himself, putting away his paper with a smile. "I run the Historical Society. You must be the new man on Polwerran Park."

Feathers had a historian's appetite for information, and when Connor mentioned some of the developments he'd worked on in the City, where every project schedule had time built in for archaeological work, he was alive with curiosity. Connor told him about the mosaic floors they'd found under Broadgate, the fort on the site of the new City Terrace Hotel, and the plague pit which had delayed the Swithunsgate build for six months.

The two men were on their third pints. Darkness was falling and Laura had left to organise lights for the tables. Below in the car park barbecues had been lit. The ring of vans shielded them from view, all Connor could see was a black hole full of smoke, lit red by the lights on the stalls, and sparks from burning wood; it was like looking down onto a Victorian painting of hell. For a brief moment he thought that was where he deserved to be, not here in the pure white light of the candles.

"How romantic," said Connor, distracting himself by picking up the light that had just been placed on their table. It was just a small candle inside a cheap replica of a storm lantern.

"Practical," Jim corrected him. "We used to have a generator but it died and they decided not to repair it. It's become a tradition."

Connor saw an opportunity.

"I write about local traditions and folklore in our staff blog. Is there anything here that might be interesting? Apart from candles?"

"Nothing recent," said Jim, "in the eighteenth century smuggling was everyone's main occupation. It became so serious that in 1787 the Revenue had to call in the army. Half the population was either hanged or transported; the trade stopped overnight. I've got some pamphlets about it."

Connor remembered the two vans passing quietly through the square in the dead of night. Maybe smuggling hadn't stopped completely.

"What about mining?" he asked.

"That goes back to prehistoric times. It created the landscape."

"I noticed a shaft on our building site. Was that once a mine?"

Jim shook his head. "That's always been farmland, apart from the quarry, and that went out of use decades ago. The shaft was for ventilation. The mines are everywhere here, and they all needed air.

"There is something that might interest you," he went on. "Probably to do with the mines. A local saying: *adits run red, cattle be dead.*"

Connor shivered. He thought of the bleak landscape with its naked heaps of mine waste, and the banks of silt in the harbour where nothing grew.

"And do they?"

"Run red? Not for a long time," said Feathers. "I remember there was a spate a few years ago, but it was only kids who'd got hold of some permanganate. The town was in uproar until they found out what it was it."

"They must have been remembering an old environmental disaster."

"Possibly. It would have been a long time ago; that rhyme goes back at least a hundred and fifty years. I found it quoted in a very early edition of the local paper, that that was first published in the 1850s. It's all online now if you want to look further."

He smiled at Connor's grimace.

"Probably not worth the effort," he said, then leaned forward and lowered his voice.

"You've probably noticed that you're not exactly welcome here," he said.

Connor nodded. "I'd assumed it was the usual suspicion of strangers. I've seen a lot of it in isolated communities."

"That's part of it," Jim agreed. "A lot of them don't like me either, and I've been here 30 years. Gordon Pascoe has been here even longer but they shun him as well."

"Even though he's the only one trying to do something about this place?"

"He's from Falmouth. An incomer. All the philanthropy in the world won't make then accept him."

"I don't suppose it bothers him," said Connor with a shrug. "Any more than it bothers me. What's the other part? The other reason I'm not popular?"

"It's your building site." Feathers spoke so quietly Connor could barely hear him. "People think it's cursed. The Prideaux who used to own it never used it for grazing. They would cut it for hay but they always sent the bales up-country to be sold. No-one here would buy it. Old Daniel must have been delighted when Gordon Pascoe bought it from him."

But it wasn't Gordon, it was someone else. Connor kept this to himself.

"Where did the story come from?" He asked. "Is that hundreds of year old as well?"

"It goes back at least to John Wesley. Apparently he refused to preach there. Local legend says it's because of the curse, but I think the reason is much more prosaic. Park an Jowl is a gloomy place, you've seen that, and Wesley was a showman. He'd want to wow his audience, and Gwennap Pit, a much better theatre, was only a few miles away."

"Park an Jowl?" Someone else had used that name. "Is that what people call it?"

"Know what it means?"

Connor shook his head.

"That might be something else you could look into."

Feathers paused for effect. There was a lull in the conversation around them and his words carried across the enclosure.

"An Jowl is the Devil. Satan. Park an Jowl is The Devil's Pasture."

Connor stifled a laugh, it was such a melodramatic moment, but looking down at the fiery red in the car park, and at the faces all round him, secretive in the candlelight, he suddenly felt nervous. He was in a world he didn't understand.

His thoughts were interrupted by a loud bang followed by a crackling in the sky. The fireworks had started. Feathers turned to watch, a childlike smile of anticipation on his face. Connor took a long pull on his pint and sat back to enjoy the show.

After the final flourish of the fireworks Feathers took his leave. Connor quickly finished his pint and made his way down to the car park. The murmur around the tables was low and menacing. They were watching him. As he took his empty beer mug back to the bar a short thickset man abruptly loomed up in front of him, nearly pushing him to the ground. The man turned to face him, arms loose at his side, waiting to be challenged. Connor put the mug on the nearest table and backed away, making sure there was no-one behind, then walked quickly out onto the road.

14

The street lights stretched in front of him, little pools of light like stepping stones leading Connor down towards the square. On his left, high on the southern slope, moonlight picked out the heavy bulk of the church tower. The sound of the fete quickly diminished, and soon all he could hear was the rustle of the breeze in the hedges and the occasional snorts of the cattle dozing in the fields. The smell of the sea was on the air, reminding him of home, rounds of golf with Stevie on the links.

He felt tense, alert for anyone who might have followed him from the schoolyard, but the road remained empty all the way into the town. Too empty, too quiet. Where were all the drunks? At the fete they were drinking hard, he expected to find them staggering loudly back into the town, but there was no-one at all. All the houses were in darkness.

Uneasy now, he was cautious as he approached the town centre, treading softly to avoid attracting attention, so that when he walked out onto the top of the square he saw the men leaning against the wall by the back entrance to the Ship before they saw him. There were two of them, both in dark jackets, one with a hood up, the other wearing a striped beanie. Parked beside them was a white Transit van. The glow of a cigarette told him there was a third man sitting in the driver's seat.

Connor continued walking quietly along the top of the square. It would be foolish to walk up to the hotel until he knew why they were there. He was half way across when at the edge of his vision he saw one of the men push himself off the wall and stroll diagonally up towards him. He was tall and athletic, with an easy stride. Connor quickened his pace. The man did the same. The moonlight caught the flash of something metallic in his hand. Abandoning his pretence of nonchalance Connor broke into a run. Just beyond the far junction was a narrow alley off to the left. It would be dark in there. Behind him he heard the sound of pounding feet as his pursuer ran after him. Then he heard the van start up.

The alley was at least 50 yards long and uphill and he was breathless when he reached the top: he'd had too much to drink to sustain this level of exertion. He found himself on a street he didn't recognise, but to his left he could see the church. Behind him the footsteps of his pursuer were echoing off the walls of the alley. He ran for the lychgate into the churchyard, then round to the far side of the church, looking for somewhere to hide. The graves, cold and monochromatic in the moonlight, were too exposed, but around the perimeter trees and bushes offered shelter. He slipped behind the nearest shrubs and made his way quickly to the far end of the graveyard, then took out his phone and called 999. The beep as he pressed the keys seemed deafening.

"Emergency, which service?"

"Police."

After a brief pause there was a click and the police operator answered.

"I'm in Polwerran and I'm being followed. There are three men."

"Where are you now?" The voice was male, calm and businesslike.

"I'm in the churchyard."

"And where are they?"

"I don't know for sure, but they can't be far away. One of them was running after me, the others are in a van, I think."

"We're sending someone to investigate. Is there anywhere you can go? A pub or café?"

"This is Polwerran. Everything is closed."

"What about friends, neighbours? Is there anyone you can call on?"

He thought of going back to the fete: he could lose himself in that crowd, but quickly dismissed the idea. He'd never reach the school unseen, and he wouldn't be safe amongst those hostile drunks. He said:

"I don't know anyone here. I'm staying in a hotel, but I can't go back there. One of these men is standing outside it."

"Very well. Stay where you are. Try to keep hidden. Someone will be there as soon as possible."

"How long will they be?"

"Soon. That's all I can say."

Connor disconnected, disheartened and frightened. The operator had sounded reassuring but he got the impression that there weren't many police in this part of Cornwall. Then he realised he did know someone. It was a long shot, but he didn't have much option. He called Julia.

Her phone seemed to ring forever before a sleepy voice answered.

"Hello?"

"Julia, it's Connor," he whispered.

"Who?"

"Connor." He had to raise his voice so she could hear him. "Don't hang up."

"What's the matter? Are you drunk?"

"I'm sober, Julia. I just can't get into my hotel."

He explained again.

"The police won't get here in time," he concluded. "So I'm going to try to get out of the town and walk back to your place. It should take me about 45 minutes. I wondered if I could sleep on your floor. I know it's a big favour but I can't stay here."

She didn't hesitate. "OK, I'll wait for you."

"That's great. I owe you…oh shit, what's that?"

He could hear a van driving up the road. It stopped, the doors slammed, and then he heard men coming into the graveyard. From the shouts he could tell they were fanning out.

"They're here. Oh fuck, they're covering both the gates."

"What gates? Where are you?"

"In the graveyard."

"That wasn't very clever of you," she said. "Listen, climb a tree and stay there. I'll be with you in about 15 minutes."

"Don't be stupid. You'll get hurt."

"Just do as I say," she snapped. "Where's the van?"

"Outside, I just told you."

"Where, exactly?"

Bewildered, Connor answered automatically. "Left hand road as you look down the hill. It's a white transit."

"Good, now move. Put your phone on silent. We'll talk by text."

He crouched and ran. Most of the trees were yew, all twigs, impossible to climb, but then he found an oak. He scrambled up, just as the flash of a torch told him one of the men was starting to search the area. He climbed until the branches were so thin they began to sag under his weight, wedging himself in a cleft and staying as still as he could. The tree was in full leaf and he would be difficult to pick out from the ground.

Through gaps in the foliage he could see the light of the torch scanning the graves and bushes below. On the other side of the churchyard were more torches. Someone rattled the door of the church. He lost track of time waiting in the tree. He was starting to get cramp in his right leg when his phone vibrated. A text.

2 mins. Where r u.

Big oak. Top end chchyrd. He replied, holding the phone to his chest to shield the screen .

How many men there?

3. 1 just below me.

Get ready to move.

Connor waited another few minutes. One of the men had positioned himself directly below him: he could smell cigarette smoke. His leg was now in agony. He bit his lip to stop himself crying out. He heard raised voices.

"Any sign of him?"

"Nah, he could be anywhere by now."

"Pavel saw him come in 'ere. He's not far away. Keep looking. If he's not in the bushes try the trees."

The words chilled Connor. There was no escape now. He forced himself to calm down and think through his options. Julia couldn't possibly do anything against all three of them. If he climbed down quietly he might be able to overcome the man below him man and somehow get past the others and into the street.

Slowly he tried to exercise his cramped leg, wincing with the pain. He was sitting astride a branch, he needed to be on the ground to stretch his muscles, it was impossible up in the tree. He could barely move: he would never be able to overcome anyone in his present state. In despair he listened for the sound of Julia's car, but the night was silent. The light of a torch was shining through the branches below him and he froze. The light moved on, but he knew it would be back.

Then, from the street outside came the sound of a car horn: three sharp blasts. A few seconds later he heard a crash, like a rubbish bin falling over, followed by the grinding sound of metal tearing against metal. A car alarm went off, an unholy wail filling the night.

What the hell was going on? Connor gritted his teeth and began slowly descending through the branches. There was no sign of the torch. Then an urgent voice, just below him.

"Connor!" Julia was on the path below him, "Are you there?"

He climbed down as quickly as he could. She grabbed him by the arm.

"Come on," she said, "my car is just up the road."

"I've got cramp," he hissed. "I can barely walk."

"Hop then. But get moving."

She ran ahead of him. He had to hobble, his leg in agony, unable to keep up. The path was in moonlight and they were horribly exposed. As the neared the gate he saw something on the path in front of them them, like a bundle of clothes. Julia stepped over it without even looking, and ran on towards the street. When Connor reached it he realised it was the man who'd followed him across the square, now unconscious on the ground, a heavy steel spanner in his outstretched hand. That had been meant for him; a blow on the head with one of those could kill.

They were out in the street when they heard shouts from the other side of the graveyard. Fear drove him on, overcoming the pain he ran after Julia. The road up the hill was straight, and there was no sign of any car, just a line of street lamps illuminating the empty carriageway. His leg gave way and he stumbled. When he regained his balance Julia had vanished. Behind him two men had appeared by the churchyard gate. They started toward him. Panicked, he ran on, nearly falling again as he missed his footing as the kerb ended at a side street.

"Over here!" Julia was a few yards down the street, standing beside a Toyota Prius with the doors open.

"I thought you had a Fiesta," he said.

"Just get in and pull the door to," she said. "Don't slam it."

He was barely in his seat when she set off, the car surging forward with a whoosh. Electric. Then came a loud, insistent beep from the dashboard.

"What's that?" he hissed.

"Seat belt warning."

"Oh for fuck's sake."

"Shut up and hang on. And tell me if anyone's following."

She was looking straight ahead, hunched forward over the wheel, her face tense. The street was barely a hundred yards long. As they approached the junction Connor squinted to look out of the wing mirror.

"No-one behind," he said.

Julia turned right and then zigzagged rapidly through the residential streets. The only sound was the whirr of the motor and the insistent beep from the dashboard. Connor was completely lost, convinced at every corner that they were going to meet the white van, but Julia clearly knew the streets and soon they emerged onto an open road. The street lights ended but Julia didn't switch on the headlamps. The moonlight was deceptive and at the first corner they nearly hit the hedge, but she didn't slow.

After another half mile Julia suddenly pulled over into the entrance to a field.

"What's the matter?" cried Connor.

"You have to call the police and cancel the callout. Tell them you're OK."

She sounded worried.

"Shouldn't we get further away before we do that? Those men might still be following us."

"No, we have to do it now. If they arrive and find that man in the graveyard we're in serious trouble."

"Jesus," Connor reached for his phone. "He's not dead is he?"

"I doubt it." That didn't sound too comforting.

"We need to get our story straight," she said. "Tell them you called me, and I agreed to help. I texted you when I arrived and you slipped out of the graveyard and met me where I'd parked. I didn't come into the graveyard and you didn't see those men again. They'll probably want to speak to me, so give them my number."

Now Connor was worried: he'd been so wound up he'd not thought at all about the consequences of what she'd done. He felt hesitant and nervous as he made the call, and the police operator was clearly suspicious.

"You said you knew no-one in the area."

"I only remembered her after I'd spoken to you. She's not really a friend. I've only seen her a couple of times."

"How do you know this person?"

Connor explained about the rescue on the beach and the operator seemed reassured: he'd obviously heard about it.

"Give me her name, and a phone number. Do you have her address?"

It occurred to him then that the operator's main concern was that he might be speaking under duress. After disconnecting they drove slowly back towards the cottage. They were approaching the gate when Julia's phone rang. She pulled over and answered, her voice tense.

Connor could only hear her side of the conversation.

"Julia Philips, Mawgan Cottage. I don't know the postcode. I haven't got it with me. I'm in my car…… No. I live in London. I'm here because my father has died and I'm dealing with his estate…. I met him on his building site. One of his trucks ran over my bike. The incident on the beach was a few days later… He called me about 45 minutes ago. He's with me now."

She handed Connor the phone. "He wants to talk to you again."

"Mr Munro? I'm cancelling the callout, but we will require a statement from you."

Connor put away his phone and they drove on in silence, but as they approached the turn into the lane towards the coast they passed a police car, coming towards them and heading towards the town, blue lights flashing, siren howling.

Connor felt a lurch in his stomach. Julia looked tense.

"They haven't got the message," she said.

"It may be nothing to do with us."

"Unlikely, it's too much of a coincidence. Let's hope those men have cleared out, taking their friend in the churchyard with them."

"They've got plenty of warning. Out here you'd hear that siren for miles."

Julia was thoughtful. "You'd think they would be a bit more discreet. It's as if they want everyone to know they're on their way."

When they pulled up outside the cottage Julia didn't move, sitting at the wheel, looking into the darkness. She seemed to be shaking. Connor got out of the car, listening for any sound of another engine, but there was nothing but the occasional shriek of an owl. Next to them was Julia's Fiesta. When Julia eventually stirred she locked the car and walked quickly into the house, ignoring Connor. He followed hesitantly, unsure if he was still welcome. He sat in the kitchen, massaging his calf, listening as she rummaged round in her bedroom and the living room. She was starting to alarm him. That man she had overcome had been armed, and was presumably an experienced fighter, yet she had left him unconscious. This was a side of her personality he hadn't expected, and his admiration of her was now tinged with fear.

When she finally came back to the kitchen Julia looked pale. She went to the sink, poured a glass of water and stood sipping it, looking out of the window.

"Thanks for that," he said. "I don't know what would have happened if you hadn't helped."

"I did what I had to do," she said. She drained the glass then turned to face him, clutching her arms to her body as if she was cold. Every part of her seemed to be shaking.

"So what was it all about?" she asked.

"I have no idea. They were waiting for me outside the Ship. When I saw them I carried on across the square, but they followed me."

"What makes you think they were waiting for you?"

"When I was in the graveyard I heard them speaking. They were specifically looking for me."

She stopped by the sink and began washing the water glass. Connor could see reflection in the window: she was looking out into the darkness, her face hard.

"What was that noise?" He asked. "It sounded like a car crash."

"It was. They'd left their van unlocked so I let off the handbrake. The hill did the rest."

"That was clever."

"It was necessity, Connor. The only way I was going to get you out of that churchyard was by creating a diversion."

She was spitting out the words, obsessively rinsing out the glass.

"And the man on the ground?"

"I could go to prison for that."

"He was carrying weapon, Julia! God knows what would have happened if he'd found me."

"But he didn't find you. I found him. He wasn't threatening me, he didn't even see me. As far as the police are concerned that's assault."

Connor now understood why she was so agitated. He remembered Billie telling him: *You can't attack someone just because he's armed. That's vigilantism.*

He tried to find something to say that would reassure Julia.

"I don't think the police will find him," he said. "His mates will have spirited him away, along with their van. They will have some awkward questions to answer otherwise. He was in a graveyard at midnight, carrying an iron bar. And I don't suppose they'd want the police sniffing round their van, either."

"They wouldn't," Julia said, looking a little less tense. "I saw what was inside."

"We'll just have to wait. If the police do find that man they won't waste time. They'll be round here by morning."

She let out a deep sigh. "There's nothing we can do now. I've made up the sofa bed in the lounge. You've got a towel. I'm going to lock up. I'll see you in the morning."

Connor lay awake for a long time. He could understand some drunkard jostling him at the fete, trying to pick a fight, but three men with their own transport, at least one of them armed, waiting at his hotel? That was calculated. Someone wanted him out of the way.

Maybe it was Pascoe, wanting to teach him a lesson after their row when they first met. Or maybe Kevin, humiliated because Connor had a better way of running the project. Either way he was in danger at the building site, where there were plenty of ways to organise an accident. He was going to have to be alert from now on. He'd have to find another hotel, he couldn't stay in Polwerran now: those men would assume that Connor had knocked their man unconscious, and would want their revenge. They knew nothing of Julia.

Julia puzzled him. Lots of girls in London learned self-defence skills: the gym was full of them, and he could imagine that Julia would have done the same. But she knew how to attack as well. She hadn't enjoyed it, which made him wonder why she'd learnt.

He tried to sleep, but when he finally fell into a doze he was looking at the body on the path, only this time it was a familiar figure, in a pit a long way below him, and he woke with a shout of terror, his body drenched in sweat.

15

The slam of a door woke Connor from his dozing sleep early the next morning. The cottage sounded empty: Julia must have gone out. He dragged on his clothes and shuffled to the bathroom to wash his face in cold water, then stepped cautiously outside. The sun was still low and the air felt crisp. Connor shivered in his shirt sleeves. Over the twittering of the birds he could hear the murmur of a conversation over towards the farmhouse; Julia was talking to Charlotte. He didn't want anyone to know he was there; beside him was the open garage, its heavy wooden door pushed back on its rollers to reveal a dark unlit workshop. He slipped inside.

Iron rails were embedded in the concrete floor, the remains of the railway used to bring out the ore. Connor remembered the photo in the boardroom at the Ship: a Victorian mine owner leaning against a railway wagon. It was here, this had been the mine. The entrance had been enlarged to make the garage. Chisel marks were visible on the walls and the roof. He found a light switch, the fluorescent tubes revealing a surprisingly large space. Along the left hand wall was a well used workbench with a drill press, a bench grinder, and a mitre saw with an industrial vacuum cleaner attached to suck up the sawdust. On the wall above were shelves with planes, spirit levels, tape measures and boxes of drill bits. Beside them was a large plywood board hung with the best collection of hand saws

Connor had ever seen. He picked one off its hook and ran his fingers along the blade. Japanese, he thought, it cuts on the upstroke. This belonged to a serious carpenter.

There was another much newer workbench at the rear, on a breezeblock wall which sealed off the mine. As he walked towards it Julia appeared beside him. She had come in silently, hugging herself to keep warm.

"What do you make of it?" she said.

She sounded more relaxed than she had been the previous evening but there was a serious note in her voice and he recognised an invitation. He put back the saw and looked around him more systematically. The new worktop was made from several thicknesses of plywood bonded together and the surface varnished. Below it were brand new drawer units, flat pack from Ikea, he guessed. Above were shelves which looked hand made, their supports screwed into a plywood backboard. Between the left hand end and the middle were three power sockets mounted on shiny steel boxes. A conduit ran between the outlets and back to a wooden box at head height on the left hand wall, just inside the door.

"This is recent," he said, running his hands over the worktop. "It's hardly been used. Whoever built must have had a major project in mind. There's already a good size bench on the left wall."

"Anything else?"

He leaned over to look more closely, and noticed a faint gap where he'd put his left hand.

"There's a break," he said.

He ran his hand towards the right hand end. He felt another gap.

"Another join." He took a closer look, up and down. Then he peered into the empty space to the right, noticing the hinge against the wall. He stood back.

"The whole bench is in three sections," he said. "The left hand is fixed. The right hand part can swing into the gap beside it. Is the middle section hinged as well? Does it pivot into the space left by the end unit?"

"That didn't take you long," she said with a note of approval.

"It's a door into the mine?"

Julia nodded.

"Now see if you can open it."

He smiled. "There's no handle, I take it."

"None that I can find."

Connor was looking himself for any way to open it. "Who put it in? Your dad?"

"Yes."

Her tone was flat.

"I'm sorry," he said. "This must be hard for you."

"We weren't close."

"What makes you think it opens?" Connor kept his voice neutral.

"If he'd wanted to block it completely he just had to brick to all up."

"Why is it so important for you to get in there?"

"I didn't say it was important."

"You didn't need to."

She hadn't lost her ability to aggravate. He said nothing, it would be too easy to get into another argument. She seemed to sense it too, touching him lightly on the arm.

"This can wait," she said. "Come and have some breakfast. Then I'll take you back to the Ship."

"I'd better walk," he replied. "After last night I don't think you and I should be seen together."

"I don't think we need to worry. Charlotte has just got back from Polwerran. Everyone's behaving completely normally. No stories about bodies in the churchyard, police cars, not even the wrecked van."

"No-one could have slept through that din," Connor was worried. "The whole town must have heard. If they're not prepared to talk about it they must be frightened. I don't like that at all. I'm going to find a new hotel, somewhere a long way from Polwerran."

"I'd find a new project if I were you. If those men find you again you'll not get much help from the locals."

"I can't," he said. "I'd have to tell my boss why, and he would bring in the police again, and that would involve you."

"I can look after myself."

"That's not what you said last night. Besides, I have a personal reason for seeing this through."

She gave him a thoughtful look. "I guessed that."

"Just as you have a personal reason for wanting to break into the mine," Connor said, before Julia could ask him any more questions.

"Are you offering to help?"

"I didn't say that, but yes I will. I could come back later today if you like, after I've organised a new hotel."

"Thanks," she said. "Let me know when you're coming. I'll feed you. And I'll drop you off near the town, it will save you half an hour's walk."

Julia dropped him off by the building site, and he set off down the hill to the square. The Sunday morning streets were quiet, no-one noticed him. As he strolled towards the Ship he wondered for the first time why he'd agreed to help Julia. He hardly knew her, she was reserved, she could be sullen, and she had martial arts skills that terrified him. But all of that made her different, unlike anyone else he'd known, and he enjoyed being with her. She accepted him and that tempered his loneliness.

At the Ship he was able to slip up to his room without being seen. He showered and changed, ruffled up the bed to make it look slept in, then used his laptop to search for another hotel. Most of them were booked for the entire summer but he was able to find a room in a Travelodge 20 miles away.

He packed, and then, to complete the charade of normality, he went down to the dining room and had a coffee and croissant. Sally wasn't on duty so he didn't have to explain himself to anyone.

It was early evening when he returned to the cottage. In the garage Julia had cleared the shelves on the back wall.

"You can see where the middle unit is attached to the wall," she said. "Those bolts don't unscrew."

She handed him a socket spanner. He put it on the nearest bolt, it just turned with the spanner without loosening.

"Proof that there's still a door here," he said, handing back the spanner.

She looked at him expectantly. "Is it?"

"Think about it. These fixings are either coach screws or bolts. If they're coach screws they go through the wood of the shelf unit and bite into plugs inserted into the wall behind. Tightening the screw pulls the shelf back against the wall. It's just like any other screw except it's got a hexagonal head so you use a spanner to tighten it rather than a screwdriver. A bolt, on the other hand, goes through the shelf unit *and* the wall, to a nut on the far side."

"Are you always this pedantic?"

"Only when I have to be. You tighten a screw by turning the head until it won't turn any more, right?"

He waited for her to reply.

"Go on," she said calmly.

"And how do you do up a nut and bolt?"

"With two spanners, of course, one on the nut, the other …. Oh, I see. You need access to both sides."

"Exactly. You can't bolt anything to a wall if you can't reach behind to put the nut on, and to get to the other side you need a door."

"Very clever," she said drily. "So why would dad bother when it would have been much easier just to screw everything together?"

Connor stood back. "I don't know," he said. "He was your dad, not mine. But this has all been very carefully designed and put together. Look at the seams on the worktop."

"I know," said Julia. "He did it to hide the door. That's why he fitted bolts. If he'd just used screws anybody would be able to remove them and get inside."

She looked far away.

"What was he up to?" she murmured, then collected herself.

"So, we've established that it does open. The question is how."

Connor set about trying. He pushed, pulled, lifted it, but the units remained firmly in place. He could find nothing that resembled a handle, or a keyhole. He took out the drawers from below the worktop and inspected the carcass minutely. He borrowed a torch and spent a quarter of an hour looking for anything that might operate a hidden catch, but there was nothing. It seemed to be a perfectly ordinary work bench.

He stood back and pondered. There was a simple explanation of this, somewhere. What had he missed? There was no mechanical way the door would open.

Ah.

He turned his attention to the power points on the back wall. Picking up a screwdriver he carefully unscrewed the last socket, nearest the middle of the rear wall, and turned it over.

"Bingo," he said.

Julia joined him. Her face was close to his and he could smell a discreet perfume on her skin.

"That's supplying the power," he said, pointing to a thick grey cable coming out of the conduit. The ends had been stripped back and wired to the sockets. Another identical cable, also wired to the sockets, disappeared through a hole in the back of the mounting box.

"But then it carries on, taking power somewhere else," he said.

"To the other side of the wall?"

"It looks like it. Now, look at this."

Beside the power cable was a thin white flex which ran straight from the conduit to the hole in the back wall.

"I wonder what that is for?" he said, in the tone of someone who already knows the answer. He stood back and followed the conduit back to the box high on the side wall.

"What's in there?" He asked.

"The meter," she replied. "And the circuit breakers."

Inside the box, beside the meter, was a consumer unit with six breakers. Four were labelled: *House Power, House Lights, Cooker,* and *Garage*. The remaining two were unmarked. The steel conduit ended just below the consumer unit, and both the thick grey cable and the white flex went up and into the back of it. Now Connor understood.

"The switch is electric," he said.

"He buzzed himself in," said Julia softly, almost to herself. "The cunning old bugger."

There was admiration in her voice, but her eyes had moistened.

Connor reached up and flicked the unlabelled switches. It was almost an anticlimax where they heard a loud buzzing from the end wall, followed by a double click. The middle and right hand parts of the workbench moved slightly. Julia walked quickly over, swung the end section into the gap on the right and pulled the middle part open. A blast of cold air greeted them.

They were in.

Julia picked up the torch and crept tentatively through the open doorway. Connor followed, wishing he'd brought a jumper. Julia flashed the beam around and found a light switch just beside the door. A fluorescent strip light in the roof plinked into life.

They were in a space smaller than the garage, narrowing towards the back, where a second wall with a door in it sealed off the rest of the tunnel. On the right hand wall was a coat rack, hanging from which was a thick wetsuit and Scuba gear. Next to it were half a dozen air tanks, several coils of brand new rope, and a box containing a hammer, a plastic bag full of carabiners, and several metal spikes about six inches long, each with a circular eye at one end. On the opposite wall was a small metal filing cabinet, an old table and a chair. Bizarrely there was also a mobility scooter with a small trailer attached. In the trailer was an underwater scooter: a short stubby cylinder with two handles and a propeller, like a truncated torpedo. On top of the filing cabinet was a battery charger. In the corner was a small dehumidifier, a green light on the top told him it was running.

"Is this what you expected?" he asked.

"I didn't know what to expect," she said, heading straight for the filing cabinet. "But I'm hoping the rest of his papers are in here."

While Julia started rifling through the filing cabinet Connor opened the inner door and looked into a dark, damp tunnel which sloped downwards. It was much narrower and the roof was lower than the space they were in. On the floor were more remains of the railway, the iron now rusted almost to extinction. Dripping water echoed into the distance. As his ears grew accustomed to the silence he could hear an indistinct booming deep in the mine. There was no sign of any lighting and the impenetrable darkness was frightening. It was an unwelcoming, dangerous place.

He closed the door and walked back to the scooter. Julia was looking at one of the files with a puzzled expression on her face.

"Tide tables?" she said.

"Recent?"

"This year."

He started examining the scooter. He'd seen hundreds like it whirring quietly along the pavements, though this one looked more substantial than most, with a heavily padded seat, a wraparound fairing at the front with a large square headlamp, and big chunky tyres. Clamped to the rear of the chassis was a ball joint to attach the trailer. The scooter looked new, but the fairing was scuffed with long deep scratches along both sides. The tyres were caked in grey mud and there was more mud on the footplate. Then he noticed tyre tracks leading to the inner door.

"Your dad was using this to drive into the mine," he called to Julia. "It's perfect: small, manoeuvrable, no fumes, and a bright headlight."

Julia glanced across at the scooter, with its attached trailer.

"He wasn't just exploring, he was carrying stuff, like that torpedo."

"Which is for use under water."

Connor was puzzled. "He can't have been cave diving, unless he had an experienced buddy. Doing it on your own is suicidal."

"He didn't have a buddy. The only person who knew he was here was Charlotte, and she doesn't dive." She put down the papers and walked over to the scuba kit. "I suspect he found a way to the sea. That's why he had the tide tables, they would tell him when it was safe to dive."

"It's never safe diving alone. If no-one knew what he was doing there's be no rescue if he got into difficulties."

Julia didn't reply, slowly flicking through the scuba gear.

"What's this?" she asked, showing Connor a bulky jacket with a bright yellow metal backpack attached.

"It's a rebreather. It extracts oxygen from your breath so you can use it again it. It means you can stay down longer. And there are no bubbles escaping so it's quieter and doesn't disturb the marine life."

"There's a normal BCD here as well," she said. "Maybe he had a buddy after all."

"I doubt it. There's only one of everything else."

"Come on," Julia was suddenly brisk. "I'm getting cold. Let's go back to the house. I'll come back to this lot tomorrow."

Out in the garage they carefully pushed the open units back into place. They swung easily and locked with a confident click. Afterwards there was no sign anything had ever moved.

"That's good workmanship," said Connor.

She gave a sad smile.

"He was a perfectionist," she said.

He followed her back to the cottage, suddenly aware of her father, as solitary as she was, hiding his work in a bleak cavern behind a beautifully disguised door that no-one would ever see. Connor would have liked to know him. How was Julia feeling, trying to understand what she had lost? He thought of his own parents, pottering through life up in Inverness, and how much the three of them took each other for granted. After what happened to Stevie they should have been closer, but they didn't seem to be. His hand was slowly turning over the Lego brick in his pocket.

When they reached the kitchen Connor asked:

"Did that help?"

"A bit," she said, leaning against the sink with a tumbler of water in her hand. The evening sun was shining through the window and her face was in shadow. "He was obviously doing something with all that equipment. Exactly what I don't know."

"Caving and diving by the look of it."

"I think I've already worked out that much. What I don't know is why."

"What makes you think you'll find out? He hid the door, no-one was supposed to find that chamber."

Julia shook her head. "I was," she said. "No-one else, just me."

"I don't understand that," Connor couldn't see her expression.

"You wouldn't," she said flatly, "it's between him and me."

"I'd like to know all the same."

Julia ignored him. From the fridge she pulled out two supermarket pizzas and a bottle of white wine. She plonked the bottle in front of Connor.

"Corkscrew in the top drawer by the sink," she said. "Glasses in the cupboard on the left."

Connor opened the bottle and poured two glasses.

"The only way you're going to find out what he was doing in the mine is by going in yourself. Am I right?"

"Don't cross examine me."

Connor held her gaze until she dropped her eyes and busied herself ripping the packaging off the pizzas with a kitchen knife.

"If you do that on your own you might never come back," said Connor.

"He managed it."

"I can't answer that. Maybe he was lucky. You might not be."

"That's my business."

"Do think he wanted you to kill yourself?"

"How dare you say that!" She had the knife in her hand, and for a brief moment he thought she might lunge at him. He

127

backed off, putting his hands up in a gesture of penitence. She looked down at her hand, with the knife pointing at him, and put it down carefully.

"Sorry," he said quietly. "That's not what I meant to say."

"You might be better off not saying anything at all."

"I'll just say this. Going into a disused mine alone is very stupid. If that's what you're intending then I'll come with you."

Julia opened the oven door and slid the pizzas onto the shelves.

"It's my life," she said.

And you're trespassing, was the implication.

"The offer is there," he said.

Julia opened the fridge again and took out the ingredients for a salad. She started ripping leaves off a lettuce. Connor found another knife and set about topping and tailing some spring onions and peeling off the outer leaves. They worked together in silence until the salad was finished. When the pizzas were cooked they ferried the food and drink out onto the patio. Julia lit some citronella candles to keep the mosquitoes away.

They had finished eating when Julia finally spoke again.

"Have you done much caving?" she asked.

"Some." He didn't let her see his relief. "I joined the potholing club at Uni, we spent a lot of time in the Yorkshire dales."

"So if we were to explore the mine how would we set about it?"

"Research it first. Find out how long is it, how deep, what's the geology, when was it last worked. Has it been mapped. Is there anything about it in your father's papers?"

Julia shook her head.

"Jim Feathers may have information," said Connor. "I'll call him tomorrow. And I'll get a checklist of equipment from the web."

"How do we make sure we don't get lost? Take a ball of string?"

"That's what cave divers do. We might be better off with chalk marks. Every time we make a decision we mark it so we can find our way back."

Julia lapsed into silence. She was looking out across the valley, but her thoughts seemed far away.

"I looked down that tunnel once when I was nine. It frightened me, it was supernatural, ghosts and giants. I swore I'd never go into a cave again."

"The darkness in a cave scares adults. It's so thick you can feel it," Connor was keeping his voice gentle. "Why do need to do it?"

"To find out. I've spent more than half my life not knowing, but now there's a chance to change that."

"Not knowing what, Julia?"

She didn't answer, giving no sign that she'd even heard his question. But there was no shrinking away, and Connor sensed that part of her wanted to talk. He tried a different approach.

"What was his signal?" He asked. She looked uncomprehending. "He wanted you to find your way into that chamber, but he didn't tell you how to do it. Why were so sure that's what you were supposed to do?"

She gave him a long, appraising look before drawing her knees up to her chin with her arms, as if she was protecting herself. Julia's self-possession was physical, she could take on anybody, but he sensed that she found it difficult to trust people, and that would make her lonely and vulnerable.

"He wrote a statement of wishes: he wanted me to scatter his ashes from somewhere called the Benjamin Steps. I'd never heard of them; there was nothing about them in any of his papers. Charlotte and Monica didn't know either, and they've lived here all their lives. It was only at the funeral that I realised what he was doing."

The moonlight caught tears forming in her eyes. She found a tissue and dabbed them dry.

"We fell out a long time ago. Utterly. He knew that there was no way I'd even listen to a message from him. But I might respond to a challenge."

"Before," she hesitated, "all that, we used to play games. He never liked just telling me things, he tried to make me find out for myself. Christmas presents weren't round the tree, he hid them, and gave me obscure clues to where they were. Finding them all could take all day."

She gave him a sad grin before her face became serious again. "This is another tease. He's telling me that the Benjamin Steps are important, find them and I might understand."

"You think these steps are in the mine somewhere?"

He avoided the obvious question, *understand what?*

"They have to be. I've looked everywhere else; the mine is all that's left."

She stopped for a moment, remembering something. "Apart from his laptop. That might tell me something, but I haven't been able to get into it to find out. It's another example of the way his mind works. I need a password to open it, but all he left me was a post-it note with *dadoes* written on it."

"Which isn't the password?"

"That would be too obvious. It's an allusion to something that we both knew. Sometimes I can almost feel what it was, but then it goes. It doesn't mean anything to you, does it?"

"Wooden rails on a wall at waist height?"

"I did look," she conceded. "But no, that would be too straightforward for him. The answer will come eventually, it always does. Meanwhile I'll start searching the mine."

She reached for her wine glass but it was empty. Connor refilled it, then took a chance.

"There's something unresolved, isn't there?" he said.

Julia gave him a quizzical look.

"That's an unusual way to put it."

She stared at him for a long time, Connor felt she was weighing him up. Then she sighed.

"I'm not going to escape you, am I?" she said, unwinding herself and standing up. "Wait here."

She walked briskly back into the cottage. Connor was still trying to work out when she'd meant by her comment when she came back carrying a small crumpled photo in a plastic frame. She handed it to him then pulled over a candle so he could see the picture more clearly. It was an amateurish family group taken against the background of the cottage, probably about where he and Julia were sitting now. A tall broad untidy looking man of about 40, grinning unaffectedly at the camera with his arms around a woman and a young girl. The woman looked like Julia, she had the same slight build, sandy hair and eyes that squinted at the sun. Julia, he realised, was the child. He recognised the volcanic glare on her face. It hadn't changed in the fifteen years since the picture was taken.

"You with your mum and dad?" he asked.

Julia nodded.

Malcolm, her father, was about what Connor had expected to see. Big and shabby, bearlike, he could imagine his daughter adoring him. Julia's mother seemed the complete opposite. She looked quiet and controlled, her confident stance and the steady look in her eyes suggesting she was no doormat. It was from her that Julia had inherited her toughness.

He was being shown this picture for a reason. Just an ordinary family by an ordinary house.

"You hardly mention your mum," he said. "Did something happen to her?"

Julia took the picture frame out of his hands and put it on the table next to the candle. They both watched it, the flickering flame making the eyes in the photo dance.

"She disappeared. Vanished. One day she drove me to school but didn't come back to pick me up. I never saw her again."

Julia's eyes were glistening in the candlelight. When she spoke again her voice was steady, but Connor could sense she was feeling for words. She wasn't used to telling this story.

"I remember sitting on the school steps waiting for her. All the other kids had gone and it was just me. Mrs Jeffries found me and took me to her study while she rang around to find out what was happening. I wanted to get out and search the town, but she wouldn't let me. I was scared that I'd let dad down.

"He was away; they were developing secret stuff at the base

and every few weeks he'd have to go to sea to help with the tests. Each time he went he'd make me promise to look after mum. It was a game, mum was quite capable of looking after herself, but I took it seriously. I didn't know what I was going to say to him. It was a few days before he got back, and we started looking for her. The police, were also looking, with gangs of volunteers, but I was sure that dad and I would be the ones to find her.

"The Navy gave dad compassionate leave, and he spent every day looking. He talked to people in the town, he was on the phone to the local press, or giving radio interviews, he had posters printed. He tried to build up a picture of mum's movements that day; on the kitchen wall he had a map of the area with Post-it notes of clues. There weren't very many. She took me to school then came back here. No-one saw the car; it was just here when Monica brought me home that evening. That was it. No-one else saw anything.

"I still had to go to school, but every evening I joined him. We usually went out, calling down mineshafts, clambering down cliffs, exploring adits we'd never seen before, but we never found anything. The police eventually called off their search, but dad didn't give up.

"Not at first, anyway, but as the days went on I could see him losing heart. He started to look thin and worried. I tried to be cheerful, I knew we just hadn't looked in the right place yet. Then…"

Julia stopped, looking hard at the photo as if there was something in it she wanted to understand.

"…he changed. He became clingy. He took over taking me to school. Before that he and Monica used to take turns. He dropped me off every day, watching until I was inside the building. He would be waiting to pick me up every afternoon. When we were out on the cliffs he kept me with him all the time. I thought he was being overprotective and I hated it. Mum and dad had always trusted me to look after myself. It led to our first row."

Tears were glistening in her eyes. Connor said nothing. Julia had to say this in her own way.

"Dad and I had been quartering the woods. They had already been searched but we didn't trust the locals to do a thorough job. We'd just got back from school, the phone was ringing and while dad answered it I changed and went out to pick up where we'd left off. When he found me he was livid, telling me never to go out alone again. He hauled me back home and shut me in my room. I was terrified, I'd never seen him like that before.

"After that we both calmed down, but I was still wary. He stopped smiling, I couldn't read him any more. And he kept me even closer, like a dog on a lead. I tried to argue but he wouldn't listen. He had changed completely. He had always told me everything, but he wouldn't explain why I was suddenly a prisoner. It was for my own good, that's all he would say.

"Then, probably a week later, when we got home the kitchen wall was blank. He'd taken down the map. 'We're leaving,' he told me. 'We're never going to find her, she's gone off on her own.' I knew he was lying, but he wouldn't budge. All the time we were packing I wanted to be out searching but he wouldn't let me. He resigned his commission and we moved to Surrey."

Julia turned to face Connor, making no attempt to hide the tears in her eyes.

"We never had a single friendly conversation after that. Not one. I made him send me to boarding school, and moved out when I went to uni. The last time I had any contact with him was eight years ago. When Charlotte rang me to tell me he had died I didn't even know he'd come back here.

"I had to collect his belongings from the hospital, and in his wallet I found this photo. That's when I realised what he must have gone through. He wouldn't have kept the picture if Mum really had left him; something else must have happened to her."

"It sounds as if he was frightened off," said Connor. "Probably by a threat to your safety."

"It looks that way, doesn't it?" Julia picked up the photo again. "If he'd just trusted me," she whispered.

For the first time Connor felt that Julia was being unfair. If her father had been getting close to a horrifying truth a threat to his beloved daughter would have stopped him dead, and he wouldn't have been able to tell Julia why without frightening her even more.

"Then fifteen years later he changes his mind," Connor found himself picking up Julia's story. "He comes back, not letting anyone know who he is, and starts exploring the mine. He's carrying a photo which strongly suggests he never believed his own story. He doesn't think she'd absconded either. And he sends you cryptic signals so that… what? You carry on where he left off? He hasn't given you much to go on."

"He wants me to go into the mine. That's all I need to know. Somewhere there will be the next clue."

"You make it sound like a game. A very dangerous one."

"Not if we go about it properly. You're the expert, tell me what we have to do."

"We take a full day, so not before next weekend. I find out what I can first, and we go very carefully. We don't wade into water until we know how deep it is, and we don't clamber over rock falls. The mine will be a maze of tunnels and shafts: the miners followed the lodes, wherever they took them. Every time we reach a junction or a shaft we mark clearly where we're going and where we've come from. We might be tired or injured so the route back to safety must be absolutely unambiguous."

"I'll bring chalk and a camera."

"And a notebook."

"OK." She took back the photo and stood up. "Now I'll make you a coffee and then I'm booting you out."

It was now fully dark, and the night creatures were filling the air with their cries. It was a very isolated spot, not a single artificial light was visible. The farmhouse was out of sight behind a high hedge. When Julia came back with the coffee he said:

"Are you absolutely sure your mum didn't run off? I'd like to be sure we're not wasting our time."

Julia took his words seriously.

"I've wondered that for years," she said. "I could have misinterpreted his actions. I was only nine, after all. But I didn't misinterpret mum."

She settled down opposite him.

"The police made me write down everything that happened that day; I kept a copy. I reread it the other day, looking for anything unusual in mum's behaviour.

"Dad was away, and Charlotte was in hospital with appendicitis, so Mum took me to school on my own. In the afternoon Mrs Jeffries took me to the Leisure Centre for some swimming practice while the rest of the class did PE. After school I waited in the yard for mum. I was annoyed, I'd bought some new bathers but mum had packed my old ones. I was going to tell her off. Everyone else had gone when Mrs Jeffries found me and took me to her office. When there was no reply from home she rang around to see if anyone had seen mum, but no-one had. Monica was back from the hospital and said she'd look after me. She was very kind, feeding me cake and laughing about the mix up over my costume. I was probably a bit rude. I wanted to go into Polwerran and start looking, but Monica wouldn't let me.

"The last I saw of mum was when I got out of the car. She reminded me to straighten my legs when diving in – I used to keep them bent, it took me ages to kick that habit - gave me a quick kiss then drove off. No lingering glances, no extra big hug, just a normal mum in a hurry, illegally stopped on a yellow line."

Connor was satisfied. The scene Julia described, her recollection of his attitude when he took her away to Surrey, and the photo in his wallet, together convinced him that something serious had happened. He doubted Julia would be able to find out about it after all this time, but she was right to try. In her position he'd do the same.

"I think you're right." he said. "Something did happen to her. I'll do what I can to help you find out what it was. We'll start next Saturday. I'll call you beforehand if I find out anything useful."

Driving back along the empty lane, his headlights boring deep holes into the night, Connor felt sorry to be leaving. His final view of Julia was of her walking back into her lonely little cottage. She was not naturally introverted, her circumstances had forced that on her, and he'd sensed her conflict before she spoke. Like him she was sociable, but unwilling, or unable, to express what she really felt. After what had happened to her that was hardly surprising. She seemed to accept him though. He would be a willing confidant, if that was what she wanted, but the hint of perfume and the warmth of her body as they sat together looking at the photo had stirred rather more basic feelings in him.

16

In the week that followed Connor was unable to find out anything more about the mine. There was nothing on the Internet. His calls to the Historical Society went straight to voicemail and Feathers didn't call him back. This was strange after the openness of their conversation at the fete. He sensed a pattern: the attempt to beat him up, the aggressive attitude of the men at the fete, and now Jim's abrupt change in attitude. Connor was interfering and that was not welcome. He began taking his own safety more seriously, keeping away from isolated areas of the site, watching the machinery for any attempt to injure him, ensuring he wasn't followed when he left for his new hotel each evening.

When he arrived back at the cottage the following Saturday Julia was already in the garage. She was wearing a heavy woollen jumper and waterproof leggings, hiking boots peeping out from underneath. On the floor beside her were two small backpacks.

"Hot coffee, water, sandwiches, chocolate," she said briskly. "We've each got a torch with fresh batteries and there are spares in the side pockets. Chalk to mark our route, a notebook and my camera, fully charged."

Connor nodded his approval. With no prior knowledge of the mine they needed to be meticulous in their exploration.

"I've borrowed some hard hats and hi-vis jackets."

Connor put on boots and jacket while Julia left to lock up the house. Back in the garage she pulled the door closed and locked it from the inside. Now they were on their own, cut off from the daylight and the cheerful sounds of the garden birds. They had agreed to do this in secret, in keeping with her father's actions, no-one was to know what they were doing. They both knew the risk: if anything happened no-one would be coming to rescue them. Julia put on the bright yellow jacket and shouldered her backpack. She gave him a nervous smile and they set off. Connor glanced at the mobility scooter as they went through to the inner door, wondering briefly if they could use it, but it was too small for two people.

The passage was narrow and they had to walk in single file. Connor had to crouch to avoid hitting his head on the roof, while his feet constantly skidded on the smooth and slippery floor. The darkness beyond their torches seemed impenetrable. The damp air was full of sounds: a constant booming in the distance, and nearby he could hear scratching and whispering. He stopped, convinced he'd heard someone behind them, and the sound stopped as well.

"What is it?" whispered Julia. She seemed as spooked as he was.

"There was a noise behind us," he whispered back. She turned round, and he heard it again. It was just the rustling of their clothes, magnified and distorted by the walls of the tunnel.

They carried on until they came to a junction: a substantial tunnel crossing their path.

"Straight on?" asked Julia. "Following the rails?"

She flashed her torch down each of the passages. They all looked identical, although the crossing passage seemed to be taller and wider that the one they were in. There was nothing to indicate which way her father might have gone.

Julia put a chalk arrow on the wall, photographed the junction and wrote a brief description in her notebook before they continued in the same direction.

The passage was long and constantly varying in width and height, sometimes so low they had to bend double, but always wide enough for the rail track, the remains of which were present along its length. They passed more side tunnels, stopping each time to photograph and record details. They had to skirt black silent holes in the floor which led down to more galleries. Littered along the way were abandoned wagons, their carcases rusting, wooden planks rotted away to nothing. There was distorted unearthly noise everywhere. A rushing like an extended exhalation, the echoing drip of water, a distant thumping.

After an hour the tunnel ended. They could no longer see the walls and roof, their torches shining out into utter blackness. The rushing sound had resolved itself into the hiss of a waterfall, resonating off the walls, impossible to pinpoint.

"This feels enormous," said Connor. "It must be the main working."

They stood together, trying in vain to get a sense of its size.

"Try taking a picture," he said. "Maximum ISO. With the flash we might just see it all."

Julia took a couple of shots, but all she captured was a dazzling white foreground and a short section of the ruined railway track receding into total darkness.

"I'll try it without the flash," she said. "I'll do a 30 second exposure. While the shutter is open we'll use the torches to provide some light. You do the left, I'll do the right."

She balanced the camera on her backpack on the ground, then pressed the shutter.

The result was spectacular. On the screen was a grainy yellow image, with streaks of brighter colour where the torches had shone. The cavern was wedge shaped, the smooth roof sloping down from right to left, where it met the floor. The narrow track for the railway was the only flat surface: to their right it sloped upwards towards a ledge below a jagged cliff about fifty feet high which made the right hand wall. The water was coming from an opening high in the far corner. There was loose rock and abandoned machinery everywhere. The railway terminated near the far wall, only a crude iron buffer preventing the trucks from rolling off the end of the rails.

"What now?" Asked Julia. They were hunched over the camera screen, heads close together, their breath visible in the cold air.

"We have a good look round here, then head back, exploring the side passages as we go."

They started by following the rails, moving carefully to avoid cutting themselves on the rusting ironwork of the wagons. Behind the buffers was an irregular gulley about three feet deep running up the entire length of the slope, hugging the wall, the rusting remains of a rack and pinion rail track fixed to its floor. Water was rushing down the far side. They climbed up to the ledge, beside the gully, away from the stream. The slope was smooth and slippery. This is where accidents happen, thought Connor. Lose your footing here and you'd slide all the way down, with every chance of cracking bones on the loose rocks as you passed. And if you were in single file, he realised as he moved to one side of Julia, you might take your companion with you. Then who would go for help?

A short distance from the top of the slope, in a substantial side tunnel, water was cascading onto a pile of rubble which had fallen from a shaft above.

"This has been filled in," Connor said, shielding his face from the freezing water. "It isn't mine debris, it's been tipped in from the surface."

"How interesting," said Julia. "Can we go now? There's nothing here except water."

They checked the rest of the ledge before slithering back down the slope and making their way out to the main tunnel.

Methodically they explored each side passage they came to. The first ended without warning in a sheer drop into an unfathomably deep shaft. They backed off carefully, the ground was slippery and a fall would be fatal. They approached the next more carefully: it went upwards and they could feel a faint breeze on their faces. They turned one corner and stopped. The passage was blocked by a door made from rough wooden planks. Light was visible around the frame. Connor pulled on the handle: the door was locked.

"This has been used recently," said Connor, examining the hinges. "These have been oiled in the last few months."

"Is this where dad was coming?"

"Unlikely. There's no keyhole. It's locked from the outside."

They retreated and followed more of the side tunnels. Most were short, excavated by the miners following the lodes until they petered out. Others quickly became too narrow to squeeze through. Unexpected holes loomed out of the ground, shafts down to deeper levels, the only access to them via rotting wooden ladders.

One tunnel disappeared into a long pool of inky black water, still and menacing. Julia sniffed the air then dipped a finger in to taste it.

"Salt," she said. "This one connects with the sea."

"He wasn't diving here, was he?" asked Connor.

"God, I hope not."

They retreated to the main shaft, and continued working back towards the entrance, checking more galleries. Most went nowhere.

"How many more?" asked Connor after they'd explore yet another short side gallery. "My batteries are getting low."

"Two more," said Julia, flicking through her notebook. "One on either side. I've got spare batteries if you need them."

The next gallery was long and narrow. The air in it felt fresh, as if it was open to the air. After five minutes it ended at the base of a round vertical shaft. Smooth pebbles littered the granite floor. They could see daylight fifty feet above them, a thick bar crossing the opening to the sky.

"I recognise this," said Julia looking up in surprise. "We're under Charlotte's garden. This is the well that never has any water. I probably threw most of these pebbles in myself."

"Let's get out of here before one of Charlotte's kids decides to add to the collection," said Connor. "A stone dropped from that height could give one of us a serious injury."

There was only one more branch to explore, a substantial

tunnel to their right. They set off, a strong breeze in their faces, the shaft soon wide enough for them to walk side by side. The booming sounds they'd been hearing throughout the mine became louder, and more distinct, and soon Connor recognised the sound of waves. Like the previous tunnels this one wasn't straight, so that they heard the sea long before they saw it. Eventually they saw daylight reflected off the glistening walls.

Soon they were standing on a narrow ledge, looking down at a small inlet about twenty feet below them. Connor couldn't see the open sea, only the regular up and down motion of the water told him that it wasn't a rock pool. The inlet was bounded by a wall of rock which started at the cliff on their right. The curve of the cliff prevented them from seeing the end of it to their left. The sides of the rock face in front of them were smeared with bird droppings. Gulls circulated overhead.

Below the narrow ledge was a short but unpleasant looking drop, whether it was onto more rocks or the water Connor couldn't see. The only way off the ledge was via a narrow downward staircase cut into the cliff face on their right.

Julia set off ahead of him. The steps were old and worn and there was nothing to hang onto as they made their way unsteadily down. They seemed to be heading straight for the water but at the last moment the steps turned and they came to a small stone landing stage built on the rocks.

"Well, bugger me." Connor looked around in wonder. "A little private harbour."

It was no more than ten feet long, ending in a further short flight of steps which led down into the water. The surface was dry, with only a few pieces of old seaweed on it: judging by the tide marks on the rock opposite it was well above the high water line. It was very cleverly constructed – the jetty and the tunnel through the cliff were completely invisible from the open water. Looking up he couldn't see the top of the cliff, they were invisible from up there as well.

"Eighteenth century I would guess," said Julia. "This must have been built by smugglers, and that trade died out in the early part of the nineteenth century."

Connor could imagine a small boat tied up at the jetty, a gang of men unloading barrels of brandy and bales of tobacco and carrying them up to the tunnel entrance.

Julia seemed to have the same thought. "I dreamed about places like this when I was a girl," she said. "I never suspected there was one right on our doorstep."

Connor was looking around, taking it all in, when he noticed a small inscription carved into the rock at head height, just above the base of the stairway: *Benjamin fecit. 1756.*

"You're right about the date," he called to her. "Someone signed his name."

She came over to look, and her eyes widened as she read it.

"The Benjamin Steps," she whispered. "We've found them."

She ran her fingers along the lettering. "You knew I would, didn't you?" She said. Connor stayed silent: she wasn't talking to him.

Now they had to find out why it was important, but there didn't seem to be any clues. Nothing on the concrete except bits of dried seaweed. The cliff behind them was sheer, there was no way up. The rocks on the opposite side of the pool were inaccessible, cut off by the wall of the cliff. They searched the rocks for anything that might have been hidden in a crack in the granite. Julia went back up to the tunnel to see if there was anything secreted around the entrance.

There was nothing. They sat on the lower steps, watching the water as it surged gently up and down with the waves.

"He didn't send you here to find something specific," said Connor.

"I didn't expect him to. It's the start of a journey."

"The only way out of here is by water," Connor said. "There's no boat tied up anywhere along here, is there? Out of sight, around the corner?"

"I had the same thought," said Julia. "There's no sign of a painter."

"There might be one tied up below the waterline."

"Then you'd need a boathook to fish it out, and there isn't one here, or in the garage. There's no boat, Connor. I think we have to dive from here."

"Dive? Where to?"

Julia didn't answer. She was peering into the water.

"There's something glinting down there," she said, pointing down into the water opposite. Connor could see nothing, just the waving seaweed below the surface, but then a larger wave than usual surged up the inlet, and in the trough that followed he did notice something bright, deep in the water.

"I see it," he crouched down to look more closely. "It looks like a rope anchor. There was a box of them in the garage."

"There's a rope attached. Going down," said Julia. "I think that's where I'm supposed to go next."

"Diving? That explains the scuba gear in the garage."

"Will you come with me?"

"My gear is in London," said Connor.

"You could try dad's. You're about his size."

"I don't like wearing other people's kit," he said.

"You would if you had to, wouldn't you?"

Connor couldn't think of an answer to that. While he hesitated she went on:

"Just try it, and if it fits, fine."

"You're determined to get me in that water, aren't you?"

"You said you'd help."

"All right," he said. He was beginning to feel part of Julia's quest. "Only at slack water, though. Fighting a tide out here would be suicide. And we're going to look pretty stupid if we drag everything down here and get kitted up only to find it's just a bit of fisherman's line."

"Don't worry," she said. "I'll investigate with a mask and fins before we kit up properly. Come on."

She stood up and started up the steps.

"Let's do it now. We've still got nine hours of daylight."

"Have you done much diving in these waters?" Connor asked as they went back into the tunnel .

"No," she admitted. "I prefer warm water, like the Red Sea. But I've got my kit with me."

"How many dives have you logged?"

"Over 100. What about you?"

"200," he said, relieved that she had a decent amount of experience. "Quite a bit in the UK. Cold water, crap visibility, currents which wouldn't be out of place in a washing machine."

"I can hardly wait."

Back in the garage Connor gathered up her father's scuba gear and took it through to the bathroom to try on. It fitted well enough. Back in the chamber he found Julia sitting at the table by the filing cabinet, her head down studying a small booklet.

"OK?" She asked.

"I'll manage," he said, putting everything back on its hanger.

"I thought you would. Today looks good. High tide is in two hours. We've got plenty of time to get ourselves set up and be ready to dive during slack water."

This was moving too fast for Connor.

"We don't rush this," he said. "If we overlook anything it could be fatal."

"We're not going to rush it," she countered. "I just don't want to hang around."

"We don't even know if any of the air tanks are full."

"Find out then. I'll fetch my kit," she left before he could say anything else.

She was impossible to argue with. He took a regulator and checked the pressure on each of the cylinders. They were all full.

17

As he assembled his scuba gear Connor kept an eye on Julia: he wanted to be sure that she knew what she was doing. He was reassured when Julia showed no sign that she was in any hurry, methodically working through the stages of assembly. She doused the strap of her buoyancy jacket with water from the garden tap before slipping it over the air tank and tightening it. That way the webbing was fully expanded before she put it together, and wouldn't loosen the moment she was in the sea. A loose tank could easily slip out of its harness, with disastrous results. When she was satisfied that the webbing was tight she attached the regulator, checking the O-ring on the tank for damage before clamping it on. After clipping the inflator hose to the jacket she held the pressure gauge with the glass facing away from her while she opened the valve. She checked the pressure, let some air into the jacket, and took a couple of breaths from each of the mouthpieces to ensure everything was working properly. It was exactly as any diver would have been taught, but there were a lot who skimped on it.

She noticed that Connor was watching.

"Satisfied?" she demanded.

"You know how important this is," he said.

The scowl left her face and she nodded soberly. It wasn't about scoring points, they each needed to be convinced they could trust the other underwater. It was going to be a difficult dive, they had never worked together before, and there was no dive leader to tell them where to go and what to do. He was right to challenge her.

Back in the kitchen they set about planning the dive.

"There are 200 bar in a full tank," said Connor. "I suggest we use 80 bar out, and 80 back. We surface with 40, that will leave plenty for emergencies."

Julia nodded.

"We go in single file and we don't let go of the rope," he continued. "If the current gets too strong we abort."

Connor remembered a current off Weymouth so fierce it had nearly pulled the mouthpiece off his face. It had taken him weeks to get his nerve back after that.

"That's what happened to Charlotte's husband Nick," said Julia. "He was diving with his brother and they misjudged the tide. Paul was rescued hours later by a fishing boat. They never found Nick."

"Poor Charlotte," said Connor. He'd wondered why she was bringing up the kids alone.

Julia had finished filling a flask with hot chocolate. She looked apprehensive.

"We'll be all right," said Connor, brightly, though he was feeling nervous himself. "Slack water."

She gave him a weak smile, then went to her room to change while Connor used the spare bedroom. When they met again in the kitchen she was wearing a black and yellow wetsuit. No-one ever looks good in a wet suit and Julia was no exception. This one was particularly libellous, suggesting entirely fictitious rolls of fat around her midriff and upper thighs. Her scowl when she saw his expression made her look like a bad tempered wasp. Connor concealed a grin as he went back to the garage and gathered his kit. Julia followed carrying a bag with the flask and a couple of towels.

They set off into the garage without another word, Julia's face still grumpy.

They used the scooter and trailer to carry the kit. Connor drove, with Julia walking behind to make sure nothing fell off.

At the end of the passage they ferried the equipment down to the narrow stairway to the jetty. The heat was intense - the sun was directly overhead and there was no wind. Connor peeled the wetsuit down to his waist to stop himself overheating as Julia put on her fins and mask and slipped into the water. She duck dived and disappeared from sight, surfacing near the open end of the inlet.

"We're in business," she called back. "The rope goes straight down to the sand, out to here, then runs back along the outside of these rocks towards the next bay."

Connor pulled up his wetsuit and put his gear on, looking forward to the cool of the water. When Julia had done the same they checked each other's kit, then Connor put his hands over his mask and mouthpiece and stepped out off the jetty. He hit the water with a crash, sank briefly then surfaced in a hissing mass of bubbles. He immediately felt more comfortable. Julia hit the water beside him. When she had sorted herself out they signalled OK to each other, an O made with thumb and forefinger. Connor pulled down on the inflator to let air out of his jacket and gradually sank beneath the surface.

This was the moment he always loved, the transition from the awkwardness of the kit on land, heavy, huge feet, to weightlessness in the sea, where all the gear made sense. The weight belt to make you sink, the inflatable jacket counteracting the weight so you just floated.

He dropped to the bottom, letting enough air into his jacket to stop just before hitting the sand, and settling into a rhythm of slow deep breaths. A moment later Julia drifted down to hover beside him. She looked relaxed, her body horizontal, arms folded across her chest, her eyes calm and alert. Her buoyancy control looked better than his. They exchanged OK signals, then slowly began to explore. The water was murky, bits of loose seaweed drifting past, the occasional fish, crabs edging across the rocks.

The rope was just beside them, dropping vertically until just above the sand, where it went through an eye, like those in the box back in the chamber, and turned horizontally to follow the bottom towards the open sea. The eye had been hammered into a crevice in the rock and felt solid.

Comfortable with the equipment Connor signalled to Julia, pointing in the direction of the rope. She signalled back OK, and they set off, Connor leading. At the end of the inlet the line turned sharp right and continued along the outside of the rocky outcrop. They were in the open, the sandy bottom sloping away on their left towards the murky grey deep. He could no longer see the surface, and the only indication of their depth was on his dive computer, which showed six metres. He took hold of the line, kicking slowly with his fins, checking periodically that Julia was still behind. The water was calm: slack water had arrived and there was no current. Connor was getting used to the unfamiliar kit and beginning to relax.

After ten minutes the outcrop ended. There was nothing but sand in front of them. The line passed through one last eye then turned left and continued out into the open water, disappearing in the murk. But there was another rope attached to the eye, leading right, back towards the cliff. He checked with Julia, she pointed right. Connor understood. If her father had been this way then they should do the same.

At first they were following the line of the rock with unbroken blue in front and to the left of them, but then the water in front of them seemed to darken, another wall of rock, with the rope heading straight towards it. Connor approached cautiously as they entered a narrow gully which turned abruptly right and became a short tunnel in the rock. He could see daylight beyond.

At the end of the tunnel the rope turned vertically upwards again. Following it they surfaced in a circular pool about fifteen feet across, surrounded by jagged rocks which obscured the view of everything except the cloudless sky. It was like the crater of a small volcano. With nothing to see from the water they hauled out onto a flat rock, shrugged off their gear and began exploring on foot, moving carefully to avoid slipping on the seaweed.

On the seaward side of the pool they could see the whole of the inlet. The shoreline swept away from them on the right, running in a half circle towards the far cliff. At the head of the bay were the remains of red brick buildings, all that was left of the naval base. Directly opposite them, no more than a couple of hundred metres away, was a house, long and low, white, with huge glass windows overlooking the water. A well-spaced pair of bright red beach umbrellas suggested a substantial patio. Below the house were steps leading down towards the water. A gleaming white cruiser, the name Loretta in blue lettering on the side of the bow, was anchored in the bay in front of the house.

Julia glanced across with a thoughtful expression.

"The line that went out over the sand," she said. "Which direction did it take?"

Connor tried to conjure up the picture underwater. "Just before we turned in here we were travelling roughly south, and the other line went off at about right angles. So it was east-ish."

She nodded. "And judging by the shadows I'd say that house was also east. So that's where he was heading."

"It looks like it. So why did he stop off here?" he asked, looking round for anything that might answer the question. Julia joined the hunt, putting on her mask to peer into the water. There didn't seem to be anything, but then he noticed a thin shiny black cable under the seaweed, just in front of where they had been standing. They started tracing it: Connor following it forward while Julia uncovered it as it went along the rock face to their left.

Connor soon found where it went: it was plugged into a small cylindrical camera pointing out across the bay. It had been wedged in place with pebbles and hidden by weed which covered the top and sides, leaving the lens clear.

"It's a camera," he called to Julia. "Pointing at that house."

"And this is the power source," she called back. She pointed to a small plastic box with a short antenna on the side. Next to it was a small solar panel.

"Wireless," he said. "If this was your dad's work there must be a receiver somewhere near your cottage. Is there anything on your CCTV?"

"I don't know," she said with a resigned shrug. "I haven't found out how to view it yet."

Connor looked back across the water. The sea was getting up and the rocks below the house were now bathed in spray.

"We'd better go before it gets too rough," he said. "We can follow the line across the bay but unless the end is tucked away in some shelter we may not be able to surface. Those waves look far too dangerous."

Back in the water they swam to where the line split. Visibility had worsened, the waves were churning up the sand, and the rope disappeared in the murk just a few feet in front of them. After a long swim over the sandy seabed they came to an isolated rock, jutting a couple of feet out of the sand, and there they found the next eye. The rope continued onto the sand beyond. Connor checked his instruments: plenty of air, depth fifteen metres, so the increased pressure would mean they would be using air more quickly now, but not excessively so. Apart from the poor visibility he felt comfortable. Julia signalled she was OK and they set off again.

The seabed began to slope up as they approached the far side of the bay. Finally a mass of rock loomed out of the murk and the line ended, tied to an eye just above the sand. Connor could feel the swell swinging them back and forth. Surfacing here could be fatal. They might be able to come up in the open water at a safe distance from the rocks, but with the water throwing them about as it was they might not find the line again when they went down. They had to turn back. He signalled to Julia. She was just behind him, swinging wildly on the line. She didn't respond immediately. Connor pulled himself closer so he could see into her eyes, to make sure she wasn't about to panic. But her expression was alert, and when he repeated the signal to turn round she gave a clear OK. She was probably feeling the same frustration that he was.

But as she turned a wave picked her up and swung her through 180 degrees, and the unexpected movement caused her to lose her grip. Connor tried out to grab her but the current had already pulled her out of reach. He immediately let go himself and kicked hard towards her. You stayed with your buddy, whatever happened. He grabbed her outstretched hand, then immediately signalled to go down. Together they dropped down to the sand, where the current would be less strong. They passed over exposed rocks and he caught hold of one.

The immediate crisis was over: they were no longer being swept out to sea, but they were still in serious trouble. They had lost the line. Surfacing was out of the question: there was no dive boat to pick them up and they'd be swept away. He remembered what had happened to Charlotte's husband. They might try to swim sideways out of the current but that was too risky; they had no idea how wide the rip was and they might not get across it before they were driven into the main channel. They had no choice: they had to get back to the line, and they had to do it quickly, before their air ran out.

The murky water was disorientating: there was nothing to tell them how to find their way back to the line. Then Connor remembered the geography of the cove. The open sea was north, his compass told him the rip was taking them north, so if they went south they should eventually find their rope . He signalled to Julia: two index fingers together, *stay beside me*, She looked alarmed but in control. Connor lined up the compass on his console: south was directly into the current.

The first few yards were easy, pulling themselves forward across the rocks, thankful that the waving seaweed was strong enough for them to hang onto. They crossed a short stretch of sand protected from the current by outcrops of rock. But then the rocks ended and all they could see was unbroken sand.

This was going to be hard. A diver tries to avoid swimming against a current: it uses too much air, you can get out of breath and that can make you panic. But now they had no choice. Connor checked his air: half a tank, Julia had the same. He signalled with a downward scoop of his hand, *drop onto the sand,* where the rip would be weakest.

They kicked out, side by side so they could watch each other. Slowly the rock disappeared behind them. Connor didn't think about how long it would take, he kept an eye on the compass while looking all the time for clues that they were still going forward. They crept over ripples in the sand, past an abandoned lobster pot half buried in the sand. The swirling yellowy water was disorientating, but the compass was his guide. He had a ghastly thought: suppose there was a magnetic anomaly, iron ore in the rocks, making his compass give a false reading. He pushed the thought away: there was nothing he could do about that.

He felt himself starting to panic: he was in an alien environment, he was reliant on a machine to breathe, to survive. Just a few feet above him was fresh air. A few kicks and he'd be free, he could throw away this uncomfortable piece of rubber in his mouth and breathe normally. His brain recognised the symptoms, he was becoming breathless, he was exercising too hard and the mouthpiece wasn't delivering air fast enough. The only way to get over it was to stop exerting, to let his breathing return to normal.

Just ahead another small outcrop materialised. He kicked harder, resisting the urge to throw away the mouthpiece, forcing his hands away from his mouth, until he reached a rock and clung on, waiting for his breathing to subside. Julia stopped beside him, tapped him on the arm and looked searchingly into his eyes. She was checking him out. He beat his fist against his chest, the signal that he was out of breath. Julia waited patiently beside him until he felt his breathing had returned to normal, then he gave the OK signal and they set off again.

Almost immediately Julia pointed. Ghostly in the distance was a snakelike shape in the sand. Then they were within touching distance of the line. He clamped his hand round it, Julia a second behind.

They both clung on, getting their breath back. Connor tried not to think of what might have happened if they hadn't found it, he had to stay focused on getting safely back to the Steps. He checked his air: 100 bar left. He'd used half of his reserve already. He signalled to Julia to check hers: 120. Girls always used less than he did. They had to get going or risk running out. Julia went first, Connor holding back to avoid being hit in the face by her fins.

The sea became calmer as they went deeper, but the sand was churning again when they reached the far side of the bay. Connor kept himself as far out in open water as possible while still holding the line to avoid the rocks, pulling himself along the line one handhold at a time. Julia stopped regularly to check he was still with her. Finally they reached the last corner into their little inlet. The final challenge was coming: getting out of the water.

The waves were funnelling into the inlet, the movement of the water becoming fast and turbulent. Connor signalled to Julia to let him take the lead. He had done this before. Waiting at the corner, he watched the rhythm of the waves, then, in the still water between surges he pulled himself round the corner and let the incoming wave push him in. When the water stopped there was a brief moment of calm and then it began rushing out, raging past him, trying to tear him away from the line. He clung on for a moment unable to breathe: the pressure of water on the diaphragm stopped it working properly. He turned his back on the flood and put a hand round the mouthpiece to shield it, and was able to gulp air.

After two more waves he was opposite the jetty where the rope turned vertically towards the surface. Julia came up beside him and together they slowly ascended. At three metres below the surface the steps were just visible in the murky water. Connor waited until an outflowing wave was just about to turn, then signalled to Julia to go. She launched herself out and upwards. At the steps she got onto her knees, took off her fins climbed out. Connor waited for the next wave then followed her.

18

He felt clumsy and awkward again as he staggered up the steps and took off his gear. Julia had already taken off her scuba set and was unclipping her weight belt.

"I never want to do that again," she said. She avoided his gaze but he could see the fright in her eyes.

"You managed all right," he replied.

"I didn't have any choice, did I?"

She was starting to shiver.

"Get your wetsuit off," he said. "The sun will warm you. Come on, I'll give you a hand."

Obediently she turned her back and he unzipped her, then she did the same for him. It was something divers always did to help each other, but this time it felt oddly trusting. Julia pulled the top of her wetsuit down to her waist. Underneath she was wearing a black one piece swimsuit. She had goosepimples and the soft downy hair on her neck and shoulders was standing erect. She looked small and vulnerable. He wanted to hug her, tell her everything was all right, but he knew that would be wrong. Julia was tougher than he was, just not as good at hiding her feelings.

"It was scary for me, too," he confessed. "That swim back to the line was hard. I was starting to panic. I couldn't get enough air."

"But you didn't panic. And you stayed with me. You're a

good man in a crisis, Connor."

Julia reached out and touched his arm, giving him a brief, shy smile, then abruptly turned to look for her backpack. A few moments later she was back with two mugs of hot chocolate.

They drank in silence, Connor sitting with his legs dangling over the edge of the quay, Julia lying on a towel beside him. He wondered if she knew just how close to disaster they had been.

Eventually she sat up.

"What do you make of it?" She said.

"Nothing that isn't obvious. Your father was interested in that house: watching it on CCTV, able to get to the shore below it by following the rope. He could do it quickly too. The scooter to get through the mine, and the torpedo to pull him across the bay."

"When we were here before all that bay was MOD land. That house wasn't built," Julia sipped her drink. "I need to find out who lives there."

As they made their way back through the mine, in a hurry to get out of the cold, Connor noticed something. The headlight had picked out a shape on the ground, tucked into a crevice to one side. He picked it up: a heavily scuffed man's leather shoe. It had been strapped up with duct tape which had ripped and the sole was flapping loose.

"This hasn't been here long," he said. "There's no mildew on it."

"Someone else must have found the Steps. Maybe they were in a boat."

"Nobody wears rubbish like this."

Julia took it from him.

"Unless he's homeless," she said, turning it over. "No maker's marks anywhere. That's unusual."

"Put it back." Connor's voice was suddenly urgent. "They might come looking for it."

"Who?"

"Let's get out of here," was all he would say.

The rest of the journey was cold and they were both shivering when they reached the cottage.

"Have a bath," said Julia. "That will warm you up. Just be quick. I'm cold too."

When he returned to the spare bedroom Julia had found him a huge fisherman's sweater that had clearly belonged to her father. He sat on the patio with a mug of hot chocolate, letting the sun warm him again, while Julia showered. When she joined him again her face was sombre.

"What did you make of the shoe?" she asked.

"I think it was made by a local cobbler somewhere in Asia."

Julia's eyes widened. "People smuggling?"

"It fits," He told her about the noise he'd heard in one of the derelict houses, and the night when the two vans crept through the Polwerran's deserted square. "Now I understand why there's a gang of thugs patrolling the streets."

"We should we be telling this to the police," said Julia.

"I will, but there's nothing they can act on."

Julia sipped her drink in silence, curled up inside another of her father's jumper as if she was still cold. "I keep thinking about what might have happened on the dive," she said.

"Concentrate on what you'd do differently next time."

"There won't be a next time. I'm sticking to nice calm warm water. Did you actually see any fish down there? I saw about two."

"It's not the Red Sea, that's for sure. But we weren't looking for fish were we? That camera was a surprise. I presume it's being recorded. Can we look at it?"

"I told you. I can't get into it. The recorder is on top of one of the kitchen units," she said. "There's no screen or keyboard. No way I can see what's on the disk. I guess dad was viewing everything from his laptop."

"You still haven't worked out the password? Why don't you find an IT guru to help?"

She shook her head. "This is between me and him. I just have to work it out."

Connor was too tired to argue. The dive had been strenuous,

and the extra nitrogen in his body always made him feel sleepy. Sitting in the sun in the warm sweater he felt ready to drop off, but Julia seemed as alive as ever.

"It's a hint," she said. "To give you an idea, he told me he'd give me my ninth birthday present when I'd worked out what CE3K meant. He told me to sing him the answer."

"Which was?"

"Dum-di-da-dum-dum," she sang the notes and looked at him expectantly. Connor shook his head.

"It's the motif from Close Encounters of the Third Kind," she looked disappointed.

"I never got into those movies."

"I can see that."

"You think this *dadoes* is along the same lines? An acronym?"

"It's the sort of thing he would use."

Connor roused himself. This was important to Julia.

"it would be something you were both familiar with," he said. "Scientific, or science fiction."

Once again he was struck by the lively relationship Julia must have had with her father, and how much she had lost. His own parents had been dull by comparison. They loved him and looked after him and encouraged him in whatever he tried to do, but he couldn't remember them ever challenging him.

"What did you do together?" he asked.

"We watched videos mainly, usually when mum was out. She hated SciFi, and she thought most of the films were too adult for a nine year old."

Her eyes went blank, she seemed to be reminiscing again.

"I keep seeing rain, and 1940s makeup."

"Sorry?"

"The video."

He tried to conceal a yawn.

"I'm not going to be able to help you, Julia. I don't know any of the books, or the comics, or the films they were made into. And even if I did I'd be too tired to think of any of them."

"Not keeping you up, am I?"

"Don't scoff. Plenty of people have this reaction to diving."

"I'll make you a coffee."

She disappeared back into the house. He could hear her clattering about in the kitchen, then a shriek.

"Idiot!"

"What?" he called back.

Julia opened the kitchen window and thrust her head out.

"Look up Philip K. Dick," she said. "Novels."

Julia came out with the coffee as he was opening up the Wikipedia entry. He scanned it quickly.

"1968," he said. "*Do Androids Dream of Electric Sheep.*"

"*dadoes,*" Julia reached for the laptop. "What else?"

"It was made into a film."

"*The* film, Connor. *Blade Runner.*"

"You really are into all this stuff aren't you ?" he said. Julia wasn't listening.

"I'm in," she said, "*bladerunner* is the password."

Julia pulled her chair round beside his so they could both see the laptop. The CCTV control screen was in two halves, a search panel on the left and the camera images on the right. There were three live views: the side door and garage from the camera high on the corner of the drive, the front of the house with the patio where they were sitting, and the view across the far cove from the wireless camera under the cliff. The sea was becoming rough, the rocks under the distant house white with spray. The big white gin palace was moving with the swell.

"At least we avoided that," said Connor.

Julia didn't reply. She was running the cursor up and down the Explorer view on the opposite side of the screen. It showed each of the last five months with the total number of hours of recording for each camera. There were 100 hours just in March.

"This is going to take forever," she said glumly. "We'll leave it for now. I'll start on it tomorrow."

She yawned. Connor suppressed a grin.

"I'll make us some supper," Julia said as she stood up.

19

Julia spent an uncomfortable night, visions of what nearly happened on the dive constantly intruding on her thoughts. She rose early, picked up her father's laptop and took it out to the patio. The morning was cold, the sun just beginning to burn off an overnight mist which was smothering the garden. She found the heavy sweater that Connor had been wearing; pulling it on she realised that he had become part of her life without her being aware of it. There was something insidious in the way he had broken through her defences. She made friends rarely, and new relationships never. She was content with her own company, resigned to life with little happiness, and she didn't care if people saw that. Connor didn't seem to notice: he took her as he found her. He'd asked her about her mother, and she'd told him; she'd never done that before. She knew with dismaying certainty that there would be more conversations like that.

She shook off the thoughts, switched on the laptop and began working through the CCTV recordings.

There were nearly three months of video. There was no index, just a timeline showing when each camera had recorded. The cameras on the house were motion-sensitive, only recording when something in their field of view moved, but the third camera, pointing across the bay had recorded continuously, hour after hour of the same image. Sometimes the sky was clear, at other times cloudy, and occasionally rainy, when a grey mist obscured the distant house. The white cruiser, the Loretta, came and went at random. There might be dramatic scenes buried in the recordings, but the only way to find them would be by working through from the beginning to the end. It would take days. After a fruitless half hour Julia switched to one of the other cameras, the one looking along the front of the cottage. It was just behind her, high on the wall over her right shoulder.

Suddenly her father was on the screen, standing just outside the French windows, running a hand through his hair and gazing about as if he was seeing it all for the first time. Julia recognised that look. His actions had preceded his thoughts, and he was wondering what he'd come out for. In the next clip he reappeared, bent over one of the planters on the patio with a watering can in his hand. He'd put on weight, his stomach was pushing against his shirt. There was a bald spot on the top of his head.

She watched for a long time as snippets of his life playing out in front of her: weeding the borders, sweeping up leaves, sitting at the table tapping a pen on his teeth as he did the crossword. She recognised every gesture, and for the first time she missed him. They could have been solving that crossword together.

There was a scene with Charlotte, both of them relaxed and chatting across the patio table. Julia tried to imagine what they were talking about, wishing there was sound with the recordings. She felt jealous of their uncomplicated relationship. She had forgotten her mission, absorbed in his life. Watching him alive was infinitely more heartbreaking than seeing him dead in the mortuary.

Then the scene changed abruptly and what she saw jolted her out of her reverie.

He was on his own at the patio table, but now he had the laptop with him. He was sitting awkwardly, the laptop to one side so he had to lean over to see the screen. He appeared to be watching a video, but Julia soon saw that it wasn't a film, he was viewing the CCTV. She looked more closely at the image on the screen and felt a tingle in her stomach as she saw what he was doing. He was looking at the picture from the camera behind his head. The message could not have been more plain: *I've angled this because I want you to see what I'm doing.* He was speaking to her.

Julia slipped her hands into the sleeves of the jumper and hugged herself as she watched the rest of the scene. His hand moved to the trackpad and the image changed. It was blurred, she could only make out three broad streaks of colour: light blue at the top, a grey band in the middle and dark blue below. She had just spent a fruitless half hour looking at the same picture. In the middle of the grey was the white rectangle of the house on the opposite side of the water.

He picked up a pencil and made a note on a pamphlet he had open on the table in front of him. One of the tide tables? Julia paused the playback and ran into the kitchen to fetch the booklets. The date of the recording was May the nineteenth. In the May edition, against high tide at seven on the morning of the nineteenth, she found a tiny pencil mark. Now Julia felt a warmth she had never experienced before, as if part of her mind had unfrozen. He'd marked the booklet, making sure she could see what he was doing, and here was the evidence. After fifteen years they had made contact.

Julia took out a tissue and blew her nose. Now wasn't the time to get emotional again. What exactly was he showing her? And why? The image he was looking at was too small and fuzzy to make out what had caused him to make the mark. Zooming in again didn't help, but then she realised she didn't need to. He'd been watching a recording: she could watch it too.

Switching to the water camera she saw it. At seven that morning a man in bathing trunks had come out of the distant house, walked quickly down the steps, and dived into the sea. Half an hour later he emerged from the water and climbed back up to the house. Julia rewound to the start of the scene and zoomed in on the man's figure. He was tall and well built, but too far away for her to make out in any detail. He was fit: even after a long swim he had climbed back up the steps as quickly as he had descended.

In spite of the poor quality of the image the easy athletic stride was unmistakeable. It was Gordon Pascoe.

She stopped the playback, leaving Pascoe's image poised in mid step, one foot in the air. This was dad's target. Ever since she and Connor had found the camera looking across at the house she'd had a notion of who it was. Someone well off, able to get permission to build a house on an unspoilt cliff; someone who must have been around all those years ago when she and her father had left the town so abruptly.

Julia went back to the tide tables, searching for more pencilled marks. There were many, and every one of them corresponded with a high or low tide, slack water, when Pascoe took a swim.

Julia stood up and hugged herself, suddenly cold despite the heat of the sun. If Malcolm had been spying on Pascoe it could only have been because he thought Gordon had something to do with his wife's disappearance. Now the scuba gear and the underwater line had a very dark interpretation. The CCTV would tell him that Pascoe was in the water, the mobility scooter and torpedo would take him quickly to the steps below the house, he could be there before Pascoe had finished his swim. He'd be able to catch Gordon while he was still in the water, alone and unprotected. What then?

Julia could only think of two answers. He might force the truth out of Pascoe by dragging him underwater a few times until he confessed, it would be like waterboarding. Or he might go further and actually kill the man. He had the setting for an undetectable murder. The currents would carry the body out into the ocean and it might be days before it was found, with no sign that it was anything other than a routine bathing accident. By that time Malcolm would have gathered up his line and the wireless camera, and destroyed the tide tables and CCTV footage. There would be nothing to suggest he had anything to do with the event.

Julia stared in horror at the image of her father on the screen.

Is that what you're telling me daddy? she wondered, *how to kill him?*

She tried to dismiss the thought. It made no sense. If he'd been planning a murder he'd never film himself doing it. She was puzzling over this when Connor called.

"I think you're right," he said after Julia had explained what she'd seen. "He was planning to confront Gordon. He knew he was ill and probably felt he had nothing to lose. He'd found out from Charlotte that Pascoe had built himself a house on an isolated cove close to his own house. He discovered that the man went swimming, where he'd be on his own. It was his best chance to persuade him to talk."

"It's still a risk. Gordon's a fit man, it wouldn't be easy to overcome him."

"It may be all he had."

"I suppose so," Julia sighed. "And now we're in the same position as he was, knowing that Gordon had forced him to leave but not knowing why."

"It's something to do with your mother, isn't it?" said Connor. "There must have been some sort of connection between them. Maybe she was a threat to him."

"How?" Julia remembered her mother, quiet and undemonstrative. How could she pose any kind of threat to a man like Pascoe?

"That's what you have to find out."

He hesitated. "There is another possibility, Julia. They might have had a relationship."

"Oh, no," Julia's response was immediate. "That's impossible."

"Be objective, Julia. Pascoe was a predator, and your mum was vulnerable: your dad away at sea for weeks at a time, you off at school, she could have been bored."

"Not all of us need a man to feel fulfilled, Connor. Some of us can manage perfectly well on our own."

"If Pascoe was responsible for what happened to her there must have been a reason."

"We were a close family," Julia said quietly. Connor was

right, she had to distance herself. She tried to remember what it had been like when her father was away.

"Mum and I sort of retreated from everyone. We stayed at home, cooked, cleaned the house, pottered in the garden. And when he came back there was never any tension. If she'd been playing away I'm sure dad and I would have noticed."

"OK, if you really think that, that's fine. Something else must have happened."

"It could have been anything," said Julia. "How am I going to find out what it was? Maybe I should do what dad was doing and catch Pascoe alone in the water."

"Do some proper research first. Find out what your mum did while you were at school. Talk to people who might have known her, like Monica Truscott. They were neighbours, they must have known each other."

"I'm seeing her tomorrow, she invited me to for a drink ages ago. But I can't ask her; she might say something to Gordon. I could try the Circle, one of them might remember."

"There's also that person she used to visit on the Park estate."

"I don't even remember her name. Maybe someone at the Circle will know that as well."

They agreed to talk again mid week, and Julia disconnected. She started to doubt herself. She reminded herself that her parents were happy. Olivia didn't get bored when Malcolm was away: she didn't need anyone else around to make her feel fulfilled. When she met Pascoe Julia had seen the attraction in him but found it very easy to resist. Olivia would not have fallen for him either.

Or had she? Am I refusing to face this because I can't bear to? she wondered. *I was only nine, what insight did I have at that age?*

These weren't questions she could answer easily. But then she remembered the way her father had looked when he told her that her mother had run away. She knew him, he could never hide his feelings. During the interminable games, working through the layers of clues, his face was an infallible guide to how well she was doing. If she was stuck she would make a guess and watch his eyes, they always gave him away, and they gave him away then. He was lying. Whatever had happened to her mother had nothing to do with sex.

She walked round to the farmhouse to ask Charlotte to take her to the Circle again. She was in the kitchen, baking cakes, her pinafore covered in flour. There was no sign of the children. She sat Julia down at the table and thrust a tray of scones towards her.

"They should remember her," said Charlotte, as Julia spread jam and clotted cream on a scone. "She gave a talk once."

Julia looked at her, startled. She remembered now: her mum typing her speech into the old computer, the zip-zip printer, practicing the words from the fanfold paper. The talk had been about carrots. *How does this…?* Her mother had rehearsed opening her left hand to show a tiny black seed, *…turn into this?* From her other hand she revealed a fully grown carrot. She was nervous and tentative, the look on her face suggesting that she had expected to produce something entirely different. Even as a nine year old Julia knew it would be a disaster.

"Jim Feathers is giving a talk the day after tomorrow," Charlotte went on. "Why don't you come along? A lot of the older members will be there."

20

Julia had never seen Monica's house before. She had passed the locked iron gates to the drive many times, but Westerly itself was hidden, set back on the hillside above the road, shielded by a high hedge. It came into view as Julia walked up the drive, flat roofed, single-storey, unaccountably painted grey, the same drab colour as most of the houses in Polwerran. An integral double garage formed two sides of a square with the side of the house. Monica's white Audi sports car was parked in front of the garage. The main door was in the side wall of the house. It was open, Monica waiting, cool in a white blouse and black trousers.

"This is nice." Julia could think of nothing original to say.

"Unexpected, isn't it?" said Monica with a faint smile as she led the way through the hall. On their right the lounge stretched along the entire front of the house. The walls were hung with vaguely abstract prints, their colours and textures chosen to match the muted blues and browns of the rest of the decor. The furniture was minimalist: two angular sofas and chairs arranged round a low table with a square vase of dried flowers in the middle. It was like the lobby of a boutique hotel.

As they continued their inspection - Monica had assumed without being asked that Julia wanted a tour - the size of the house became apparent.

"Six bedrooms, all en-suite," Monica recited.

On their way to the back of the house they passed a small study, empty except for an uncluttered desk with a small framed photo of the three grandchildren. At the rear was a kitchen-diner, the polished oak table large enough to seat a dozen people. Monica opened the double-doored fridge and took out a bottle of white wine.

"Glasses in the cupboard above the sink," she said.

As she took out two wineglasses Julia made a guess:

"This house is just an investment, isn't it?"

"Absolutely. When the Park is finished it will be worth a fortune. Come on, let's go upstairs."

"Upstairs? I thought this was a bungalow."

"You'll see."

Intrigued, Julia followed Monica back to the entrance hall. Behind a locked door was a staircase which led up, not to an upper storey but to the open roof.

As they emerged into the open air Julia was impressed in spite of herself. The whole of the roof was a flat open space bordered by glass panels which protected it from the wind while allowing uninterrupted views of the sea and the surrounding countryside. To the east was the church in Polwerran, its tower the only tall structure for miles around.

Near the front of the roof was a glass-topped table with half a dozen metal chairs. While Monica poured the drinks Julia looked out towards the sea. Mawgan Cottage and the farmhouse were invisible behind the trees. A memory came back to her. The farm had always been hidden from up here.

"I've been here before," she said. "There used to be a derelict house where we are now. Charlotte and I played in it until you told us to stop."

"It was dangerous." Monica lit a cigarette. "It collapsed a couple of years after you left."

Julia remembered the smell of sodden plaster and the crunch of rotten floorboards under her feet.

"There was a mineshaft as well, in a corner of the garden. It sloped down, you could walk into it. We always wanted to explore it, but neither of us had the courage."

"Just as well, you might never have come out again. I've had it blocked off. Malcolm did the same with the shaft behind his garage. Did he ever take you in there?"

"Never, it was absolutely off limits."

Julia was suddenly wary; Monica's glance at her while they were speaking was less casual than it looked. *Does she think I've been in since?* she wondered. She took a sip of wine, conscious for the first time that there was a purpose to this meeting. It wasn't social, they hardly knew each other. Julia had her childhood memories of Monica: Charlotte's mum, calm, efficient, but not particularly welcoming to others. Even now she still didn't seem to have friends: she'd been noticeably alone at the funeral and at the fete, where she'd only spoken to her grandchildren and Gordon Pascoe.

"What will you do when you sell this house?" Julia asked.

"Whatever I want." There was grim satisfaction in her voice. "I'll have no mortgage, no loans, just a steady income. I've worked for this."

Julia was surprised. Monica struck her as well off already: big house, expensive clothes, smart new car.

"Just by selling this house? Is it worth that much?"

Monica shook her head. "Don't forget the Park. When that opens we're all going to make a lot of money."

"What will you do? Retire? Or will you stay with Zenith?"

"What else is there to do round here?" Monica seemed to avoid the question. "I'll see what happens. For the moment my job is to make sure nothing jeopardises the project."

Julia caught a warning in Monica's voice.

Monica topped up Julia's glass.

"Did you find what your father was asking you to look for?"

"The Benjamin Steps?" Julia kept her tone neutral; she had been expecting the question. She was going to say nothing that might find its way back to Gordon Pascoe. "Not yet, I'm still going through his belongings."

"You haven't got much time. Your term starts in three weeks. What will you do then?"

"I'll come back." Julia looked down towards the cove, hidden behind the trees. "I will find them. Dad never set me anything that was impossible."

"He did like his riddles, didn't he?" Monica smiled. "I suppose that means you might not be selling his house just yet."

Julia was fully alert now.

"I haven't got probate," she said. "It's not mine to sell."

"But it will be."

Julia glanced at her without saying anything. Monica flicked ash from her cigarette.

"We're taking on new staff," she said. "We need places for them to live, and there's very little suitable housing in Polwerran.

"You want to buy it?"

"We could make an arrangement," Monica said. "Rent it until it's yours to sell."

"I'm not sure I want to sell. I might keep it. I might be one of those who make a fortune when your park opens."

"True," said Monica, reaching for her wineglass. She'd giving herself time to think, Julia realised. She thinks I'm negotiating with her. "We would naturally take that into account."

"Not now, Monica," Julia had to stop this. "I'm waiting until it's legally mine before making any decisions."

Monica didn't seem particularly surprised. "Of course. I do need to find a property though, so if you change your mind you will let me know, won't you?"

"Of course."

"Good." Monica topped up the glasses. "Now tell me about Hackney. I hear it's become quite fashionable."

Julia knew the evening was over. Monica had said all she wanted to say. When half an hour later Julia began making her goodbyes she didn't object.

Walking down to the cottage Julia felt uneasy. Monica had reiterated how important the Park was going to be. Had Malcolm's return, his spying on Pascoe, put it at risk in some way? Julia couldn't see how. He'd had been looking into something which happened 15 years before, the Park hadn't even been thought about then.

It didn't matter. Her own priority was clear: to find her mother, scatter both sets of ashes from the Benjamin Steps and leave, never to return.

Pascoe knew the answer, but she had nothing with which to confront him. For the first time she wished her father's challenge to her had been a little less obtuse.

21

At the Circle the following evening the cafe was occupied by middle aged women. The TV was off, there were no shrieks of children playing, just a low murmur of conversation which faded away as Julia and Charlotte walked. More hostility. Julia ignored them, walking confidently to the far end of the room where Laura Jeffries was once again seated to command the room.

"Come to hear Mr Feathers?" With a gesture Laura invited her to sit down.

"I thought it might be interesting," said Julia. "And I needed to get out of the cottage."

Next to Laura was a large lady with a mass of grey hair and wide blue eyes which fixed Julia with a stare like a cat assessing a pigeon. Julia knew that look, it had terrified her many times before.

"Peggy Stevens." the woman thrust a hand towards her, her glare unwavering. "I remember you, always whispering. Louder than talking, you know. People don't realise that."

"You run the library." Julia had a vivid memory of tiptoeing towards the desk to take out a book, feeling like Oliver Twist asking for more.

"Used to until it closed. Retired now. Must be difficult for you in that bungalow, going through all your father's belongings," said Peggy.

"It's got to be done," Julia took the plunge. "But it does bring back all sorts of memories. I find myself thinking about mum. I remember so little about her. Dad was big and lively; mum was a bit overshadowed. I wish I'd known her better."

"Nothing you can do about it now," said Peggy.

"Did she have any particular friends here? Someone I could talk to?"

Julia was watching the two of them as she spoke, and sensed that they were deliberately not looking at each other. There was a definite pause before Peggy spoke again.

"She kept to herself," she said. Laura was looking down the room.

"I remember her practicing a talk," said Julia, as if she the memory had just come back to her. "It was about carrots."

"Vegetables." Laura corrected her. "She talked about growing your own vegetables. We were having difficulty recruiting speakers at the time, poor Mr Feathers was giving a talk just about every month. He needed a break, so Olivia volunteered."

"She was terrified," Julia forced a smile. "She wasn't a natural public speaker, was she?"

"I can't really remember," said Laura. "We've had a lot of talks over the years."

"I do remember," said Peggy. "Poor delivery, mumbled all the time, but she managed to interest several of the members. She handed out a lot of seeds. Most of the girls gave up when they found out how much work was required but one or two persisted. Olivia was very good, she kept in touch with them, helped out where she could."

Julia had an idea. "Did one of them live on the Park Estate? I remember she used to visit someone there."

Laura shot a warning look at Peggy but she wasn't watching.

"That would have been Eliza Jones," she said. "Poor thing."

"Eliza!" exclaimed Julia. "I remember now. I always thought it was such an old-fashioned name."

"She soon tired of the idea, too much work, but Olivia persisted. Eliza's garden was much more fertile than any of the others. But Eliza was a drug addict, like many on the estate, and that took over her life. Olivia still visited, but by then it was only to keep an eye on little Jason, poor kid."

"Wasn't that Social Services' job?"

"Of course, but they were overstretched. They were happy for Olivia to help out."

Laura interrupted her.

"Time to go, Peggy," she said, then raised her voice over the hum of conversation.

"Five minutes everybody."

Everyone in the room stood up, chairs scraping on the wooden floor, gathering coats and bags and shuffling towards the door. Julia joined them, silently cursing Laura. The moment had passed.

The meeting room took up most of the upper floor. It was panelled in light oak, with windows high up on three sides. Blackout blinds cut out the light. Julia looked round for Charlotte but couldn't see her, so she took a seat towards the back. The room filled up rapidly but no-one sat near her.

Jim Feathers' theme was old Polwerran in pictures. He'd scanned the photos and was showing them with a laptop and projector. The room was warm with all the bodies, and getting warmer with the heat of the projector and in the semi darkness Julia was soon struggling to stay awake. The subject didn't interest her: sepia pictures of men and women in Edwardian dress posing stiffly in front of shop doorways, horses and carts, hay ricks and fishing smacks. She recognised one picture: the staff of a school standing in from of a blackboard. There had been a copy of it on the wall in Mrs Jeffries' study.

Eliza Jones. Another tentative clue. Something had happened to her. Julia tried to conjure up a face, but she had no memory of the woman or her child, only of visiting the house.

Which wasn't there any more, just a concrete slab covered in well-established weeds. It had been pulled down many years before. Connor and that big man Kevin had been puzzling over it that day.

The lecture ended, the lights went up, and there was more than one surreptitious yawn from the audience. Julia waited until most of the members had left, then made her way to the front, where Feathers was unplugging his laptop.

"I remember you," he said when she introduced herself. "You and Mr Munro rescued those two children on Mawgan Cove. That was courageous of you. The currents here claim so many lives."

There was nearly one more, she thought, remembering the dive.

"I was wondering if you could help me. I lived here when I was much younger. My mother was…"

"Olivia Philips," he interrupted, looking closely at her for the first time. "I see the resemblance now."

"You knew her?"

"Slightly." He seemed suddenly nervous, quickly thrusting the leads into his laptop bag.

"If I wanted some background on the time, where would I look?" Julia persisted.

"I wouldn't look anywhere."

He lowered his voice.

"Things happened then that no-one will talk about."

"She was my mother," Julia hissed, dismayed at his guarded attitude. He'd spoken freely to Connor when they'd met at the fete. "I want to know."

"She was a troublemaker," he replied. "Don't you make the same mistake."

"What mistake? What was she doing?"

"She made accusations but she had no proof. The fire…" he stopped in mid sentence, as if he realised he'd said too much. He scooped up his bags and scuttled out of the room before she could ask him anything more.

Julia made her way slowly to the front entrance to wait for Charlotte, alarmed by the feelings she was stirring up. Her mother making accusations, against whom? Pascoe, the Circle's benefactor? That might account for the hostility.

"Do you know anything about a fire?" Julia asked as they drove back to the farm. "I was asking Jim Feathers about Eliza and he was starting to tell me. Then he changed his mind."

"I don't know anything about that time," said Charlotte, keeping her eyes on the road. "I was the same age as you, remember."

"What about since then? A lot happened: Mum disappeared, something happened to Eliza Jones, the fire... what fire? Did someone die? If so it would be part of the folklore."

"You'd think so. But I've never heard anyone mention it."

"They still won't," Julia was puzzled. "Everyone is suddenly going very quiet. Jim looked frightened, so did Laura. Peggy was ready to talk, but Laura stopped her. I might give her a call."

"If they're not talking it's for a reason," said Charlotte. "Think about that."

Julia looked at her in dismay.

"You as well? You think I should stop looking?"

Charlotte brought the car to an sudden halt and turned to face her. "I know it's difficult, but you're not going to bring her back."

"I can give her a proper funeral."

Charlotte looked away.

"What is it?" Asked Julia. "Has someone been speaking to you?"

"You could hurt a lot of people," Charlotte avoided the question.

"How hurt do you think I've been?" Julia exploded. "Where's my family? Gone, fucked up by someone living here."

"I have three children, Julia."

She spoke very quietly and it was a moment before Julia realised what she meant.

"Who spoke to you?" she asked, more gently this time. But Charlotte shook her head, started the engine and drove back to the farm without another word.

22

Julia locked the cottage door and closed the blinds to shut out the night. The evening had reminded her of her isolation. She was an outsider, scratching away at something frightening. Those around her just wanted to live and prosper, regardless of who they might damage in the process. They were no better than the foxes and weasels, killing to feed themselves and their families. The sounds in the night were the desperate scramble for the safety of the nest, the sudden pounce, the final screams of dying prey. The uncaring struggle for survival had infected the people as much as the animals around them.

In the kitchen she found her father's whisky and poured herself a glass, diluting it with water, remembering Connor's warning about drinking it neat. Back in the lounge she curled up on the sofa. The scotch had a sharp, peaty taste, challenging and disconcerting. It wasn't relaxing, it made her think. It suited her mood.

The sensible thing to do was to follow Charlotte's advice: stop. Pack up and leave. No-one was going to help her, how was she going to find out what happened all those years ago? Just collect his ashes from the crematorium and scatter them from the Benjamin Steps. That had been his wish, she would have no further obligation to him.

Julia took another sip of whisky. She *did* have an obligation. Not to his words, to his intention. By finding the Steps she had uncovered his obsession with Gordon Pascoe. His behaviour in front of the CCTV camera was clear: he had wanted her to find out. He hadn't been certain he'd live long enough to finish what he'd started, he was encouraging her to do it for him.

What, exactly? He had left no clue to that. Julia was convinced of only one thing: Pascoe knew what had happened to her mother, but she couldn't think of any way of finding out more. Pascoe wasn't going to tell her, even if she caught him on his own in the water she didn't have enough information to force a confession from him.

It was 10 o'clock; Connor would still be up. She called him, but his phone was switched off. She left a message, finished the whisky and went to bed.

The following morning Julia collected the ashes from the crematorium. The urn, surprisingly heavy, stood in the corner of the lounge. To take it to the Benjamin Steps she would need company, there was no way she was going into the mine on her own. She immediately thought of Connor. He hadn't called back, but it was too soon to call him again.

She looked for something else to occupy herself. All her father's belongings were packed away, the house was clean, as were the yard and the patio. Only the garden remained, everything except the lawn overgrown and ragged through years of neglect. Julia hated anything to do with plants, but she also detested untidiness and the straggly hedges were starting to annoy her.

The old petrol powered hedge trimmer was in the garage, covered in dust, unused for years. Julia lifted it onto the old bench, primed the fuel and heaved on the starting cord. The engine turned but did not catch. She pumped more fuel and tried again. Still nothing. After five minutes fiddling with the controls Julia knew it was never going to start. She looked around for an alternative, but all she could find was a pair of secateurs and some loppers, neither of which would tackle a hedge. It was pointless buying a replacement, perhaps she could hire one? It would mean driving to Truro or Penzance to find a hire shop.

Julia looked back at the machine and a question popped uninvited into her head. *What would dad do?* The answer was immediate. He would fix it. He was an engineer, he understood machinery, and he had repaired this particular machine many times. Julia had helped him. The problem is always with the fuel: if it's left in the tank petrol eventually evaporates from the 2-stroke mixture and the resultant fuel is too rich in oil to start. It clogs up the fuel lines and fouls the spark plug. To get it functioning again you have to strip it down and clean the engine. It sounds impossible but is actually straightforward.

She could visualise her father at the workbench with the trimmer on its side, beside it a sheet of newspaper with the components laid out in the order they had been removed, screws, washers, tiny springs, the choke butterfly, gaskets. Malcolm peering at the instruction book, open at an exploded view of the engine, his eyes flicking between the diagram and a tiny widget between his thumb and forefinger as he worked out what it was and where it went.

That was what she would do. She changed into an old pair of jeans and T-shirt. Back in the garage she laid out a newspaper next to the trimmer, rooted through the boxes of tools to find the instruction book, and gathered the tools she would need. She worked slowly and methodically, making it a ritual, deliberately calming herself down. *If you hurry you'll make a mistake*, Malcolm had warned her, *do it carefully and you'll only have to do it once.*

Fifteen minutes reading and rereading the instructions told Julia what she had to do. Only when she was sure did she pick up a spanner and start dismantling the motor. It would take all her concentration to strip it down, clean and reassemble it. A single part lost or broken and the machine would be useless. Slowly, unhurried, she worked in a trance of concentration, her world her fingers, the tools and the little motor. She forgot about Gordon Pascoe, the Circle, probate, Connor, Charlotte, even her father.

When the machine was finally reassembled Julia came back

to reality, as if she'd been hypnotised and the hypnotist had clicked his fingers. She heard the birds singing again, and the rushing of wind in the trees. She took the trimmer out onto the hard standing, filled the fuel tank with a fresh mixture, primed the engine and pulled the starter cord. The machine spluttered uncertainly for a few moments then broke into a roar, briefly enveloping her in a cloud of black smoke before settling down to an irregular tickover. Julia let it run from a few minutes, revving it occasionally to make sure the blades were working, then switched it off in a little glow of satisfaction. She could hear her dad's approval.

Julia spent the rest of the day slicing branches off the trees and trimming the hedges. It was going to be a long job: judging by how much she completed in half a day it was going to take a week. It was boring, reminding her of why she hated gardening, and there was nothing to stop her mind wandering.

As the days wore on her thoughts turned increasingly to Connor. He hadn't called. At first she was annoyed, he'd broken his promise. Julia was used to boyfriends who couldn't find the courage to say goodbye so didn't say anything at all; she knew she could be intimidating. But Connor wasn't a boyfriend, they'd only known each other a few days, yet she trusted him. He was wary of her, but he was no coward.

After three days Julia could wait no longer and called the building site.

He wasn't there. No-one would tell her when he'd be back. His hotel told her he'd checked out. She called Layzells, his employers in London: they wouldn't tell her anything either.

Was he injured? Or dead? Had he been sacked? No-one would tell her anything.

Julia was stymied. Her only means of contacting him had been his phone, which he wasn't answering. They hadn't exchanged home numbers, or email addresses. There was no way she could get hold of him.

Something had happened to him, she was sure of that, but there was absolutely nothing she could do about it.

The weather turned wet, dank grey mists descended on the valley forcing Julia indoors, increasing her feeling of isolation and loss. Where was he? With nothing else to do she turned to school work and began rewriting lesson plans. She was just finishing two days later when Charlotte knocked on the door. She backed in, closing up an enormous golf umbrella, looking harassed as she shook water out of her hair.

"Filthy weather," she said. "The children are going mental. I'm taking them away: they're going to stay with their aunt in Somerset. You'll be all right on your own here for a few days, won't you?"

"Of course," said Julia, with more enthusiasm than she felt.

"Is there anywhere you can go until I get back?"

"I'll be all right here," Julia saw a troubled look in Charlotte's face. "What about you?"

"I can't keep the children away for ever."

Julia gave her a quick hug. "I understand. As soon as I've finished I'll go back home. I promise," she replied.

Charlotte drove away after breakfast the following morning, and Julia was alone in the valley. The rain had finally stopped and she was able to return to the garden. By mid afternoon an untidy pile of cut leaves and branches was standing at the top of the lawn. Julia stopped hacking and wheeled the shredder out onto the patio to reduce it all to compostable waste. A stack of plastic bags of chippings steadily replaced the pile of branches. After an hour she'd filled all the bags and began carting them down the garden to the compost heap tucked away close to the fence. The silence after the grinding racket of the shredder seemed absolute, only gradually did Julia become aware of the cries of the seagulls and the territorial singing of the woodland birds.

Then a different sound caught her attention. Something scraping. She was on the patio, it seemed to be coming from the side of the house, outside the front door. Julia stayed very still, the sound stopped for a moment, then started again. Irregular footsteps, someone loitering, someone in heavy boots.

Julia suppressed an urge to run round and tackle the intruder. He would be ready for her, the noise of the shredder would have told him she was there. And he might not be alone. Instead she slipped into the lounge, quietly pulling the patio door shut and locking it. The front and back doors were already locked, she was safe inside the cottage. The laptop with its CCTV monitoring system was on the coffee table.

Opening it up she saw, on the far side of the hard standing next to her Fiesta, a heavily built man. He was looking towards her front door, his face down so all she could see of his head was a striped beanie hat. There was something in his hand, long and fuzzy, she couldn't make out its shape. He knew he was on CCTV: the cameras were clearly visible and he kept his face hidden. Then he swung his arm and threw what was in his hand towards the house. Julia heard a soft thud as it hit the door. Julia put a hand to her mouth as she guessed what it was, fighting the panic and she watched to see what he did next.

Slowly he turned and walked away towards the farmhouse, the CCTV following him until the path curved out of sight. Julia waited another half an hour, watching the monitor, scanning the garden from the kitchen and the lounge, keeping out of sight as much as she could. When she was convinced no-one was waiting for her outside she quietly opened the front door. She thought she was ready for what was there but she still gagged. On the door was a heavy smear of blood. On the doorstep was the body of a cat, its throat cut, eyes and mouth wide, still showing the scream of terror as the knife took its life.

Julia closed and locked the door again, standing in the hallway, fighting down the urge to throw up. Gradually her stomach settled. She found a roll of plastic bags in the kitchen, put one inside another for extra strength, turned it inside out to act as a glove, then quickly opened the door again and picked up the remains of the cat.

Her phone rang.

More intimidation? Was the man in the beanie watching from the woods, waiting until she ventured out? Her hand were busy, the phone was in her pocket, she let it ring while she pulled the bag over the body.

She took a bucket of warm water from the kitchen and began mopping the door. The phone rang again, again Julia ignored it. The third time it rang while she was tying up the bag with the body inside. Furious, *why couldn't they leave her alone?* she fetched it from her pocket and pressed answer, but at that moment the bag split, the cat dropped onto her feet and blood smeared onto her jeans.

"Fuck!" she screamed.

"Are you all right?" a tinny voice from the phone. Connor, at last.

"No, I'm not all right," she shouted. "I'm covered in blood. Where the fuck have you been?"

"Blood? Are you hurt?"

"Someone has thrown a dead cat at my door."

"Oh no, Julia, they've started on you as well. We need to talk."

"Then why didn't you call me? I needed you, and you just buggered off."

"I didn't bugger off, I've been in hospital."

"They have phones in hospitals, don't they?"

"I just told you… oh, forget it. You're not listening. I'll find another way of dealing with it."

Abruptly he disconnected. Julia threw the phone onto the hallway mat and finished clearing up the remains. She knew she was behaving badly but her temper had its own momentum, immune to reason. She bagged the body again, this time in one of the tough rubble sacks from the patio and put it in the boot of the Fiesta, then scrubbed the door and threshold clean. When every trace of the cat had been washed away she threw her blood-stained clothes in the sink to soak, showered and changed. Then, very deliberately, she lay down on the carpet in the lounge, stretched, and began deep breathing, gradually relaxing the muscles in her neck, her back, her arms and legs, gradually emptying her mind of the horror she had seen. When at last she felt calm she picked up her phone and called Connor back.

"Tell me what happened," she said without preamble.

"I was beaten up outside my hotel." Now she noticed that his voice was muffled, if he had something in his mouth. "I was in hospital for a couple of days, and now I'm on sick leave. Your number was on my phone, and that was stolen."

"You could have got it from your company records. The claim form for my bike."

"I did. But that's personal information and it took me days to persuade them to give it to me."

Julia hadn't thought of that. Her anger began to subside.

"You said you wanted to speak to me," she said.

"Not over the phone. Can we meet?"

"It depends where you are."

"I'm at the top of your drive."

"What? How long have you been there?"

"About an hour."

"For god's sake, Connor, why didn't you just press the buzzer?"

"I did, but you didn't answer. I tried to phone you but it's taken this long to get a strong enough signal."

"Did anyone see you?" Julia was thinking of the man with the beanie.

"I don't think so. I'm in the woods, out of sight."

"Come down the footpath, but keep your eyes open. I'll unlock the bottom gate when you arrive."

Julia dropped the blinds in the kitchen and lounge, angling the slats so that no-one could see in, then went quickly down to the pond and stood by the gate. It was late afternoon and the sea breeze was starting to blow, rustling the leaves in the trees. They seemed to be whispering to each other, secrets she would never know.

There was the sound of shuffling feet and a quiet knock on the gate. Julia opened it and Connor eased in. His face was swollen from a bruise on his right cheek, and there was a livid cut on his forehead. But his eyes were calm, with a determined look she hadn't seen before.

"You do look a mess," said Julia, closing the gate behind him. "Let's get inside."

They walked side by side up the slope of the garden, Connor slow and stiff but he stood tall and his face gave no hint of pain. Once inside the cottage he lowered himself carefully onto the sofa in the lounge.

"This is an unexpected pleasure," she said drily. "They told me you'd left Polwerran Park. Someone else had taken over."

"That's true. I'm on sick leave."

"What are you doing here then?"

"I want to find out why I was beaten up. They've tried twice now."

"It was the same men?"

"Positive. One of them wore a striped beanie. I'd recognise him anywhere."

Julia suppressed a shudder. The man who'd thrown the cat had been wearing a beanie.

"I've frightened someone," he went on. "I don't know who, though we can both guess, or how, but it's connected with the Park in some way. I've been trying to find out more of its history, and I think that's what has spooked him."

"How do you know it's not Kevin Fisher, or one of the others on the site? You have upset a few people."

"That was my first thought," Connor agreed. "But then I found this."

He reached into his jacket pocket and pulled out a small buff envelope. As he leaned over Julia noticed a vivid cut, with several stitches, on his ear. His hands were shaking slightly.

"I found it amongst my clothes as I was leaving the hospital," he said. "It's got my name on it, but I don't remember receiving it."

Inside the envelope were a single rail ticket and a photo. The ticket was a first class open single from Truro to Paddington. Julia glanced at him in puzzlement.

"One way ticket. *Get out and don't come back*," he explained. "If you don't, there will be consequences…"

He gestured to the photo. Julia went cold as she saw what it was: her own face, a head and shoulders shot, but it was damaged, burned through with drops of acid. One eye was completely missing, just an irregular brown-edged hole in the paper.

"*The girl gets it,*" she said. "But you haven't stayed away, have you? This could actually happen. Thanks for that."

"I'll keep out of sight," he said.

"It's too late for that. Your man with the beanie was here less than an hour ago. He was responsible for the cat. He probably saw you as he left."

Connor shook his head. "The taxi dropped me half a mile away and I came the rest of the way over the fields. No-one saw me."

"Let's hope you're right," she looked gloomily out of the window. "You still haven't explained why you came back."

"Because there's something wrong. I need to find out what it is."

"It's not your problem any more. It's for your successor to deal with."

"Jackson? He's about 18, he's not going to challenge Gordon Pascoe."

He was silent for a moment, then began again, talking almost to himself.

"If Gordon had been sensible and had a quiet word with my boss - *Sorry, Tony, but it's not working out with Connor, we have to replace him before we have a strike* - something like that, I'd have accepted it. Another step down the career ladder. But he didn't, he decided to make absolutely sure I'd leave, and it's had the opposite effect. Now I want to know what he's so determined to suppress."

"Dragging me along with you."

"You're already part of it. Your dead cat was a present from the men who beat me up. Gordon wants us both away from here."

He stood up and stretched, arching his back with a grimace of pain.

"It stiffens up if I sit too long," he said, pacing slowly across the room.

"You've just confirmed his second mistake," he said. "I was just rooting around for an interesting story to put in a blog post. I was speaking to Jim Feathers until he stopped returning my calls; he'd obviously been warned off. That left me with no-one to talk to, so no story. But Gordon went too far again, giving me that photo. It reminded me that your dad was also digging into the past. Now you tell me he's trying to frighten you off as well.

"The two are linked, Julia. Your father's investigation has something to do with the Park."

"He was trying to find out what happened to mum," Julia reminded him. "But mum couldn't have had anything to do with your project: it hadn't even been thought of then."

"Not so. It was first proposed 16 years ago, it took until now to get the funding. But I said the Park, not the project. I think there might be a problem with the land itself."

"It's more likely to be Gordon trying to hide something dodgy from his past."

"We don't know," Connor conceded. "But whatever it is we have a much better chance of uncovering it if we work together. We need to find out what your mother was doing when she vanished."

Julia gave him a long look then sighed. "Ok, let's see what we can do together."

Connor took a deep breath, and some of the tension went out of him.

"Where are you staying?" she asked.

"A B&B in St Ives."

"That's not going to work. We can't spend all our time communicating by dodgy mobile connections. You'd better stay here. I've got a spare room."

He looked at her in horror.

"That's stupid, Julia. It would tell the whole world what we're doing."

"No-one will see you. You'll have to keep off the terrace, but everywhere else is private."

"What about Charlotte?"

"She's away for a week. When she gets back I'll tell her what we're doing. She can keep a secret."

Connor was still doubtful.

"It's still a risk."

He looked down at the envelope with the acid-stained photo.

"If we're going to work together we have to be together. This is not negotiable," she added, seeing the mulish expression on his face. "If you want my help this is the way we do it."

He stared at her, then broke into a faint grin.

"You're as stubborn as I am," he said. "I'd better get my luggage."

"I'll take you."

Ten minutes later the Prius crept silently down the drive, Julia at the wheel while Connor lay out of sight on the back seat. When they were clear of the town Julia stopped and he moved to the passenger seat beside her. She asked him about his beating up.

"I'd been working late," he said. "When I got back to the hotel the main car park was full and I had to park in the overflow. It was unlit and a long way from the main building. That's where they were waiting for me. Two in an old black BMW and the third, well I don't know where he came from, but he was behind me. He kicked my legs away and I was on the floor. I don't remember much after that. They could have killed me, but I was lucky: another car pulled in. The three of them scattered, piling into the BMW and driving off. I found myself in an ambulance heading for the hospital. They kept me in for a couple of days, I had a bump on the head and they were checking for concussion, but I was OK. I was signed off work for three weeks, the firm sent a car and took me home to my flat."

This is what I stopped in the graveyard, thought Julia.

After two hours they were back at the cottage. Connor sat in the lounge while Julia made up his bed; he looked exhausted, and when Julia came back after making up the spare room she wasn't surprised to find him asleep on the sofa, his battered face gentle and peaceful. She prodded him awake. He looked around startled, as if unsure where he was.

"Go to bed," she said. "You've got a room."

He got slowly to his feet.

"House rules?" he asked.

"Keep your bedroom locked, your wash bag and towel out of the bathroom in case anyone drops in and wants to use the loo. If anyone does turn up get into your room and lock it behind you. We'll make up the rest as we go along."

"OK," he said. "And thanks for putting me up. You didn't have to."

"I did, Connor. It was inevitable."

Julia saw the puzzled expression on his face.

"You can use the bathroom first," she said, hurrying into her bedroom and closing the door before he could ask anything else.

Inevitable. The word terrified her. She had made him to stay because she didn't feel safe on her own, but she had invited in a different danger. The man who had draped a towel over her shoulders and sat silently beside her after the accident on the cove, who had asked her about her mother and she had told him. He just understood; he knew how to be with her. The heroics: rescuing the children, staying with her on the dive, made her admire him. This was far deeper, far more destructive.

Julia sat down on the edge of the bed, waiting for the sound of his bedroom door closing. The events fifteen years before had ensured she would never be happy, but she had found a sort of contentment, accepting her life for what it was. It got her to work every day, it kept her calm and focussed and independent.

Until now. Now her contentment was doomed, like a sandcastle on the beach awaiting the unstoppable approach of the tide.

23

"Your mum wasn't popular, she made accusations, apparently about a fire, then she disappeared. Something happened to Eliza, her friend," Connor said after Julia had told him of Monica's hints, her visit to the Circle, and Charlotte's warning.

It was the following morning. He looked refreshed, his face a little less swollen, his expression eager.

"It's not much to go on, but it's a start. Let's see what we can find from other places. I'll go back over the project files, you look into the fire. Feathers didn't want to talk about it, so it's significant. Try the local paper. All the back issues are online."

"Seriously? It's just a local rag. Ninety percent adverts."

"You'd be surprised. What's the name of it?"

"The West Cornwall Weekly Mail."

He took out his phone. "There you go," he said a few swipes later. "Every issue for the last 150 years."

He showed her the screen.

"That will keep me busy for a while," she said, gathering up her laptop and taking it out to the terrace. The sun was up and the air still, the trees motionless. In spite of her gloomy mood she was glad to have company, the valley seemed less remote today.

She switched on and navigated to the newspaper archive. The website was primitive, just a list of editions, each with a link to a set of scanned pages. None of the content was indexed, the only way to find an item was to guess when it happened and work backwards and forwards through the pages until she found it. It was going to be like wading through the CCTV footage again.

Julia started with October 1995, the month her mother disappeared. The story was news for weeks. The police and teams of volunteers had been searching the woods, the cliffs, beaches, the old mines, but nothing was found. There was no clothing, none of her belongings, no signs of a struggle. The last person known to have seen her mother was Julia herself when she was dropped off outside the school. After she drove off no-one saw her mother again.

The car. Julia glanced across towards the drive, remembering. It had been a 1970 Citroen DS Pallas. Dad had loved it, her mum hadn't: she used to say it was like driving an armchair. Julia thought it was brilliant, particularly the way it sank as if the tyres were deflating when the engine was turned off. People stared at it: there weren't many like it in Cornwall and in Polwerran it was unique. So how had mum managed to drive from the school, through the town and out to the cottage without a single person seeing it? Narrow minded peasants, Julia thought bitterly. Of course they all saw it, they just weren't going to tell anyone, not even the police. Olivia had been an outsider, what happened to her was nothing to do with them.

Looking up from the screen to rest her eyes Julia noticed a buzzard circling high above, wings motionless as it scanned the ground for prey. Surveillance was everywhere. On the far side of the valley the trees in their full summer leaf could be hiding an army of watchers. Maybe she should be joining Connor in the safety of the back yard.

Julia shrugged off the thought. She was being paranoid. Concentrate. She began working back through the issues looking for any mention of a fire. On the way she found a piece on a fundraising dinner, with a photo of a younger Gordon Pascoe presenting a cheque to Monica Truscott, who was then the Treasurer.

On the same page was a report of a fire, but it was just an

outbuilding on a remote farm, no-one was injured. After that Julia found fires reported almost every week. Arson seemed to have been a local speciality. Fires in hay ricks, cars on the street, even an attempt to burn down the junior school. Julia remembered that, they had a day off while they cleared up the mess. The classroom smelled of smoke for weeks.

Then, in the issue for the first week in July, Julia found what she was looking for. A blaze on the Park Estate, the fire so intense the two bodies were unrecognisable, only identifiable from dental records.

Eliza Jones and her two year old son Jason. Eliza, her mother's friend.

"I've found it," she told Connor. He was in the back yard, exercising on her yoga mat, sweating from the effort. "Poor girl, what a hideous way to die."

"Was anyone arrested?"

"No. The police wanted to talk to the rent collector, but he disappeared. They appealed for other witnesses; it looks as if none of the neighbours would talk."

Connor stood up and went to the table where his laptop was open.

"I'll check the fire brigade records, they always publish the results of their investigations."

After a few minutes searching he found the report.

"Definitely arson," he said, skip-reading the conclusions, "The fire started in the hall, just inside the front door, which wasn't locked. That's where they found the bodies, at the bottom of the stairs. The blaze was unusually ferocious, suggesting it wasn't just a random attack."

"Cause of death?"

"They couldn't decide. There was evidence of drug usage, but the bodies were too badly burned for anyone to reach a definite conclusion."

"I thought they could find traces of DNA anywhere these days," said Julia.

"A hot enough fire will destroy anything. Body tissue

vaporises and blows away in the smoke."

He closed the laptop.

"Which is convenient if you're trying to cover up something else entirely," he added. "Did your mum have her own suspicions, I wonder?"

"It's possible, we just don't know," Julia said. "It could have been murder, but it could also have been an insurance fraud that went wrong, a kids' prank that got out of hand, even suicide. "

"It was something deliberate," Connor was emphatic. "Pascoe forced your dad to leave, and now he's trying to make the two of us go as well. There's something he doesn't want us to find. Eliza died in dubious circumstances and soon afterwards, your mum vanished. I'd say that the fire, which no-one wants to talk about, is at the heart of everything."

"Including your own beating up?"

"That I don't know," Connor said quietly. "There are one or two odd aspects of Zenith, maybe they didn't want me digging too deeply. Firstly, Pascoe isn't the only one with a stake in the company: 40% has been owned from the start by an offshore company called Apricot Holdings. I can't find out anything about them, they're registered in the Cayman Islands. I've got a friend in our Legal Department who's got some unorthodox contacts. He might unearth something.

"Secondly, I've been looking at the accounts for around that time. In 1994 Zenith went from comfortable to barely solvent. Cashflow became very tight, there was a big increase in loan repayments and professional fees. The fees were probably for consultants helping them put together the business case for the park, but there's no obvious reason why they'd be taking out massive loans."

"It could be something else entirely. They own the pasty business, don't they? Maybe that was expanding."

"Good point. I'll keep digging, see what else I find. Oh, by the way, have you even heard of someone called Leigh Henderson?"

"Should I have?"

"He was director of Farwest 80. They're the company which initially sold the land to Zenith. I can't find out anything about him. I've looked on Linkedin, Facebook, Google, but there's nothing; he doesn't seem to exist."

"I could ask Charlotte. She knows everybody."

"Best not. She might ask someone else and you can't be seen to be digging. You might try Peggy Stevens though, she seemed to be sympathetic. And she might know more about Eliza."

Julia's call went straight to an answering machine. Julia hung up without leaving a message.

"Nothing," she said. "We really are on our own, aren't we?"

"We always knew that."

Catering for Connor meant that Julia needed more provisions, so after lunch she threw some shopping bags in the boot of the Fiesta and set off for the supermarket. The lane was twisty, high stone walls making it difficult to see more than a few yards in front or behind. It was safer by night, when the light from headlamps warned you of another car long before you saw it. In daylight all that was visible was the short stretch of road between the bends, so for a while she wasn't sure if she was imagining the dark shape behind her drifting into view on the occasional length of straight road. Gradually it came closer, a large black saloon. Julia was driving as a safe speed, ready to stop if she met a car on one of the narrow stretches of road. The car behind was catching up, making no attempt to keep at a safe distance. Julia slowed, if she had to stop he would run into the back if her. Now she could see the driver, a dark face. The car was a BMW, just like the one Connor had described. It came closer, now she couldn't even see his radiator, just the driver, his face expressionless. He seemed to be on his own. Julia kept her nerve, trying not to be intimidated. Maybe it was another aggressive driver trying to overtake. There was a straight section of road ahead, she would see what happened then.

As they entered the straight Julia kept well to the left, slowing to give him room to pass. The BMW swung out onto the wrong side of the road and pulled alongside, but instead of accelerating away he kept pace. Julia slowed, so did he. She could hear the deep growl of his engine. Julia continued to slow, the other car did the same, maintaining station alongside her. At the end of the straight was a sharp bend, there was no way two cars could round it together. And if they met anything coming the other way, like the milk tanker…

Abruptly Julia braked hard, taking the other driver by surprise, but as he shot ahead he swung into her path, forcing her off the road and towards a gate. Julia felt the judder of the anti-skid system as the car lurched to a halt, just short of a stone wall. The BMW accelerated away. Julia looked after it in horror. If she had been less alert she might have been killed. This wasn't a kid high on drink or drugs, it was a deliberate attempt to run her off the road.

Julia forced herself to start again, to get off the empty side road and into traffic, where she'd be safer. She drove fast to the outskirts of Truro, watching for anyone following her, but the black car was nowhere. She found a space in the busiest part of the car park and sat unmoving for ten minutes until she felt calm again. Then she began shopping, doubling her quantities so they'd have enough food for a fortnight. It would see them to the end of their investigation.

Driving back down the lane Julia met no more cars, but her hands were shaking as she pulled up at the cottage.

"What happened?" Connor asked when he saw the expression on her face as she unloaded the groceries.

"I met your black BMW," she said. "He tried to run me off the road."

She described what had happened. He listened in horror.

"We haven't got much time have we?" he said when she finished. "They'll try again, and soon."

"I'm staying until we've got an answer," said Julia. "I've stocked up, there's no need to chance another meeting on the road. You can help me put it all away."

Julia was too tense to sleep that night. Her encounter with the BMW had shaken her more than she had realised. She tried to read, but couldn't concentrate. On her own she would have gone into the lounge to watch a DVD, but she didn't want to disturb Connor. Trapped again. She dropped into a fitful doze, again replaying the scene with the black car, only now she could see the driver and it was her father, laughing as he swung the steering wheel and the two cars collided, locked together as they hurtled towards the blind bend that ended the straight, her father crying out "NO!"

Awake again and sweating, Julia realised the cry had been real. It had come from Connor's bedroom. It had happened before, when he had slept on her sofa after she'd rescued him from the graveyard. Something troubled him. He'd never acknowledged it, but it was there all the time, in his anger and in the way he spoke about the park, as if he had a personal compulsion to see it through.

Another sound, a faint scuffling in the yard. It seemed to be coming from directly below her window. Julia froze, holding her breath as she tried to identify the sound, mentally checking that she was safe. The window was closed and locked. Connor had told her the house was secure, but the scratching outside didn't reassure her. The rustling stopped and the night lapsed into silence before it started again. Now Julia recognised it, even though it was fifteen years since she'd last heard it. She slid quietly out of bed and eased back the edge of the curtain. Moonlight gave the yard a ghostly look. There was nothing moving, the source of the noise was out of sight directly below her and she did not dare open the window. She waited, as she had always done. Sooner or later he would show himself. For a creature of the night he was remarkably unsubtle, never bothering to hide, noisy enough to be heard at the other end of the garden. She didn't have to wait long. Soon a small dark shape crossed the yard from under her window to the far wall. A hedgehog, rootling through the dead leaves for insects. Its waddling gait used to make her giggle. Now she smiled as it pottered unconcerned along the foot of the wall, heading towards the open space outside the back door.

Your mum's best friend, her dad had said. *He eats the slugs before they can eat her lettuces.*

He'd been making a ramp so the hedgehogs could get onto the raised beds. Julia had been watching to see if it worked, standing on a chair so she could see out of through the window…

The raised beds. The vegetable garden. She'd been able to see it from her bedroom.

"Oh God," she said out loud. "I should have thought of this before."

From the other end of the cottage came the sound of the toilet flushing and the click of the bathroom door lock. Throwing on her dressing gown she went out into the hall and switched on the light. Connor was rounding the corner, moving stiffly in his pyjamas, and stopped in surprise.

"I've remembered something," she said. "I think it's important."

He looked at her blankly, and she saw how tired he was. "I won't keep you long," she said. "Come into the front room. I'll light the gas."

"Mum's vegetable garden was at the back, where you've been working." Julia began as they sat in front of the artificial coals, Connor upright in one of the armchairs, wrapped in a silk dressing gown, his phone on the armrest beside him. Julia sat beside him, cross legged on the floor. "It was a lot of work, four big raised beds to look after; she was there every day. Then one day when I arrived back from school it was all gone. The plants, the canes for the beans, everything. It was all flat, Dad was walking backwards and forwards with a machine like a lawnmower with a big plate on the bottom. It vibrated, it made my teeth chatter."

"A compactor," said Connor automatically. "Did they replant it somewhere else?"

"No, they just dug it up and put down paving slabs."

"When did this happen?"

"I'm trying to remember. It was warm and sunny, and Dad built a barbecue in the corner immediately afterwards. He christened it straightaway, so it must have been summer."

Julia remembered sawing through the charcoaled skin of the first sausages. It had been vastly more exciting that the limp string beans her mother used to serve.

"We were here two years," she went on. "It couldn't have been first summer because mum exhibited at the Circle, so she must have had a garden then. So it was the second year, 1995. It happened before the end of term, so it was around June or July."

Connor's face was becoming increasingly serious. "Around the time Eliza died," he said slowly. "Did they tell you why they'd done it?"

"They may have done. At the time I didn't care: barbecued sausages were much more fun than vegetables. It's only now that I'm starting to wonder. She was in that garden every day. Why did she suddenly abandon it?"

"Perhaps they knew they were moving and decided to keep it as a holiday let. A veg garden wouldn't be much use then."

Julia shook her head. "They would have told me if we were about to move. It was a feature of navy life, we never settled anywhere."

They sat in silence, the only sound was the hissing of the gas. Connor was leaning forward to catch the heat from the burner.

"I'm sorry," said Julia. "I've kept you up. You should be in bed."

"It doesn't matter." He kept his eyes on the fire. "I don't sleep well."

"I've noticed."

He gave her a sharp look. "I don't wake you up do I?"

"No," it was only a small lie. "But I'd like to know what's bothering you."

He looked back to the fire and Julia sensed he was trying to decide whether to speak, but at that moment there was a beep from his phone. They both jumped, staring towards the screen.

"It's your CCTV. I found an app."

Connor studied the image. "Just a hedgehog."

"A hedgehog is too small to set off the PIRs," Julia leaned

over to look. "Rewind it."

They sat close together as he replayed the last few minutes.

"There," she said. They were looking at the picture from the yard, the front door on the left, the garage in the background, and bushes on the far right. In the shrubbery was the indistinct shape of a man's head. He seemed to be watching the door, then he retreated out of shot.

"He's still here." Julia's voice dropped to a whisper.

"There's nothing we can do," said Connor. "You can't go out now, he might not be alone, and he mustn't find out I'm here."

"He's not trying to break in, is he?"

"He won't succeed. I checked your security. The doors are solid, the locks are all insurance grade, the windows are all double glazed with laminated glass. This house is seriously well protected."

Julia pulled away from him, glancing at the windows. The blinds were drawn, it was impossible for anyone to see them.

"I'm starting to hate this place," she said. "What's he doing?"

"Letting you know he hasn't gone away," said Connor. "He knows you'll see him on the CCTV. It's just more intimidation."

"It's succeeding."

"Forget him. Concentrate on your mum's garden. You're right, it is important. We need to establish why she dug everything up. Did they say anything about what they were doing?"

"I don't remember." Julia was trying to push away the image of the man peering at them from the bushes. "I spent fifteen years trying to forget, I can't bring it all back just like that."

"OK, Let's go at it in a different way. What possible reason could there be? Did your mum get bored, or start doing something else, so she didn't have time for the garden?"

"She wasn't the type to get bored, and she saw things through. She wasn't impulsive. If she was planning to stop gardening she'd have waited until the season was over. They might have decided to reorganise the whole garden but again they wouldn't do it while everything was still growing."

"She wasn't ill or anything, something physical which meant she wasn't able to do the work?"

Julia shook her head. "None of that."

Connor was looking into the fire. "Well, if it wasn't your mum it must have been something to do with the garden itself. Maybe some of the crop died."

Julia looked up at this. "There's always something that doesn't grow, or shrivels up unexpectedly. One year it will be the lettuce, another the potatoes, it's part of life. But if something affected the whole crop…"

"Just what I was coming to." Connor's face was grave. "To affect the whole garden something would have to go wrong with the soil. All of it."

He gave her a bleak look.

"The only way that can happen is through the water that feeds it. Your parents abandoned their garden because the water went bad."

Julia felt a shiver which had nothing to do with the cold of the night.

"The water in your garden comes from the mine." Connor continued in a monotone, as if he was struggling to react to what they were saying. "Oh bugger."

"It's not just here, is that what you're thinking?"

"There's a story that the Polwerran Park land is cursed. There's never been anything specific, just a lowering cliff which intimidates everyone who sees it, and an ancient story about John Wesley refusing to preach there. But this might be proof that there really is a problem with the land."

"Your park is a mile away, Connor," Julia's rational self was reasserting itself. "You can't assume that our water comes from your spring."

"The shaft we explored goes towards the town for at least a mile," he reminded her. "And in that cavern was a substantial stream, which might be from the spring."

"That's still supposition. There's no proof."

"We'd better get some then." Connor was suddenly brisk. "I'll speak to the hydrologist who monitors the spring. Tom Mather. He can run a dye test: pour something bright and fluorescent into the spring on site and see if it comes out here."

"Can he test the garden as well? If the soil did become contaminated the evidence should still be there, under the flagstones."

"Good idea. We'll dig out some samples. I'll collect some water from your stream as well. He'll have them analysed in a couple of days."

"So," Julia was calculating, "in a few days we should be able to know if the ground was once poisoned, and whether or not the poison could have come from your spring. That would be a result."

"Not a happy one, but yes," said Connor.

"What else? Is there any way of checking for poison actually on the Park?"

Connor thought for a moment. "The spring is buried for its entire length. The only place we might find something is where it drops into the old ventilation shaft to the mine below."

They looked at each other.

"In Eliza's garden."

"Where there's no soil anymore, just solid concrete."

"No soil, no evidence. That's convenient."

24

Connor rang Mather the following morning while Julia prised up one of the paving slabs in the back yard and shovelled soil into a plastic box.

"There's nothing wrong with the spring," said Mather after Connor had asked him for a dye test. He sounded defensive. "We check it regularly, I can show you the schedules and the results. There's never been a problem."

"This isn't about your work, Tom. If there is a problem it's intermittent, and very infrequent. There's something obscure going on."

"Bring the samples in; I'll have the result tomorrow." Tom still sounded anxious. "I can inject the dye the day after, but it might be several days before you see the outcome of that. Water seepage can be very slow."

Julia was sealing the boxes as he rang off.

"If we're going out let's make a day of it," she said. "We can drop off the samples and carry on to the beach. It will be better than staying cooped up here. We could try Perranporth. The beach is huge, there will be thousands of people, no-one's going to notice us. And you can exercise in the water for a change."

Connor grimaced at the thought of spending the day surrounded by trippers but he could see Julia's point. Being able to spend the day not worrying if someone was spying on him was very appealing.

"We just have to get out of here without being driven off the road by that BMW," he said.

"I've thought of that," she said. "He won't try anything if there's a witness, so we wait for another vehicle and tag along behind. But we'd better be quick, he comes along at around ten. Come and help me make a picnic."

"Who comes at ten?"

"The postman in his little red van."

He followed her into the kitchen, surprised at her mood. Despite their oppressive night she seemed almost skittish.

Punctually at ten they were parked in the trees near the top of the farm track. Soon the post van trundled down the lane, heading towards Pascoe's house and the farms beyond. Julia drove out through the gate and waited. Connor was out of sight lying on the back seat. This was the difficult time, stopped for no apparent reason just outside her own gate she would attract the attention of anyone passing. An anxious ten minutes passed before the van came back and Julia was able to slot in behind it. They reached the main road with no sign of the black car. Her satnav directed Julia to the industrial estate outside Falmouth where Mather had his office.

"My God!" exclaimed Mather as Connor walked into his office. "What happened to you?"

"Somebody doesn't want me to do what I'm doing. Take it as a warning, Tom. Keep this quiet."

Mather gave him a quizzical look, inviting an explanation, but Connor didn't elaborate, handing over the samples and leaving with a brief thank you.

He was pensive in the car as they drove on to Perranporth.

"How could it happen?" he asked. "How can water be pure for years, become lethal, then clear again?"

"No idea." Julia didn't take her eyes off the road. "All sorts of odd things happen underground. Does it matter?"

"I need a convincing case if I'm to stop the project, and that includes some plausible physics to explain what happens."

It was noon when they reached Perranporth. With their towels, beach mats and the cool box they looked just like all the other holidaymakers. They passed windsurfers and kitesurfers sitting by a café on the edge of the sand waiting for the breeze to pick up. The main beach was busy but they found a quiet spot in the shelter of the dunes. They changed and headed for the water, Connor self-consciously wearing a wetsuit to hide his bruises, his legs so weak it felt as if he had weights around his ankles, Julia patiently walking beside him. He waded in tentatively, keeping within his depth, bobbing as the waves threatened to submerge him. Julia stayed with him, watching.

"You go off," he told her. "I'll be all right here."

"Later," she said. "Let's see you swim."

"Are you mothering me?"

"Just get on with it."

He grunted, seeing the schoolmistress in her. He kicked off, barely managing five metres before putting his feet down again. He waited until his limbs had stopped complaining and tried again, with the same result.

"Bugger," he said.

"What did you expect?" Julia said. "This is going to take a while. Try it a few more times then we'll take a break."

Half an hour later they trudged back up the beach. Connor lowered himself carefully onto the beach mat.

"I have got some work to do," he said, taking a swig from the water bottle in his backpack.

"You'll get there," said Julia. "It's only bruising."

From her bag she fetched a Kindle and settled down to read, turning so that her back was towards him. I wonder what she reads, he thought. An e-reader gives no clues, and the only physical books in the cottage were her father's, in packing cases. He knew very little about Julia. She didn't volunteer anything, and he didn't enquire. He was her guest and nothing more, and yet he felt they understood each other. She was sad, often grumpy, but so was he. They could be grumpy together, and his intuition told him that was quite unusual.

There was something else as well. She had said his staying

with her was inevitable. She hadn't explained what she meant but he could guess, and the thought thrilled and terrified him at the same time. He glanced across at her tiny bare back, crossed by the single string of her top tied in a bow, then looked away quickly, aware that he had been prying.

They remained on the beach for the rest of the afternoon, Connor spending as much time as possible in the water, slowly strengthening his muscles, Julia watching all the time. When evening came and the air cooled they dressed and took their belongings back to the car.

"Let's stay here a while longer," said Connor as they loaded everything into the boot. "Have fish and chips on the cliffs. There's no reason to go back just yet."

Julia agreed and half an hour later they were sitting above the beach watching the last of the surfers bobbing on the swell. Dog walkers were strolling along the hard sand below the high water mark. The sun was starting its slow descent towards America.

"It's not a bad place, is it?" he said.

"It's even better during a storm," said Julia. "You can hardly stand against the wind, and the noise of the waves makes it impossible to think."

A large dog bounded across the grass and deposited a stick at Connor's feet. He picked it up and threw it towards the middle aged man he took to be its owner, wincing as his muscles complained at the unexpected effort.

"I couldn't live here though," Julia went on. "I'm a Londoner now. I need the buzz."

They ate in silence for a few moments, then Julia turned to him. He tensed, seeing a determined look on her face, guessing what was coming.

"Something troubles you," she said.

"You mean apart from being beaten up and losing my job?"

"You know what I mean. Who's Stevie?"

"Ah." His hand went to the Lego brick in his pocket. "Have I been shouting?"

"Stevie, No. It's like a warning."

"It was," he said quietly. "But he never listened."

He took out the brick and held it in his open hand. Julia looked down at it, puzzled, before returning her gaze to his face. It was an invitation to talk.

"Stevie was my brother," he said. "Three years older than me. He was an architect, brilliant, they used to compare him to Foster and Hadid. His buildings are all over the world. He didn't just do office blocks and shopping centres and concert halls, he'd do anything that interested him: golf courses, leisure complexes, he even won an award for a car park. And he was fascinated by theme parks. We both were."

Understanding spread on her face.

"As boys we had this grand vision, the Ultimate Experience, full of rides that no-one had ever thought of before, most of which would probably never work. He had all the ideas and I could build, so when he sketched them I made models in Meccano, or plasticene, sometimes in Lego."

He looked down at the brick. There was a faint imprint of the plastic in his palm, where he'd been holding it in his clenched fist.

"The last remaining part of Killer Junction," he said. "Two trains approach a signal at 50 mph, one at right angles to the other. One had green the other red but neither slows down. They miss each other by exactly three inches."

"Stevie never lost his fascination. While he was at college he developed a concept for the greatest theme park in the world as his final year project. It was fabulous, a lot more beautiful than our original designs, and a lot less lethal. A model of it was exhibited at the Royal Academy Summer Exhibition. One of the councillors here saw it, and invited Stevie to produce a design for a project of theirs, which became Polwerran Park. When the project was approved, many years later, Stevie's firm, Layzells, were asked to be the architects and project managers, and that's where I come in.

"I studied architecture as well, and got a good enough degree, mainly because I understood the technicalities, but I didn't have Stevie's flair. I got a job in Layzells' project management division, which suited me, and worked my way up. I'm now a senior team leader."

Connor paused. He'd lived every day with the memory of what happened next, never speaking of it to anyone. But he knew Julia would understand, and he wanted to tell her; he wanted the intimacy that sharing the story with her would bring.

"It was two years ago, May 14, a Wednesday. I was working on the Swithunsgate development. You'll know it as the Icicle, the Upside-Down Building. It won Stevie the Sterling Prize. We were on the site together, his mind already on his next project. He wanted to design something that looked unfinished. He loved the shapes in a building under construction: the metal rods sticking out of concrete pillars, the walls made up of rough tubes of concrete which line the foundations, the way a block appears to grow like a crystal, the lift shafts shooting upwards, behind them the floors, then the walls, then the windows, so that lowest floors look as though they're ready to be occupied while they're still pouring concrete at the top. He wanted to design an office block that looked just like that, just like work in progress.

"At that time the Icicle was just a 50 foot hole in the ground. We were standing next to it; Stevie sketching and photographing everything. He'd seen a pattern in the ironwork at the bottom of the pit and was leaning over to get a picture but I warned him to keep back: the barrier was flimsy. I'd been trying for weeks to get Conco to replace it.

"Then my phone rang: Accounts chasing up a missing timesheet. I had to turn away to take the call and I heard the screech of metal and the warning bark of one of the guard dogs. When I looked back there was a gap in the barrier and Stevie wasn't there any more."

"Oh, Connor," said Julia. She reached out to take his hand, picking the Lego piece out of his palm, running her fingers over it then putting it back, closing his fingers around it.

"He was in my charge and I failed him."

"The barrier wasn't your fault. The contractors were responsible."

"Of course they were, but they denied it, and as they're also the biggest in the country no-one challenges them, not if they ever want to work again. I tried, and I ended up on their blacklist. Unemployable in London. If this contract hadn't come up unexpectedly I'd be out of a job by now."

Julia was silent for a while, releasing his hand and staring out to sea.

"It's so destructive," she said eventually.

"Losing someone?" He thought she was thinking of her relationship with her father. She shook her head.

"Guilt," she said. "Let me ask you something. If you had that moment again, when your brother was beside you on the site and your phone rang, what would you do that was different?"

"Lots of things. Not answer the phone, move away from the edge, be more insistent with the contractors."

"That just hindsight. If you'd known what was going to happen you'd have done something else."

"Does it matter? You're implying it was inevitable. That just makes it worse."

Julia scrunched up the greasy fish and chip paper.

"Now you're telling me you feel guilty because of who you are. I can't help you there."

She stood up.

"You're not as careless as you think you are," she said. "When we first met you were ranting at a driver because he was about to let his truck turn over as he unloaded his cargo. You shouted at everyone else because they were risking lives sending the rubble through the town. The way you've described your arguments with that contractor in London you almost lost your job over safety. You spotted the kids in danger in the water. You stayed with me on our dive.

"And you came back here," she finished. "You're the least negligent people I've ever met."

For some reason her words made him angry. Stevie was dead. Nothing could change that.

"You're telling me to get over it."

"I'm saying what I think."

Julia walked quickly away, Connor scrambling to follow her, but she was already at the car by the time he caught up. They drove back to the cottage in a heavy silence, Connor sitting in the back. He knew he was being childish. As they drew close to the farm and it was time to lie down out of sight he leaned forward and touched her briefly on the shoulder.

"Thanks," he said.

They were back at Perranporth the next day. Connor had just managed his first continuous fifteen minute swim. Feeling pleased with himself he towelled himself dry then checked his phone. He'd missed a call from Tom Mather. He called back, walking away from the dunes, there were people all around and he didn't want to be overheard.

"We've got the test results," said Tom. "Are you somewhere private?"

Connor looked around. A beach ball bounced past, pursued by a small boy. He waited until the boy was out of earshot.

"Go ahead," he said.

"The water sample is OK. A few impurities, but you could drink it if you had to."

This was the stream trickling down the hill in Julia's front garden. Connor wasn't surprised to learn it was safe: he'd seen birds drinking from it. But Mather's tone suggested that was the end of the good news.

"And the soil?" he ventured.

"Lethal. Enough arsenic to kill an elephant. In each sample."

"My God," said Connor. Julia had been right.

"Where did it come from?"

"What was once a vegetable garden. You wouldn't want to be eating any carrots growing there."

"Believe it or not you'd be safe. Most plants are very selective about what they absorb from the soil. You'd probably get a funny taste, but you'd have to swallow the earth itself to poison yourself."

"The garden was abandoned years ago," Connor said. "Now we know why."

"It happens," said Mather. "I'll email you the full analysis report this afternoon. Do you still want to run the dye test?"

"Definitely. And I want to be in the mine when you do it. If I see the dye at least I'll know I'm in the right place, even if it takes a few days to seep through to where we found the soil. I'll take some more samples from the rock as well. There might still be traces of arsenic."

They agreed on 11 the next morning. Julia was unpacking their lunch when Connor rejoined her.

"It's dramatic, but it's still flimsy," he said after explaining what Mather had told him. "An adult wouldn't eat soil."

"You're forgetting the toddler," said Julia. "He'd have eaten anything, and that concentration of arsenic would kill him within hours."

"Unless he was treated promptly. What was his mother doing? Why wasn't she rushing him to hospital?"

"The police found evidence of drugs in the house. Maybe she was out of her head."

"We'll never know," said Connor as he sat down, lowering himself gingerly onto his towel. "But we do have another piece of the story."

"I'm not sure about that," said Julia. "My garden was polluted, that's the only fact we've got. Tomorrow we may be able to link it to the Park. Even if we do, we still don't know what it means. It might have been an isolated incident, an industrial spillage maybe."

Connor shook his head.

"The poison wasn't some specialist chemical, it was arsenic, it's common in these mines. There was a time when they extracted it in preference to tin: It was used it as a cosmetic, would you believe. A skin whitener.

"Then there's the legend that the land is cursed. The old rhyme, *"Adits run red, cattle be dead."* Plus all the effort that someone is expending in trying to frighten us both off."

"I see what you mean," said Julia reluctantly. "Let's see what happens tomorrow. If we do see dye in the mine, we'll have to raise the alarm, even if it does eventually come to nothing."

"I don't think it will. But I'd still like to know what might have caused it. Water is usually always clean or always dirty. Flooding can mess with the quality but this isn't related to rainfall. We've just had the worst storms for years and the water is still good enough to drink."

"I've been thinking about that," said Julia, wiping her mouth with a paper napkin. "I know what might be happening. The physics of it. It was something that Dad told me which gave me the idea."

She put the napkin down and sat looking at it for a moment, her mind elsewhere. Connor waited for her to continue.

"There's a lake in Madagascar where the water level drops when it rains," she began, her voice brisk. Connor was intrigued.

"Dad teased me with it for a day before he explained how it happens. Beside the lake is a fold in the rock like an inverted U. Trapped inside the fold is a thin layer of mud. When it rains the water seeps into the mud and turns it into a siphon, drawing water up from the lake and onto the surrounding land."

"A syphon? The sort of thing that makes your loo flush?"

"Exactly. If you fill a tube with water, put one end in a tank and the other at a lower level, the pressure of the atmosphere will force water up through the tube and empty the tank. In dad's example the lake was the tank, the mud was the tube, and water was pulled up through the mud and flowed away down below the edge of the lake."

Connor was beginning to understand.

"Something similar could be happening in the rocks under here. In this case the tank is a mine working gradually filling up with contaminated water. Somewhere below it is the spring, normally clean. In between the two is an upside down U of permeable rock. As the mine fills up so does the U until it spills over and poison flows into the clean water below. The syphon effect ensures it continues to drain until the level in the mine drops below the base of the U, when it stops. Then the cycle starts all over again."

"I get it," Connor said. "It might take years for the contamination to build up, and only a few days to drain. A week or so when the spring is deadly, after years when you could drink from it all day long. No wonder Mather's tests never showed a problem."

He sighed.

"If the spring does become deadly, even for just a few days, the project is finished."

"Why? They can just get a supply from Western Water."

"They'll never agree. We'd be pouring away millions of litres of precious drinking water every day. There's a drought, they can barely supply their existing customers."

"Why not recycle it? Fill everything up once and then pump it back from the bottom to the top."

"It would be far too costly. Even if Western agreed we'd need an extra reservoir, pipes and pumps. And we'd need permission to change the design. The delay would cost us the Aquantas deadline, and that would push the start date back two years, by which time the funding grants would have expired."

He looked gloomily out to sea.

"The project is dead, Julia. There's no other source of water."

Julia looked at him in amazement.

"What's right in front of you, Connor?"

He took a moment to realise what she was talking about. It was the sea, of course. Salt, undrinkable and corrosive. Until you desalinated it. That was expensive, but maybe there could be a renewable source of electricity, solar, or wind. That might attract a subsidy...

Julia was watching his face. "You once told me that project management was all about problem solving. This is just another one, isn't it?" she said.

25

"He was back last night."

On the laptop screen was the same man, a scarf concealing the lower part of his face, casually walking round the front and side of the cottage, peering through the windows and pulling at the doors. The timestamp on the recording said 3:15 am.

"He wants me to know he's still watching."

Julia closed the laptop.

"I'm not going to be intimidated. How are you feeling?"

"I'm not fit enough to go into the mine," he said. "I need a few more days."

"Which we haven't got. You'll be all right with the scooter."

"It's you I'm worried about. If you're injured I won't be much help."

"I know that. We'll just keep it simple. Go in slowly, wait for the dye, take our samples, and come out again. We won't rush. I've made sandwiches and flasks of coffee in case we have to stop. "

Connor tried to smile.

"You make it sound like a picnic," he said.

They finished breakfast then loaded the trailer with backpacks of food and hot drinks, a crowbar, trowels and plastic boxes for the samples, rechargeable torches and a battery powered LED floodlight on a tripod which Julia had found amongst her father's tools.

Julia locked up the cottage, pulled the garage door closed and locked that as well. They were alone now, cut off from the outside world.

There was only room on the scooter for one, so Connor drove with Julia walking behind. It was easier going with the headlamp beam showing the way, but the darkness behind them was absolute and Connor was again unable to shake off the feeling they were being followed. Past the turnoff to the Benjamin Steps the floor deteriorated, the ground littered with mud and small rocks.

"Some of this is fresh," said Connor as he manoeuvred between the piles of rubble. "The roof here isn't stable."

They crept forward, keeping their noise and vibration to a minimum, watching all the time for more rock falls, until they reached the cavern. The cascade of water was at the top of the slope, beyond the ledge.

Connor pointed the scooter up the slope and squeezed the throttle. It started to climb laboriously.

"Go up at an angle," said Julia, trudging along behind. "You'll put less load on the motor. We don't want to drain the battery."

Connor agreed. The battery charge meter had dropped noticeably since he started climbing.

At the top of the slope Connor parked the buggy and switched off the headlight. Now the only light was from their torches, illuminating circles in the blackness. The cascade was a few yards into a tunnel, a continuous stream of water running down through an untidy pile of rocks, bricks, slabs of cement and bits of rusting machinery which had been tipped in from a vertical shaft in the roof. Freezing water was splashing onto their faces and hands. There was no sign of any coloration in the water.

Connor checked his watch.

"Any moment now," he said.

"If we're in the right place."

"We'll soon find that out. Let's take the samples while we

wait. A bit of activity will warm us up."

He reached into the pile of rubble and grasped a rock, flinching as he plunged his hand into the icy water. The rock held fast. He tried another, with the same result.

"All the loose material must have been washed away," he said. "We'll need the crowbar."

"I'll fetch it," said Julia, setting off to retrieve it from the trailer. Connor kept his torch flicking over the water, scanning for the bright red dye. Julia came back at a run, without the crowbar.

"There's someone else here," she said. "I saw torches at the bottom of the cavern."

"That's absurd. Who could it be? Cavers?"

"Come and look. Quietly."

They crept back to the ledge, lay down on the cold stone and peered over.

"Four torches," muttered Connor.

Then an authoritative voice.

"Mr Munro. This is Gordon Pascoe. I want to talk to you."

"Fuck! How does he know we're here?"

"He must have followed us."

"He couldn't have. We locked the garage."

"It doesn't matter. He's here, and we're in trouble."

The torches were flicking over the sloping floor and the walls, searching. Pascoe spoke again.

"Pavel, stay by the tunnel. Make sure no-one gets out. You two come with me."

"Pavel," said Connor quietly. "He's the one with the beanie hat. Pascoe had brought his hard men. He's not here to talk. Shit! All we've got is a crowbar. We can't win a fight against them all."

"Yes we can." Julia's whisper was fierce. "We're on higher ground, and we're surrounded by loose rocks. You can do a lot of damage with stones."

"I'm waiting, Munro." Pascoe's confident voice was mocking. They peered over the edge. Three of the torches had moved a little distance from the entrance.

Julia started shrugging off her hi-vis jacket.

"Those men are undisciplined," she said. "I saw that in the graveyard. This is a spooky place. We can panic them. You stay here, keep Pascoe talking, but don't let him see you. Take the floodlight to the far end of the ledge and turn it on, it will distract him. I'll try to get behind them, then I'll start throwing rocks. When I do that you join in. We keep up a barrage, we don't give them time to think."

Julia's resourcefulness was reassuring. "Take the crowbar as well," he said. "Throw it horizontally, with a spin. It could do a lot of damage."

As Julia dropped the jacket Connor caught sight of a red streak across one arm.

"The dye," he hissed. "This is the right place."

"And the wrong time." Julia said grimly. She picked up the crowbar. "Whatever happens don't let them reach this ledge. If they do we lose. Don't wait for me. Throw rocks, lots of them."

She slipped away into the darkness. Connor could just see the glimmer of her torch as she made her way slowly down the water-filled channel. He squirmed to the back of the ledge then carried the lantern to the opposite side of the cavern. He angled it towards the torchlights below him, switched on, picking out the figures of Pascoe and the two others, then scrambled away. His back was aching by the time he was lying down again. He wasn't nearly fit enough for a fight. This one would have to be short. He began gathering rocks.

"What are you doing here, Munro?" Pascoe's voice came from below. "You're not even on the build any more. Why are you giving orders to my contractors?"

"What orders, Mr Pascoe?" he yelled back.

"Don't fuck with me. You gave Mather a job to do. On whose authority?"

"My own. He's helping me test a theory about the spring. I want to find out if it goes bad. Does that interest you?"

"The spring? Going bad? What the fuck are you talking about?"

His voice changed.

"Marko, shoot that light out," he barked. "I can't see a fucking thing up there."

Jesus, thought Connor. They're armed. A bullet ricocheting off the bare rock could go anywhere.

"I wouldn't do that," he shouted. "Unless you all want to die. An explosion could bring the whole roof down."

"This place is solid granite," said Pascoe. "Nothing is going to collapse. Marko, get rid of that light!"

Reluctantly one of the men took out a pistol, aimed and fired. The noise was so loud it hurt, crashing around the chamber, seeming to get louder before it finally died away. A few loose stones fell from the roof and skittered down the slope, but the light stayed on. He fired a second shot, and missed again. Pascoe seemed to lose patience and grabbed the gun, took careful aim and fired. There was a clang and the lantern went out. Now all Connor could see were the three torches, dancing like fireflies, forming a line and starting steadily towards him. He felt for his pile of stones, picking one up, waiting for Julia to start her attack. She'd better be quick, they'd be at the top of the slope before long.

When Julia's attack didn't materialise Connor knew he had to act. He picked up a heavy rock and pitched it two handed towards the nearest light, like a throw-in. His injured muscles protested at the exertion, but it had its effect. There was a scream of pain from one of the men and a torch spun through the air, going out as it hit the ground.

Pascoe must have spotted Connor because there was another deafening shot and a bullet hit the wall behind his head. Connor crouched and ran towards the far end of the ledge, picking up more stones as he went. Pascoe had given away his position: he was in the middle of the line, his torch the more powerful of the remaining two. Connor took aim and with both arms hurled a large rock at him, then dropped back and shifted his position again. A curse from Pascoe told him his aim had been good. A third light came on, the injured man had been carrying a spare torch.

Connor threw more stones in quick succession, the torches telling him where to aim. Then he heard a loud metallic clang and more confused shouting. Julia had finally joined in with the crowbar. Connor continued bombarding with anything he could put his hands on. He could hear the crash of stones as Julia kept up her volley. The line of torches started to waver, no longer climbing the slope towards him. Pascoe was shouting at his men to stay calm. Connor began aiming directly at him, put him out of action and the others would scatter. His arms and upper body were in agony but he kept up the assault and was soon rewarded by a howl from Pascoe. The torch appeared to fall from his hand, rolling onto the ground and shining uselessly at the far wall.

"Someone get that gun," he called out. He was clearly injured, he'd dropped the torch and now the pistol. Connor switched his aim to the other torches, and after a few moments they all turned, flashing on the rails at the bottom of the cavern, then moving towards the exit tunnel. Rocks continued to rain on them as they fled.

Suddenly it was quiet, the only sound the rush of water, the torch on the ground the only light. Connor slid quickly down the slope. He had to get to the pistol before Pascoe. The stone floor of the cavern was slippery and he couldn't balance, his muscles were too stiff. He slid most of the way on his backside. But when he reached the base of the slope Julia was already there, waiting beside the rail track.

Near the bottom of the slope Pascoe was lying, propped on his elbow, his left ankle at an unnatural angle below him. He was sweating, his face twisted in pain. Connor knelt beside him and began to frisk him. Pascoe tried to shake him off.

"Fuck off," he said. His voice was hoarse. "You don't know who you're dealing with."

"We're the only ones who can get you out of here, Mr Pascoe," said Connor calmly, as he continued feeling for any further weapons. "We'll leave you here if you want. It might be some time before your friends come back, though. Can you stand?"

"I wouldn't be on the floor if I could. Look what you've done to my ankle, you bastards."

Connor ignored him and beckoned Julia away.

"That's a nasty fracture," said Connor quietly. "We have to get him out."

"How? We can't carry him. It must be a mile to the entrance."

"What about the scooter?"

"There's no room, and he can't sit in the trailer," said Julia. "The vibration could damage his ankle permanently. We have to go back and call an ambulance."

"Not both of us. We can't leave him alone."

"Why not? He can't go anywhere."

"Don't be so sure," Connor glanced over at Pascoe. "We don't know where he came in, do we? I don't want him getting away."

"All right," said Julia. "You go. You know how to drive the scooter. Just be quick. I'll wait here."

"What if his men come back?" Connor seemed to hesitate.

"That's a risk we have to take. I don't think they will come back after the fright we gave them, but if they do we've always got the gun."

"Have we? Where is it?"

"Over there somewhere," she pointed off into the gloom beyond Pascoe's body. "We'd better find it. I don't want him getting hold of it again."

She swept the torch round. The ground was littered with loose stones. They saw the crowbar and a discarded torch, but no gun. They scanned wider, methodically drawing every widening circles, checking that it hadn't fallen behind any loose rock on into a hole in the floor, but there was no sign of it.

"I'll get the scooter," said Connor. "The headlamp is much brighter than any of these torches."

He trudged back up the slope, his back in agony. He flopped clumsily onto the scooter and turned it on, the light of the headlamp picking out the grey roof of the cavern as it sloped down towards the lower level. He was just setting off when there was an urgent shout from Julia.

"Turn off the light, Connor, quickly!"

"What's the matter?" he called back.

"Just switch it off! There's someone else here."

Frantically Connor tried to find the switch. It was stiff, and it took a moment to push it to the off position. The headlamp went out, and the cavern was in complete darkness. Connor scrambled out of the seat and crawled a few yards from the scooter, then sat down to wait, unsure what to do next. If there was someone else, and that person had picked up the gun, all they could do was sit tight. It was stalemate. Anything that he or Julia did would invite a shot, but the flash of the pistol would give away its position and result in a hail of rocks. It was going to be a case of whose nerve broke first.

The utter blackness was disorientating. He couldn't tell which way was up and which way was down. The ground on which he was squatting was flat, the sound of water was all round him, echoing off the walls and roof. He started to imagine things: someone was coming up behind him, the gun pointed at his head. He didn't dare check, but tried to make himself smaller. He thought he saw a flicker of light, at the edge of his vision, but it might have been his eyes playing tricks.

Then he heard Pascoe speak.

"Is anyone there? Give us some light for Christ's sake." His voice was weak and frightened.

Connor remained silent. The voice had come from in front of him, and below. Now he knew he was facing down the slope.

"Where are you?" It was Pascoe again. "Just say something, will you?"

He seemed to be breathing heavily, as if he was struggling with something. A moment later there was a glimmer of light, a tiny beam. Probably a keyring, only strong enough to see a few feet by. Then his voice came again, urgent and frightened:

"Who's there? Is that you?"

Connor froze. Who was he talking to? He couldn't see the

light any more.

Pascoe was talking to someone, then let out a wail of terror, followed by an almost inaudible sob. There was a second of silence, then a shattering gunshot. As the sound echoed through the cavern Connor covered his head, unable to think, waiting for the inevitable beam of light to scan the floor and pick out Julia, and then himself.

It didn't happen. As the echo died away there was no further sound from Pascoe. Connor lifted his eyes cautiously, straining to see anything in the darkness, wondering how long the standoff would last. He caught another brief flicker of a light somewhere below him. He picked up a stone and threw it at the light, then scuttled to his right, in case he'd given away his position. Just in time: a brief flash of light picked out the scooter and a shot echoed through the cavern. Connor threw another stone, the sound of another crash told him that Julia had done the same.

Then nothing. The darkness remained absolute, the only sound the rushing water. It was now a test of patience. The gunman could stop them leaving, but only by staying where he was. Connor had the advantage of height. He felt for a large stone and threw it down the slope, another two handed throw-in. As it smashed to the ground he heard it dislodge more debris and the rush of a rockfall echoed around the chamber. He let it die down, waited a few more moments, then did the same again. The chances of hitting anyone were remote but that wasn't his intention; he wanted to unnerve his opponent, to show him the weakness of his position.

It worked. After the fifth stone there were two shots, the sound of the pistol moving rapidly towards the entrance as if the gunman was running away. A minute later Julia called out.

"He's gone," she said.

Connor switched on his torch and found the scooter. He drove slowly down the slope, the wheels skidding on the wet rock. The headlight picked out Pascoe lying on the floor, no longer propped on his elbow. As he approached Connor could make out a dark patch of liquid creeping out from under the body. Pascoe's eyes were open, looking sightlessly at the roof. A small scorched hole was just visible in the centre of his jacket. There was no sign of the gun. Julia came up, hugging herself, her face a blank. She roused herself, squatting down and putting her face close to his.

"He's definitely dead," said Connor.

"Of course he's fucking dead," said Julia. "I'm just checking on something."

She stood up. "Come on," she said. "Let's get out of here before anyone comes back. How fast does that thing go?" she pointed at the scooter.

"I don't know exactly. A lot faster than walking pace, though."

"Good. Someone might be waiting for us in the tunnel, so we need to be going as fast as possible."

"Unhitch the trailer. We can come back for that. Now let's see if we can both fit on the scooter."

Connor perched on the very front of the seat, and Julia was able to sit behind him with her feet on the wheel arches and her arms round his waist. The headlight illuminated a large circle of wall with the deep black hole of the tunnel in the centre. He squeezed the throttle and the scooter shot forward, the tunnel entrance becoming larger and larger until it swallowed them up.

Connor kept at full speed throughout, recklessly fast, the scooter bouncing off the walls, almost overturning as they hit scatterings of rubble, but they met no-one and in a very short time they were back in the garage. They staggered off the scooter, unlocked the outer door and stepped into the sunshine. Julia hurried to the cottage, and soon after Connor heard her retching in the bathroom. As he called the police Connor checked his watch: they had been in the mine for less than an hour.

26

Connor was taken to Truro police station, where he was questioned by two detectives, a sergeant and a constable, both with strong Cornish accents and lazy eyes which belied their intelligence. Connor had resolved to be open about what he and Julia had done. He would talk about his own motivation, but not about hers. That was for her to say.

It didn't last. *How did you know your way around the mine?* They asked. *Had you been there before?* That led him to explain his helping Julia find the Benjamin Steps. *Why were they so important to her?* and so it all came out: her father's Statement of Wishes, finding the door into the mine, finding the cavern, the Steps themselves. More probing questions and he was describing the mystery of Julia's mother, the scuba expedition, and their discovery that Malcolm had been watching Pascoe's house.

He and Julia were obvious suspects. He reminded them that there had been others in the mine, there would be blood on the ground from the cuts they had suffered. Tom Mather could vouch for why they had both been there. They could check his clothes for evidence of a gunshot, they would find nothing.

He couldn't say the same for Julia, and for the first time he realised that he only had Julia's word that there had been someone else in the cavern after the three men had fled. The sergeant noticed his hesitation. *Why did she send you away to fetch the scooter?* They were giving him the opportunity to blame Julia.

She didn't send me, he replied, that was my idea.

They kept him overnight, in a cell smelling of disinfectant and vomit. He couldn't sleep: lying down was painful, when he was able to doze drunken shouts from the other cells woke him again. He sat on the edge of the bunk in despair. If Julia had killed Pascoe he'd never see her again, he'd never want to see her again. And if she hadn't killed him, who had? Did it mean that Gordon wasn't responsible everything that had happened? Had their whole investigation been a waste of time?

Next morning the police took him through the events yet again. His mind was confused from lack of sleep and they deliberately tried to make him contradict himself, suggesting he'd changed his story when he hadn't. He managed to keep his composure, and after a relentless hour they stopped, abruptly shifting their questions to the stone throwing. Dangerous: an injury from a rock could be construed as GBH. Whose idea had it been? Why did you decide to do it? What came first, the shooting or the stone throwing? Connor found this easier to answer; he stayed calm, thinking carefully before answering.

"There were three shots before I threw anything, two from one of his men and one from Pascoe. Our aim was to panic them into scattering. Nobody was seriously hurt, I heard some yelps, but only Pascoe was injured, and that happened when he fell over. Whether that was because we hit him or one of his men crashed into him I don't know."

"Wasn't it foolish, taking on an armed gang?"

"What else were we supposed to do, dial 999?" Connor was barely controlling his temper. "We were trapped. We had no alternative."

After that the interrogation was an anticlimax. They seemed to accept he was telling the truth; and mid afternoon they took his statement, gave him back all his belongings except his phone, he was getting used to losing these, and released him on bail. Connor was still a suspect, told not to leave the area. He took a taxi back to the farm.

There was a huddle of media outside the gate: a van with a satellite dish, several cars, and half a dozen reporters and cameramen who surrounded the cab as it drew up. Connor shielded his face from the flashes as the car inched forward and onto the drive, past a solitary policeman manning the gate.

The cottage was out of bounds, blue police tape across the bottom of the drive, so he told the taxi to stop at the farmhouse. The low drone of a heavy duty generator and the spasmodic crackling of police radios disturbed the peace of the valley. As he stood uncertain in the yard, all his belongings were in the cottage, he noticed the Land Rover parked by the farmhouse: Charlotte was back. She came rushing down the steps of the farmhouse, stopping in surprise when she saw him.

"Where's Julia?" she asked, looking across towards the cottage.

Connor's anxiety increased: Julia obviously hadn't been released. He tried to sound reassuring. "She's OK. The police are still talking to her."

Charlotte looked lost, her hands flapping at her sides. "I came back yesterday," she said. "He's dead, isn't he?"

"There's been an accident," Connor tried to keep his voice neutral.

"The police are interviewing everybody. What's been happening?"

"I can't say. They ..." he left the sentence unfinished, then tried to divert her attention. "All my belongings are in the cottage. I've got nowhere to stay."

Charlotte gave him a speculative look, and he remembered that she hadn't known he was back.

"What happened to your face?" she exclaimed suddenly.

"I met some friends of Mr Pascoe."

She kept silent, inviting him to elaborate, but he said nothing.

"You'd better stay here," she said eventually, her natural hospitality reasserting itself. "The kids are away for a while longer. I'll make you up a room. I'll do the same for Julia, just in case..."

"We'll have to wait. That's all we can do," said Connor

gently, putting a tentative arm on hers. They had never been friendly and he wasn't sure how she'd respond but she grasped his hand gratefully.

"A room would be welcome," he went on. "That's very kind of you."

Charlotte led him into the farmhouse kitchen and sat him at the oak table. The dog looked up hopefully from her bed only to lie down again when she saw it was the wrong guest.

"I don't suppose you've had anything to eat," said Charlotte. When he shook his head she took a chicken pie from the fridge and put it in the oven to heat up. He was left on his own with a mug of tea while Charlotte went upstairs to prepare the rooms.

They ate together in silence, both preoccupied by the horror of what had happened. Connor could still hear Pascoe's howl and the single deafening shot which ended his life. Then his own terror, knowing that somewhere in the utter darkness was a murderer with a gun.

He went to bed early but couldn't relax, lying on his bed gazing sightlessly at the ceiling. The idea that Julia was the murderer had wormed into his mind and he couldn't shift it. His mind worked it all out: she had enticed Pascoe into the mine by telling him anonymously that Connor was going to be there. The pistol was a bonus, she had found it without telling Connor, then while he was collecting the scooter she taken her opportunity. He was too tired, his mind too confused, to analyse this rationally. All he could think was that he had lost: Julia was going to be convicted, and there was nothing he could do about it.

They hardly spoke at breakfast the following morning. The dog growled whenever Connor looked at her, as if she held him responsible for Charlotte's unhappiness. I don't want to be here either, he wanted to say. How long would the police hold onto the cottage? He couldn't get to his clothes, any of his notes, or his laptop. All he had was what he was wearing. Charlotte must have realised the same, because after breakfast she said:

"I'm going into Truro for some shopping. Do you want to

come with me? Or would you like me to get you anything?"

"I'll stay here if you don't mind," he said, unwilling to face the media pack by the gate. "Could you get me some clothes from Marks? And a phone. Just get something cheap, pay as you go, with a data package."

"Write down what you want, and your sizes. While I'm out you can use the parlour, and borrow our laptop if you like. It's a bit old and I don't know what the kids have put on it but it should still work."

The parlour was a large old fashioned sitting room at the opposite end of the house, bright, with windows on three sides. Bookshelves laden with old encyclopaedias, atlases and leather-bound sets of Dickens and Walter Scott framed the fireplace. On the mantelpiece were cut glass vases with fresh roses, family photos in silver frames, and an old pendulum clock, its deep ticking the only sound in the room.

The desk was by the front window, its tooled green leather surface framed by a narrow rosewood strip. Connor sat, gazing out at the trees, trying to block out the horror of what had happened to Pascoe. He had to find something else to occupy his mind. Reluctantly he began sketching the report he knew he'd have to write, the one that would stop the Park project, probably for ever. He still didn't have complete proof that the water was a problem, but he had both ends of the trail. The dye test had already shown that the spring water, flowing below Eliza's garden into the blocked ventilation shaft, reached the cavern in Wheal Mawgan. Outside the entrance to the same mine was Olivia's garden, which had been poisoned. All that was missing was evidence that water from the spring could seep from the cavern to the entrance.

He had a thought. The dye might already have reached the garden. The police wouldn't let him in to check, but there was another way to find out. The trickle from the mine, which ran down the side of the garden, flowed into the main stream at the bottom of the valley, and that wasn't cordoned off. He hurried out, down the yard to the path and past the cottage towards the cove.

He was disappointed. The water was still clear. The change of air had given him another idea, however. If there was a known problem with the land, something more specific than an old legend, someone might have mentioned it in an objection to Zenith's application for planning permission. All the details would be on the council's website.

Back in the parlour Connor opened up Charlotte's computer. The keyboard was sticky with blobs of jam and solidified ice cream but it worked, and he soon found the planning website. He ignored the outline consent given in the mid 90s, concentrating on the detailed application which had been lodged just three years ago. It had attracted over two hundred objections: e-mails, Word documents and handwritten letters, all scanned and filed as PDFs.

He worked systematically through the list, noting the name of each objector, and a description of the objection. Most raised practical concerns: traffic, the lack of cafes, hotels, shops and petrol stations to support the thousands of visitors. Others thought the money would be better spent on schools and hospitals. Environmentalists were concerned about air pollution from the cars and coaches. There were those who objected to the scheme simply because it was Gordon Pascoe; it would make him rich but the town wouldn't see any benefit.

Then there were the religious objectors. There were about twenty, all broadly similar: the land was cursed, anyone defiling it would be damned for all eternity, remember John Wesley and his refusal to preach there. One repeated the old saying: *Adits run red, cattle be dead.* Connor read all these arguments carefully. They were from families with long memories, they'd lived in the area for generations. If any of them knew of a specific problem they would have said so, but no-one did. The arguments were all vague, repeating the old stories without any evidence to back them up.

If these long established families knew nothing then it was likely that no-one else was aware either, or at least, no-one with an objection to the park. What about those in favour, like Gordon Pascoe? Connor thought back their confrontation in the mine, the shouted exchange with Pascoe. *The spring? What the fuck are you talking about?* Gordon had been sincere, Connor heard it in his voice.

He looked up in disbelief. Pascoe hadn't suspected the water either.

It seemed all their assumptions were wrong. Julia's dad spying on Pascoe. Gordon trying to intimidate Julia. Connor's beating up. None of it made sense any more.

Connor started doodling. Everything had to make sense, he just hadn't found out how. The possibilities stretched out before him like the channels in a river delta, endlessly splitting and recombining. Was Pascoe still the villain, trying to conceal something completely different? The intimidation, was that Pascoe or someone else, the person who killed him? Who was it? And why? Was it linked to the water?

Connor stood up, crumpled the paper into a ball and threw it into the waste paper bin. Keep it simple, he told himself, construct a hypothesis and see where it leads. Don't make it any more complicated than it needs to be.

Pascoe died in the mine, his killer knew he was there. Pascoe was ignorant of any problems with the water. First assumption: his killer was not ignorant. Connor had no direct evidence for this, but it felt right, it pointed to a motive. Someone was protecting the secret.

Who? No-one knew, it seemed. Not the townspeople, they'd have objected to the planning application. No-one on the Council. Not Pascoe.

Then he stopped. There had been someone: Prideaux, the farmer who'd originally owned the land. It had been in his family for centuries, he would have known all there was to know about it.

But Prideaux wasn't the only one: in 1980 someone had bought it from him.

Glimpsing an opening, Connor went back to the laptop to refresh his memory. In the original purchase documents he found the name: Leigh Henderson, and the company, Farwest

80. They had bought the land for £10,000, obtained planning permission for housing, and sold it seven years later to Gordon Pascoe for a million. Henderson had made a lot of money at Gordon's expense.

On impulse, Connor looked up land prices in 1980, when Farwest had bought the Park. He quickly found what he was looking for.

"Gotcha," he murmured.

The million pound profit was spectacular but the most telling feature of the transaction was the original £10,000. As arable land Park an Jowl should have been worth at least £50,000. Prideaux had sold it for a fifth of that, and farmers, of all people, know the value of land.

Agreeing to that price was an admission that he knew there was something wrong with it.

That wasn't all. Henderson had shown he was a sharp businessman. He too would have found out the value of the land, and would have been very suspicious of such a good deal on what looked like ordinary farm land. The implication was clear: Henderson also knew that the land was tainted, and used that knowledge to drive down the price.

But he revealed nothing when he came to sell the land to Gordon Pascoe.

It was starting to make sense. Henderson had known about the water. In 1995 the water polluted and Olivia disappeared, apparently murdered after seeing the evidence for herself. Fifteen years later Julia's father, then Connor and Julia herself were all threatened, apparently by Pascoe. Who in turn has been murdered by somebody unknown.

Leigh Henderson. There could be no other explanation. Henderson was still protecting the secret.

Leaning over the computer had stiffened him up again body, and Connor stood up to stretch his back, barely noticing the pain as he realised what he had achieved. He had a candidate.

All he had, however, was a name. Henderson as a person didn't seem to exist. The only mention he could find was in the Companies House records for Farwest 80, and the only information that gave him was the registered address. Farwest was wound up immediately after it sold the land to Zenith; the chance of finding out anything more about it was slim.

Then his mind caught another whisper. Something much more recent: the 40 percent of Zenith that Pascoe didn't own. It was held by Apricot, registered in the secrecy of the Cayman Islands. Another untraceable person with a financial interest in the park. Henderson again?

Suppose Henderson hadn't just taken his million and disappeared. Suppose he still had an interest, a stake in Zenith through Apricot. Zenith was on the verge of becoming very valuable indeed. A keen businessman like Henderson might well want to be part of it.

Connor reached for his phone and called Jim Feathers. He might have heard of Henderson, and now that Gordon was no longer a threat he might be prepared to talk.

"Terrible news about Mr Pascoe," Jim's tone was excited rather than downhearted. "I heard you were there at the time."

"Not really," Connor didn't want any questions on that subject. "Jim, does the name Leigh Henderson mean anything to you?"

Feathers thought for a moment. "No, it doesn't. Should it?"

"Not necessarily." It was disappointing, but not unexpected. "I came across it in an old file. I've got another question: remember our conversation at the fete? You mentioned an old saying: *adits run red, cattle be dead*. You'd actually seen the water turn red. Can you remember when?"

"It happens all the time. Every couple of years there's a new scare, but it always turns out to be a false alarm. As I told you before, it's kids tipping laboratory chemicals into the mineshafts for a joke."

Or it might be someone creating the expectation that it's a harmless prank so that when the real thing happens no-one takes it seriously.

"Has anyone ever asked you about it?"

"Tourists ask all the time," he said with a sigh. Then his voice sharpened. "There was someone local as well. It was years ago.

Olivia Philips. Your friend Julia's mother."

Connor felt a jolt.

"Where is Julia, by the way?" Feathers said. "They're saying she had something to do with Gordon's death."

"Don't ask me," Connor was sharp. "I haven't seen her for days. I don't know what she does with her time."

"I thought…" Jim seemed to realise he was being tactless. "Sorry. None of my business."

"That's OK," Connor said evenly. "Do you remember what Olivia wanted exactly?"

"She asked about the saying. There had just been another episode, she wanted to know if it was important. I told her it was always happening. I don't think she entirely believed me because then she asked if I had a map of the mines."

Connor felt the hairs on his neck stand on end.

"I'd just given a talk to the Circle about local industry in the nineteenth century," Feathers went on. "She hadn't been there but she'd heard about it. I'd mentioned the railways that were installed in the bigger mines. Her home was near the main shaft of Wheal Mawgan and she'd seen rails embedded in the concrete outside. She must have realised it was a substantial working and wanted to find out where it went."

"Were you able to give her a map?"

If there had been one he and Julia wouldn't have had to trek into the mine again, and Pascoe might still be alive.

"No, these mines have never been surveyed," said Jim. "Then she asked if there had been any mining on the Park estate. I gave her the answer I gave you: there had been a ventilation shaft near the bottom of the site."

"What did she say to that?"

"Nothing. I terminated the conversation: I was probably a bit rude, but no-one wanted to be associated with Olivia. She was trouble. Always looking for injustice, and there was plenty of that to keep her occupied. She made herself very unpopular."

It took a moment for Connor to realise what Jim was saying.

"Olivia was already unpopular when she came to see you?"

"Very," Jim was emphatic. "She had been banned from the

Circle. Gordon Pascoe nearly withdrew his sponsorship because of her. She made some very serious accusations against him."

Connor was scrambling for his notepad as Jim talked.

"It was about a fire," Jim continued.

"The one that killed Eliza Jones?"

"You know about that? She thought Gordon had done it himself to cover up his own negligence."

"Negligence? In what respect?" Connor hadn't expected this.

"She said that Eliza's house was shoddy. Damp, draughty, the electrics didn't work, and the water heater was dangerous. Olivia had noticed Eliza and her boy looking ill. She suspected carbon monoxide poisoning."

"So when the house burned down..." prompted Connor.

"Olivia thought it was a cover up. She told the police about the carbon monoxide, they looked into it but found nothing. The fire has been so strong it destroyed any evidence of a faulty installation, and any trace of poison in their bodies."

"What did you think?"

"I didn't have an opinion, it wasn't safe. You never knew who was listening."

Connor shuddered as he went back to his scrawled notes. He could imagine what it was like, a small, forgotten community completely dominated by one man.

"Can I get the timing straight?" he said. "The house burned down in June 1995. When did Olivia ask you about the adits, and the map?"

"A couple of days after my lecture, in the middle of October."

Connor found his note on the sequence of events.

"Four months later. Just before she disappeared."

"Less than a week. I never saw her again."

Connor looked thoughtfully down at the paper.

"Thank you Jim," he said. "That's very helpful."

They disconnected. Another piece of the puzzle was in place.

27

Charlotte scraped Connor's uneaten breakfast into the waste bin with a look of disgust. "I'm going out for the day, you'll have to look after for yourself. I'll be back later this afternoon. If you do decide to eat there's food in the fridge."

Connor had spent another night barely sleeping; he'd woken with a headache which the heat of the kitchen and the smell of frying food was making worse. He escaped to the cool of the parlour. On the laptop he checked the BBC website: the police were treating Pascoe's death as suspicious, but said nothing more. No mention of a suspect. He didn't know if that was reassuring or not.

He heard the back door slam and the revving of the Land Rover as Charlotte drove off. He was alone, with only the unfriendly dog in the kitchen for company. On the laptop was his unfinished report: he still had to write a section on alternative sources of water. It was academic, there was enough in what we'd already written to frighten off the investors and kill the project, but he felt the need to explore the options, just in case. Julia had suggested desalination; it was a subject he knew very little about. He began researching the technology; how it worked, what it cost, whether there were grants to offset some of the expense, gradually sketching out an alternative project plan.

The laptop pinged: a new e-mail. A reply from his lawyer

friend in the office.

No clue yet as to ownership of Apricot, but I've found a bank record from 2004 showing a transfer of $55,000 from Apricot to Farwest (Holdings) Ltd, also Cayman registered. I can't find out anything about them either. The financial info comes from an unofficial source. It's reliable but it cannot be quoted. Sorry I can't be more helpful.

At last. This was a breakthrough. Henderson's company had been Farwest 80. With such a similar name Farwest (Holdings) had to be his as well. Connor went back to Zenith's accounts. In 2004 they paid shareholder dividends of £75,000. Apricot's share would have been £30,000. At the prevailing exchange rate that was around $55,000.

His surmise was correct. Apricot had paid the whole of its dividend to a company belonging to Henderson. The inescapable conclusion was that Henderson also owned Apricot.

That meant that Henderson was still an active participant in Zenith.

There was another ping from the laptop.

One more thing. Three days ago Apricot sold its entire holding in Zenith to GlobalParks.

He e-mailed back.

When exactly?

11:30am.

Connor stared at the screen. Apricot sold out half an hour after Mather began his dye test. Now he knew the whole story. The fire, Olivia's death, Malcolm's pursuit of Gordon, the attacks on himself and the threats to Julia, and why Gordon had to die.

And he knew Henderson's true identity.

The sound of a car engine roused him. Charlotte must be back earlier than expected. He closed the laptop and was heading for the door when he heard the car drive off. So it wasn't Charlotte. He waited. There was a bark from the dog, then silence. Connor moved swiftly towards the kitchen. Bella had recognised a friend.

He hardly noticed the heat as he opened the kitchen door. Standing by the table, the dog by her side, its tail lazily dusting the floor, was Julia. She was still in the thick jumper she had worn into the mine two days before. Her face was grey, her eyes rimmed red, swaying slightly as if she was having difficulty staying upright. She looked at him, defeat and despair in her eyes.

"Surprised to see me?" she asked.

"I thought they'd thrown you in the deepest dungeon," he said. He walked forward quickly and wrapped his arms around her. She stood unresponding as he hugged her, then he felt her trying to free her arms. He let her go, thinking she was pushing him away, but she reached up, curled her arms around the back of his neck and pulled him close. She didn't look at him, laying her face against his shoulder. He understood. This was the intimacy she'd been fighting ever since she'd invited him to stay at the cottage. The inevitable, she'd called it.

When she released herself Julia finally looked directly into his eyes, her gaze naked and accepting.

"I'm trusting you," she said.

"I know." He still had his arms around her back. "It's not easy is it?"

She nodded, and Connor knew he had said the right thing. Julia was tough and gruff and ballsy but her physical toughness wasn't matched by any emotional independence. Solitude didn't come naturally to her, but relinquishing it to share with someone else was going to be a struggle. Realising that he felt a sense of responsibility he hadn't felt since Stevie's death.

He let her go, and immediately Julia put a hand on the table to steady herself.

"You need to sleep," he said.

"Not yet. Tell me what's happened. When did they let you out?"

"The day before yesterday."

"Lucky you. Have you any idea what's going on?"

"I think I know the whole story. There's a lot to tell you.

You'd better sit down before you keel over."

"Not in here, it's stifling. Let's go outside."

They stood for a moment in the yard by the back door, breathing the cool fresh air. Charlotte had left a carousel of washing to dry; the breeze had blown a child's bathing costume onto the steps up to the garden. Julia retrieved it, fingering it for a few moments, a puzzled look on her face, before pegging it back on the line. They walked on to the kitchen garden where they found a wooden bench. The sea was visible over the roof of the cottage. A dinghy race was in progress, white sails almost stationary in the light breeze. Beyond them in the middle distance a white cabin cruiser was moving slowly by. A tanker was hull down on the horizon.

Julia sat with her hands clenched, alert despite her fatigue, inviting Connor to start.

"When we were in the cavern," he began. "I was keeping Gordon occupied while you tried to get behind him and his men. Did you hear any of our conversation?"

Julia shook her head.

"He told me something crucial. He wanted to know why I was in the mine, so I said we were investigating the water."

"I thought we were keeping that to ourselves."

"It was a bit late by then. And anyway I wanted to hear his reaction."

"Which was?"

"The key to the whole story, Julia. He had no idea what I was talking about."

"Of course he knew." She was scornful. "That's why he followed us. He was going to make sure we didn't tell anyone else."

"He was sincere, I could tell it from his voice, and it fits with something else. Remember the fete, and that fat little grandchild of his who accused everyone of cheating in his race? Gordon had promised him one of the first rides when the Park opened. He wouldn't have done that if he thought the boy would be in any danger."

"He wouldn't," Julia agreed reluctantly. "But if this isn't about the spring we've been wasting our time, haven't we?"

"I didn't say that. It is definitely about the water, it's just that Gordon thought it was about something else."

"Stop being clever and just tell me."

"OK. Someone killed Gordon while we were investigating the mine. That's not a coincidence. There has been another person actively involved with Zenith ever since it was set up, and that person killed him."

Connor explained what he had discovered about Henderson and Farwest 80, the profit it had made from selling out to Zenith, and the evidence that Henderson was still involved in Zenith.

"Henderson knew the land was tainted when he bought it. That's how he was able to negotiate such a good price," he concluded.

"For a long time that didn't matter, the spring was irrelevant, buried deep underground: when they built the housing estate they took water from the mains. But when the MOD announced that the base was to close, and the Council published a regeneration plan based on tourism, Gordon, completely innocently, had the idea of using the spring as the basis for a theme park. Now imagine you're Henderson. You've got a problem. Do you tell Gordon? Do you tell anybody? Prideaux is dead now so no-one knows what you know. There's a fortune to be made, but only if you keep quiet and take precautions against being found out. Pollution events announce themselves: *adits run red, cattle be dead* is a local saying. Henderson knew it to be true, so he devalued it by ensuring that every couple of years there would be a false alarm, children apparently tipping chemicals into the mines. If the real thing occurred no-one would take any notice.

"By the middle of 1995, with everyone except Henderson ignorant of what might happen, the Park concept was gaining acceptance. Zenith hadn't yet raised enough money, their ideas weren't exciting enough to attract investors. Stevie's plans were some time in the future. But they had agreement in principle, and with that Zenith was about to become very rich indeed.

"Then there was a fire on the estate. Eliza and her son died, their house completely destroyed. That fire is central. It wasn't an accident, it was deliberate, the blaze so ferocious there was no evidence left to suggest who did it or why. But it got Pascoe out of a tight spot and it led, ultimately, to your mother's disappearance."

Julia looked up sharply.

"Mum? What did she have to do with it?"

"I spoke to Jim Feathers. He told me that over that summer Olivia thought Eliza was showing symptoms of Carbon Monoxide poisoning. After the fire she told the police, but she couldn't prove anything. It made her unpopular; she was accusing Pascoe, main sponsor of their Circle, of criminal neglect. He would have withdrawn his support if she hadn't stopped."

"Carbon Monoxide," Julia was puzzled. "Not the water?"

"Henderson was the only one who knew anything about the water. If the fire was covering up anything it was Carbon Monoxide poisoning. If that could be proved it would raise serious questions about Gordon's fitness to build and manage anything as important as a theme park. The whole project would be under threat so they destroyed the evidence. Gordon organised the fire to cover up a faulty boiler installation.

"Your mum seemed to give up. She had no evidence, no-one would listen to her. Jim told me she wasn't seen in Polwerran for weeks."

Julia was fully alert now, her eyes were red but there was no trace of fatigue. Connor continued.

"Then she had another idea. She called Jim Feathers just after he'd given a talk about mining technology: the engine houses, steam power, and the underground railways used to transport ore to the surface in the bigger mines. Olivia wanted to know how far the mine behind her garage extended. There were the remains of rail tracks in her garage, which suggested it was an extensive mine. Jim didn't have any maps, but he did tell her something useful: there had been a ventilation shaft at the bottom of the Park Estate."

Now Julia was able to pick up the story.

"She'd make the connection between the poisoning in her own garden and Eliza's death, just as you and I did. She'd never thought of it before: the two houses were a mile apart, there was no reason to suspect there was any link until Jim gave her the idea that her mine might run under Eliza's house."

"Now Olivia was a danger to Henderson all over again. If she could prove that arsenic-laden water could be cascading through the Park the project was doomed. She had to be stopped."

Julia looked out across the roof of the cottage as she tried to take in what he was saying. The little flotilla of dinghies was still engaged in its slow motion race, the tanker on the horizon had almost disappeared, in between the cabin cruiser had changed course and was now moving out to sea. She looked across at Connor, sitting beside her. His eyes were alive with excitement. This isn't a game, she thought.

"So this is all Henderson's doing. That's what you're saying. Mum died because Henderson had to protect his secret from everyone, including Gordon Pascoe. But when dad came back he started spying on Gordon. On the CCTV he pointed him out to me. Why would he do that?"

"Henderson knew what Olivia was pursuing, but couldn't run the risk of Gordon finding out. So Gordon was persuaded that Olivia was still looking into carbon monoxide theory, maybe she had new evidence, and had to go. Gordon was implicated in the fire, he was vulnerable and open to manipulation."

"And now, after 15 years, Henderson decides to kill Gordon. Why?"

"That's where you and I become part of the story. We'd become suspicious of the water and arranged the dye test. Gordon was about to discover the truth. He'd never risk the lives of his grandchildren, so he'd pull out, and the project would collapse. He'd then realise that Henderson had conned him and he'd be livid. He knew all about Henderson's role in the fire, and Olivia's death. If he chose to talk Henderson would be in serious trouble.

"Henderson knew there was a risk this might happen, and had made plans. Half an hour after Tom Mather injected dye into the spring Apricot sold its entire holding in Zenith. Soon after that Gordon was dead. Henderson knew the game was up, so he got rid of the main witness to all he had done, took what money he had, and ran."

He was interrupted by the sound of a diesel engine on the drive below, revving in low gear before cutting out. A car door slammed.

"That's Charlotte," said Julia, jumping to her feet and walking quickly back to the farmhouse. "I'd better say hello."

Connor stayed where he was, unwilling to intrude on their reunion. Julia hadn't yet reached the conclusion that he had; he was unsure how she would react when she did. He waited, watching the boats out at sea. When Julia came back she was almost running.

"The police are taking DNA samples from everyone in the town," she said. "They're onto something. I don't have much time."

"Time for what?"

"Once your Henderson is in custody I'll have lost my opportunity. I have to get there first."

"So you know who you're looking for?"

Julia didn't reply: she was looking round her at the neat rows of carrots and onions, and the walls of climbing beans, understanding spreading on her face.

"Yes I do. Call the police," she said. "Tell them to call the coastguard. I'll be on the beach."

Connor was mystified.

"Look out to sea," she said. "The cabin cruiser that's been hanging around ever since we've been here. It's the Loretta; it's waiting to pick someone up."

The cruiser was moving slowly back the way it had come. Connor walked quickly back to the farmhouse to find his phone. Julia was already running down the drive.

28

Julia stopped running when she reached the edge of the wood, moving into the trees to the side of the path. She found a fallen log where she could sit unobserved while she watched the cove. The beach was deserted, the woods around her silent. She waited, desperately tired as the adrenaline drained from her body, her feet aching from the heavy boots, her dirty clothes starting to itch.

Leigh Henderson. A name that could either be male or female. There was only one person who fitted Connor's description, and that was a woman.

As she waited Julia thought about what she had to do. Stop the woman reaching the boat if she could, obviously, but there was something much more important, and considerably more dangerous. To succeed Julia would have to go against all her training, all her instincts, and let Henderson take control. Only then would she feel confident enough to tell Julia what she wanted to hear. That was her hope. If it went wrong Julia might not survive.

A movement on the cliff caught her attention. A familiar figure in a blue shirt and white slacks was striding quickly down the left hand path. Julia kept completely still as the woman reached the shingle bank, crossed to the middle of the beach and disappeared down the seaward side. Now out of sight Julia ran fast across the flat scrub, where the helicopter had landed all those days before, and up to the top of the bank, cursing the boots as they crashed through the shingle. Once over the brow Julia jinked to her left and rolled forward in a move to unsight her opponent, in case she was waiting with a gun in her hand.

It wasn't necessary. The woman had disappeared, the beach was deserted.

Julia looked round, bewildered, then realised she herself was exposed. She slid back down the landward side of the bank and ran for the cover of the rocks at the right of the cove. She had to be quick, finding her quarry before the dinghy arrived. Julia made her way carefully down towards the sea. At each outcrop she stopped, creeping forward, ready to pull back, but she met no-one. When she reached the water's edge the half-submerged rocks formed an impassable barrier, and she turned back, carefully examining every cleft and fold in the cliff as she went. The woman was here somewhere.

Julia heard it before she saw it: the echoing drip of water coming from deep inside a gap in the rocks. Cautiously she sidled along the shingle until she found a narrow slit, barely wide enough for a person to squeeze through, tucked under the cliff and completely invisible from the sea. The hollow plopping was louder now, there was a substantial chamber inside. Julia waited, listening. Rushing in might be fatal, the tight entrance would make her a very simple target for anyone waiting inside. Then she heard quick footsteps, inside the cave, becoming fainter. The woman was going deeper into the hillside.

In her pocket Julia still had the torch she had taken to the cavern two days before. She flicked it on and squeezed through the narrow gap, into a damp cavern with a man-made tunnel beyond. After a hundred yards it joined a bigger tunnel where she could stand upright. From her left came the sound of the sea. Julia recognised the shaft leading to the Benjamin Steps. She moved cautiously towards the top of the stone stairs, then stopped to take off her boots and socks. The clump of heavy footwear would give her away and she needed surprise.

The woman was standing at the far end of the jetty with her

back to Julia, talking urgently into a phone, repeatedly clenching and unclenching the fist on her free hand. There was a tote bag at her feet. Julia was puzzled that she'd managed to get a signal, but then she realised it wasn't a phone, it was a walkie talkie. She was speaking to someone on the yacht.

It would be easy to overpower her. She was unaware of Julia's presence. The gun would be in the bag. Four quick strides, a chop to the side of the neck. Easy. But that way Julia never find out what she needed to know. Instead, she moved quietly forward until she was about six feet behind the woman.

"Hello Monica," she said.

Monica swung round, her eyes widening in alarm.

"Julia, what are you doing here?"

She picked up the bag and held it protectively against her chest. She looked down at Julia's bare feet. Julia could guess her thoughts: no-one walks through a mine in bare feet, so Julia had taken off her footwear for a reason. Julia ignored her. She intended to behave as if this meeting was completely natural.

"This is the place we talked about, The Benjamin Steps, where dad wanted me to scatter his ashes. There's an old signature in the concrete."

She pointed to the wall behind her. Monica didn't look, keeping her eyes fixed on Julia.

"I never knew." Her tone was offhand. "We always called it Smugglers Quay."

Julia leaned back against the rock.

"Dreadful news about Gordon Pascoe, isn't it?" she said. Monica nodded warily.

"We worked together for many years. It's all a shock."

"It was a shock to me as well, I was there when it happened," said Julia. "The police thought I'd done it."

"You poor thing," said Monica. "You do look awful, when was the last time you slept?"

"They kept me for three days, but I didn't do it and eventually they believed me."

She kept her eyes down, avoiding Monica's glance but watching for any sudden movement. Monica said nothing, but

Julia saw she had become tense.

"I wish I knew who it was though."

"That's for the police to discover," said Monica. She seemed to be recovering from the shock.

Julia was silent for a while. There was no sound but the slapping of water against the concrete wall beneath them.

"Did you know that dad was spying on Gordon?"

"What?" Monica looked surprised.

"He had a CCTV camera pointing at the house. I've watched the recording, hours and hours of nothing. Well, almost nothing."

Monica was listening with an expression of polite interest, but one hand had moved out of sight behind the bag. The moment was coming.

"I think that Gordon had something to do with mum's disappearance," Julia went on. "He frightened dad away when he thought he was about to find out the truth. Dad stayed away for fifteen years, he only came back when he knew he was ill. He didn't have much time, so he planned to confront Gordon and extract the truth from him before his heart finally gave way."

"You worked all this out in the basis of a CCTV camera?" Monica was incredulous.

"Oh, there's more to it than that." Julia didn't elaborate, letting the silence between them lengthen. Monica seemed unperturbed. The dinghy was on its way; soon she'd be on the Loretta heading towards safety.

"I've found out most of what happened," Julia went on. "Mum didn't run off. She was murdered. She discovered that Eliza Jones's garden had been contaminated with arsenic. Eliza and her boy became ill, they may even have died from the arsenic, but we'll never know because all the evidence was destroyed in a fire. It looked like arson. If the poisoning became public knowledge then Park an Jowl would lose its value. No estate, no theme park, just a field with a dark reputation. Olivia had to go."

Monica's expression didn't change, but her hand was

slipping down into the tote bag. Julia tried to keep her voice calm.

"There's a problem with the theory: Gordon had no idea the water could be dangerous. He told his grandchildren they'd have the first rides in the park. He wouldn't do that if he knew they could be in danger, would he? And he wouldn't kill my mother for raising the issue. He'd want to find out if what she was saying was true, and if it was he'd never agree to anyone using the spring, especially for a water park."

"You wouldn't say that if you knew him."

"Possibly," Julia conceded. "But there was someone else, someone who did know about the water: the person who sold him the land in the first place. He used the name Leigh Henderson, but no-one can find out anything about him. Or her."

Monica shrugged. The schoolmistress in Julia recognised a practiced nonchalance: Monica had been expecting the implied question.

"Gordon is dead, Julia. Let it rest."

"Is mum at rest?" Julia moved a step forward. Monica retreated, stumbling as her foot struck the wall of rock behind her.

"You think I had something to do with it?"

"I know you did. You were Leigh Henderson. You bought Park an Jowl and sold it to Zenith, knowing it was lethal. An unpredictable time bomb. It must have been a shock when Eliza and her little boy became ill, Gordon might have found out, if my mum hadn't been obsessed with a faulty boiler. You just had to let him go on believing he was to blame. You knew what happened to mum's vegetable patch, so when she finally began wondering if there was a link between her mine and Eliza's garden you were ready."

"Is that all you've got? There was a chance the two were linked? It's nonsense, Julia."

Julia took another step forward.

"So why are you running away?" she asked. "Are you scared of what a DNA analysis might reveal?"

"You're waiting for the Loretta," she said when Monica didn't respond. "She's been out there for the last hour. Off to a new life. I suppose you'll be comfortable; you're good with money, you'll have something stashed away. Not as much as you'd hoped, but these things happen. A villa somewhere warm, a pool, expats to drink and play bridge with, very nice. A bit shallow for me, but maybe you'll like it.

"But what about the nights? When you're on your own, with only the memory of everything you did to get there. Mum's horror when she realised you, her friend, had tricked her. Gordon's terror as you kissed him goodbye, will you be able to block all that out for ever?"

"Sentimental nonsense Julia. There's nothing you can prove, even if it were true."

"We both know it's true. And I can prove you lied about mum. The day she disappeared you picked me up from school and took me back to the farm. You said you hadn't spoken to her that day, you'd been at the hospital with Charlotte."

"She had appendicitis."

"I remember. It must have been difficult for you, your daughter ill, then having to look after me, but you were very kind, asking me what lessons I'd had, how I'd got on at the Leisure Centre, joking about how I'd got the wrong bathing costume. Mum had bought me a new one, it was red, but she forgot to pack it, so when I opened my satchel I found my towel wrapped round the old blue one. I remember wondering at the time how you knew that. I didn't tell you, I didn't tell anyone, I was too worried about Mum."

"You had the wrong bathing costume?" Monica looked perplexed. "Is that all?"

"It's enough," said Julia. "The only person who could have told you was mum. So you did see her that day."

Monica sighed.

"I knew you'd be a problem," she said, swinging the tote bag to one side to reveal the dull metal of a small pistol, pointing straight at Julia's chest. Without taking her eyes off Julia she put down the bag and the walkie talkie, then straightened up, putting both hands on the gun and raising it to eye level.

"Back Julia," she said. "To the bottom of the steps. I know all about your combat skills."

Julia stepped back slowly and carefully, controlling her fright. She had engineered this moment, deliberately allowing Monica to take control. Everything in Monica's stance: the two handed grip, holding the pistol at eye level, arms slightly bent to take the recoil, told Julia that she knew how to handle a gun. The muzzle was now pointing at her face. One mistake, a stumble, a sudden movement, and Monica would pull the trigger. At this range she wouldn't miss.

"You didn't kill her, you just arranged for her to die," said Julia, speaking slowly to conceal the difficulty she was having breathing.

"I can guess what happened. Charlotte's illness was just what you needed. You saw mum when she arrived back from school. You invited her for coffee or lunch, later when you were back from the hospital, but when she came back you weren't there, you were still by Charlotte's side, the oh-so-concerned mother. Mum was met by Gordon's thugs. What did they do? Throw her down one of the mineshafts?"

When Monica didn't react Julia went on:

"Then there was Eliza and her little boy. I hope they were dead when you set fire to their bodies. The little boy in particular, how old was he? Two? Three?"

"That was all investigated. You can't prove anything."

"I don't need to prove it. I know, and so do you. But you've got to live with it."

"Don't preach, Julia. Have you any idea what it's taken me to get to where I am? The housing estate, the pasty business, the Park. Whose ideas? Mine. Who found the money to set it all up? Me. And all the time having to pretend it was someone else."

"You weren't pretending, it suited you," Julia was scornful. She remembered Laura Jeffries' words about Gordon: just a minor crook who unexpectedly became a successful businessman. Here was the explanation.

"You let Gordon think he was responsible for Eliza's death. He covered it up because he really thought he'd killed them."

In the distance Julia could hear, very faint, the putter of an outboard motor. Nothing from the adit above, no sound that might indicate that the police were on their way. When they found the beach was empty would Connor realise where she was? She was going to need another rescue.

"We both know that, but that's not why I came here," she continued. Monica's eyebrows went up: Julia had caught her interest. But the gun remained pointed at her face.

"You know this area, you grew up here. You know the cliffs, the beaches, the footpaths. And you know the mines. This one in particular. You explored it when you were a child, you told me. You know places in there that no-one else has ever found. I think that in one of those places you hid mum's body."

Monica tried to smile, but it came out as a grimace.

"I want to give her a proper funeral," Julia went on. "I need to know where to look. I'll settle for a hint, something you can deny ever having said."

Monica's eyes opened wider. "You've got guts, I'll admit. But I've got nothing to say to you, and you're not in any position to bargain."

Below them the water lapped gently against the steps. The drone of the outboard motor was getting nearer. Monica noticed it as well.

"Not long now," she said.

Did they know exactly where Monica was, and how to get in? Had she given them GPS coordinates, or had she planned to use the walkie talkie to guide them in? If so it might distract Monica long enough for Julia to overpower her. Monica seemed to know what she was thinking.

"It's Sam. He grew up here, used to be a fisherman. He knows where to find me."

In the distance Julia picked out a new sound, a vibration which she felt in her stomach, the subsonic thump of helicopter blades. Too late, the outboard was already there. A black inflatable, huge in the narrow channel, a single crewman at the helm, inching forward between the jagged rocks. An older man, handling the dinghy with ease. He had a painter in his hand, ready to step out onto the quay. He saw Monica with the gun pointed at Julia, but his expression didn't change.

Then he stopped, looking down at the water with an inquisitive look which gradually turned to horror. Threads of red were drifting out of crevices in the rocks, curling gently like smoke before breaking up in the swell. Gradually the entire surface of the inlet was turning crimson.

"It's happening," he said.

"For god's sake what's the matter?" Monica called out.

"It's the old curse," he said. "The adits are running red."

"It's just dye, Sam. Now help me on board. We don't have much time."

But Sam wasn't listening. He clambered to the back of the dinghy, falling over in his haste, reversed the engine and backed out, grazing the rock as he went.

"Come back you idiot!" Monica screamed at him in frustration.

Seeing her distracted Julia dropped to a crouch, ready to hurl herself at Monica's knees. But Monica had seen her.

"STAND UP! NOW!" she barked, swinging the gun down to point at Julia's head. Julia had no choice, she straightened up slowly.

They were alone again, the sound of the outboard rapidly diminishing as the dinghy sped away. In the silence that followed Julia didn't move, keeping her eye on Monica, waiting for her to calm down.

"How did you know it was dye?" she asked eventually. "Did Gordon tell you? And then you led him into the mine so he could deal with Connor. You took him to the one place where you could murder him and have someone else take the blame."

Monica didn't answer. She reached down for the bag and took out the two-way radio.

"Get that fool back here," she spoke. "We put that colouring in the water, we were running a test. And tell him to hurry or we'll all be in prison."

She dropped the handset into her bag.

Suddenly there was a wind, whipping up a choking cloud of dust and dried seaweed, then the deafening roar of rotating blades and the howling shriek of a turboshaft engine. A police helicopter had swept over the cliff and was hovering overhead. The harsh crackle of an over-amplified voice.

"This is the police. Put down the gun. I repeat, put down the gun. Do it now."

Monica finally lost her composure, her hair whipping across her face, obscuring her vision, her hands beginning to shake. Julia cringed: one accidental squeeze of the trigger and it would be all over. But then the arms dropped, and the pistol fell to the floor.

"Step back," the crackling voice again.

Calmly Monica took one pace back and put down the bag, all the time looking at Julia.

"I'm going now," she said, raising her voice over the roar of the helicopter. "If you want to find your mother, you just have to wait by the cross."

"Wait for what?"

"The inevitable."

Monica moved to the far end of the jetty, slipped off her shoes then walked casually down the steps and into the water. When she was up to her armpits she ducked under, her hair spreading out like grey seaweed before slowly disappearing into the depths.

29

It was later that evening. The air was warm and still, the sun golden as it sank towards the horizon. The police had left for the day and the generator was silent. The valley was at peace for the first time since Gordon's murder.

The police had finished searching Mawgan Cottage, Julia was able to move back in. She was seated on the sofa in the lounge, leaning forward, elbows on knees, hands clasped in front of her. She was deliberately not looking at Charlotte, rigidly upright in an armchair opposite. Connor watched, aware of the tension between them, unwilling to interfere. The business between the two of them was unfinished.

"How much did you know?" Julia demanded.

"Don't talk to me like that," Charlotte bridled. "You're not a teacher now."

"Monica could have killed me today."

"That's your fault. You tried to stop her. You should have left that to the police."

Connor knew she was right. Julia had been reckless.

"Monica knew what happened to mum." Julia was unapologetic. "If the police arrested her before I spoke to her I'd never find out. If you'd been more open beforehand I might not have needed to."

Charlotte shook her head.

"I couldn't have helped you. She told me nothing."

"You didn't ask. You might have been a bit more curious about her behaviour. When we were driving back from the Circle you warned me to stop investigating or people would get hurt. Monica told you to say that, didn't she?"

"Yes, she did," Charlotte spoke reluctantly. "But anyone else in Polwerran would have said the same. They were all protecting Gordon. His project was going to save the town."

"She was using him as a shield, and you never saw it."

Julia looked away in disgust. Charlotte turned to Connor.

"She never confided in me." There was an appeal for understanding in her voice. "We weren't close. When she came to the farmhouse it was only to see the kids."

"What was her relationship with Gordon?" Connor spoke tentatively, knowing the question was intrusive, but it was important.

"They were lovers, everyone knew that. It was something else I had to live with."

She thought for a moment.

"Why did she kill him? It wasn't love, or passion. She calculates everything."

"The murder was calculated as well. She saw Tom Mather testing the spring and knew straight away that he was looking for a link between the poisoning of Olivia's garden and the water in the Park. That would be the end of the project. No Polwerran Park, no millions in profit. Gordon would quickly see how she'd manipulated him. He'd known nothing about the spring, remember. Suddenly everything shows up in a different light. Eliza's death, Olivia's disappearance, Malcolm's return, the intimidation which Julia and I faced. They didn't happen to protect him, but Monica. He'd never trust her again, and she knew it.

"That made him a liability. He knew things about her that she wouldn't want made public, such as what really happened to Olivia. She had to shut him up, and then disappear herself before anyone realised what was happening The Loretta was a clever idea: in a couple of hours she'd be in international waters, safe from arrest.

"What I don't understand is why she waited three days before trying to leave. She should have done that straight away."

"The Loretta was in Falmouth for engine repairs. She was always breaking down," said Charlotte, distracted.

She spoke again to Julia, a plea in her voice.

"Monica couldn't have killed your mum as well, Julia. She was with me at the hospital all day."

Julia glanced at her wearily.

"You still don't get it," she said. "Monica is a manipulator. Gordon's thugs did it for her. There was plenty of time to arrange it. Mum would have warned her about the mine water, they were next door neighbours. But mum didn't made the connection with the Park until Feathers gave his talk to the Circle three months later. By that time Monica was ready. Gordon already hated mum because of her accusations about Eliza's boiler; Monica just had to tell him that she hadn't stopped her campaign against him, she'd uncovered new evidence. That would force him to act."

"It happened here, Charlotte, in this valley," Connor added. "Monica admitted that to Julia when she hinted at where the body is."

"The police searched everywhere. We all did, and nobody found anything."

"This mine is a labyrinth," said Connor. "Parts of it are inaccessible behind falls of rock and flooded passages. The police had to weigh up the need to find the body with the safety of their search teams. Monica knew that, and she knew the mine better than any of them. She found a place where no-one would look."

Horrified recognition was beginning to show on Charlotte's face.

"She never let me near the mine. She said it was too dangerous."

"And the Park?" Julia's voice was harsh.

"What about it?" Charlotte looked apprehensive, sensing a trap.

"When mum and I visited Eliza's house on the estate, you would never come with us. Why was that?"

"Mum didn't want me beaten up, you saw those kids."

"Not because you might poison yourself?" said Julia. Charlotte looked startled. "There's always a plausible explanation which doesn't involve her."

Charlotte turned to Connor.

"She'd never let the Park go ahead knowing what might happen. She wouldn't be that cold-hearted."

Julia shook her head.

"Tell her about the shares," she said to Connor.

Charlotte looked at Connor, a bewildered expression on her face.

"Monica had a forty percent share in Zenith. She'd held it since the time Zenith was founded, but immediately after she and Gordon saw Tom Mather investigating the spring she sold it. She was cashing in, Charlotte. She knew what was coming and was salvaging what she could."

"And if the Loretta hadn't been in dock she'd have got away with it." Charlotte said heavily, as she stood up to leave. "Now she'll have to stand trial. My life will be hell all over again."

"Stand trial?" asked Julia. "She walked into the sea. She's gone."

"The helicopter tracked her. The police boat picked her up. Typical. She could kill anyone except herself."

Connor followed as she made her way out. At the front door she turned to him.

"It's not easy living here," she said. "But it's home. I belong here, the kids belong here, the farm has been ours for centuries. We have nowhere else to go. Try to make Julia understand that."

She turned and trudged heavily back to the farmhouse.

"They're all the same," said Julia when he returned. "They only think of themselves; regardless of what happens to the rest of the world. I can't stand this place any more: I want to go home."

"Nothing's stopping you. You could go tomorrow."

"I might," Julia uncurled herself and stood up. "But first I want to work out what Monica was trying to tell me, and for that I need a drink."

"We're going to do it now?"

"Yes."

She walked quickly from the room, returning a minute later with a tray carrying her father's whisky, a jug of water, and two glasses. She put the tray on the coffee table and sat next to him.

"This helps me think," she said, pushing the bottle towards Connor.

He poured a slug and topped it up with water.

"What did she say? Wait by the cross? It isn't much to go on," he said.

"It's more than you think. She was telling me that mum's body can be found. It's around here somewhere."

"She might have been playing games."

"No," Julia poured her own drink. "I'm a teacher, I know when someone is lying. Monica knew she'd lost when the helicopter arrived: when she spoke to me she was expecting to walk into the sea and never be seen again. She was genuine. Mum's body is in the mine. *Wait for the inevitable,* she said."

"Something inevitable is going to reveal where she hid Olivia's body."

Connor took a sip. He remembered the first time he drank it, on the terrace watching the bats, the evening of the rescue.

"Where do we start?"

"We guess, and see what we come up with."

"OK," Connor thought for a moment, trying to push away the fatigue. "The body is buried somewhere and the rain will eventually wash away the earth to reveal it."

"Or it's under the shingle and a storm will do the same."

"…it's under a rock out at sea and the current will eventually free it."

"…it's in the woods hidden by undergrowth and a dog will sniff it out."

Julia stopped.

"This isn't working," she said. "Let's forget about the body for the moment. What's inevitable?"

"Death and taxes," Connor said with shrug.

"Night and day."

"Sunrise."

"Moonrise."

"The phases of the moon."

"High tide."

"Time and tide."

"Tomorrow."

"Next week."

"Next term."

Connor stopped.

"Your turn," said Julia. She'd finished her whisky and was pouring another.

"No. Go back," said Connor. "We had it. We're by the sea, where people live and die by the ebb and flow of the tide."

"What's the tide got to do with the mine?"

"You are slow," he said. "Think of when we first explored it. All the places we couldn't get to. The vertical drops down to who knows where, the tunnel beyond the cascade, the locked door."

He paused.

"And the flooded shaft."

"Full of sea water," Julia said slowly. "The level would rise and fall. Is that what Monica meant? That shaft is passable at low tide?"

"It won't be as simple as that. The police would have checked. But the height of the tides varies with the time of year as well, with the biggest range at the equinox. I bet the police didn't look into that."

"They wouldn't need to. The equinox is in September and Mum disappeared in late October."

"That's not the point. Monica spent years exploring the mine. She would have noticed the changing level in that shaft. If it was passable at the equinox she'd have checked it; maybe she found a dry chamber beyond the flooded section. That's a useful piece of information. If she wanted to use it later she wouldn't have to wait six months for it to empty again, she could just put on scuba gear and swim through."

"It's worth investigating," said Julia. "It would explain why mum was never found. We should tell the police."

"It's still speculation. They'll want much harder evidence before they act on this. And why did Monica tell you to wait by a cross?"

Julia jumped up and hurried to the door. "Because the cross marks the shaft. I'm going to get my camera," she called over her shoulder. "When we were exploring I photographed every junction."

A minute later Julia was back on the sofa flicking through the thumbnails. She slid across to Connor so they could both look at the pictures of the submerged passageway. Her head was touching his shoulder.

"There," said Connor. "Bottom left."

Julia zoomed in. At the start of the passage, just above ground level, a simple cross about three inches high had been scratched into the granite. White chalk had been rubbed in to make it stand out.

"That's it," said Julia, "That's where she is."

"Now we do have something to tell the police."

Julia was staring at the image. "We got there, dad," she whispered. "We found her for you."

Her body started to shake, tears forming in her eyes. Connor gently took the camera from her hands and put it on the table, then put his arm around her shoulder, not moving or speaking. There was nothing adequate he could say. Fifteen years of anger and hurt and not knowing had come to an end for Julia. The terror of facing Monica's pistol. The horror that her mother must have felt when she realised Monica's betrayal. And her father's anguish as he saw the love in his daughter's eyes turn to hatred.

Julia cried a long time, stopping only when she was too exhausted to continue. She lay down in his lap, her eyes closed, her breathing becoming slow and deep. Finally she had found sleep. Connor kept his protective arm over her. There would be more occasions like this: Julia was not going to find closure for a long time, but he would be with her.

He felt his own eyes closing; he too would soon be asleep. And for the first time in more than a year he knew he would not dream of Stevie, and what might have been.

30

It was winter. The sea was as grey as the cliffs, the wind whipping spray off the waves and throwing it against the rocks. Spume like dirty bath suds floated in the air. On the Benjamin Steps, sheltered from the worst of the wind, two figures made their way cautiously down to the jetty. They were dressed in heavy black coats and walking boots, carrying bulky canvas bags in their gloved hands.

Julia put her bag down on the concrete and took out a plain clay urn. She removed her gloves, unscrewed the lid and moved to the water's edge. The wind swirled around her and Connor held out a hand to steady her as she scooped out a handful of gritty ash. She waited for a lull then tossed the ash into the water where it sank quickly out of sight, leaving only a thin film of dust on the surface, undisturbed by the movement of the waves. She threw another handful, then a third, then stopped and motioned to Connor. He took a second urn from his pack, opened it and offered it to Julia. She took a handful and repeated the process before inviting him to do the same. Slowly, unhurried, they threw the ashes onto the water, the two sets of contents mingling and dropping together to the sea bed. When the urns were both empty Julia stood for a long time staring at the water, tears in her eyes. Bits of ash were lodged under her fingernails. Connor stood quietly beside her.

"He didn't get it," she said eventually. "He thought the most important thing was to protect me. It wasn't. We did things together, and we would have seen this one through together. I thought he knew that."

"He was in an impossible position. He could be forgiven for miscalculating. But he knew he'd made a mistake, didn't he? He tried to make you understand. Would you have preferred it if you'd never found out?"

"I'll never know, will I?"

They made their way carefully back through the mine to the garage. Julia swung the hidden door shut, the click of the locks echoing off the walls, now bare of tools. The cottage was empty, sold and awaiting completion. Julia still had a key but didn't go in, slipping the garage key through the letter box.

At the farmhouse they said a brief goodbye to Charlotte. She was in the garden, talking to the workmen constructing a cover to seal the well that never had any water. The police forensics team had revisited and found minute traces of blood at the bottom, DNA evidence of where Olivia had fallen to her death.

The taxi was waiting at the end of the lane. Their route back to Truro took them past the building site, the main gate chained shut, the cranes and portakabins gone, graffiti colonising the fence like ivy. Negotiations over a new water supply were proceeding, a new contractor was being sought after the collapse of Zenith. It would be years before the project could restart. At the bottom of the hill the town square was grey in the wintry half light, dust on the fountain turned to smears of grime by the sweeping rain. The Ship squatted down against the stormy weather.

Outside the town the pasty works showed the only sign of life, the car park full, steam coming from the chimneys, a heavy truck pulling into the road ahead of them. In place of Gordon's face was a new logo, and under the words *Pascoe's Pasties* an addition: *a division of Worldfoods.*

As the taxi speeded up to join the A30 Connor slipped his hand into Julia's. Neither looked back.

Acknowledgements

I would like to thank all those who helped in the writing of this book, in particular Andrew Davidson, Martin Dickson, Jim Kelly from Golddust, Jane Metter, Caroline Natzler, and Vanessa Nicolson. Special thanks to David Cliff for the cover design.

Finally to Viv for all her support and encouragement.

Printed in Great
Britain
by Amazon